Love at Christmas

Anne Greene

Love and Blessings!

Anne Greene

i

A CHRISTMAS BELLE

BY

ANNE GREENE

And, lo, the angel of the Lord came upon them, and the glory of the Lord shone round about them: and they were sore afraid. And the angel said unto them, Fear not: for, behold, I bring you good tidings of great joy, which shall be to all people. For unto you is born this day in the city of David a Savior, which is Christ the Lord.

(Luke 2:9-10-11)

I heard the bells on Christmas Day, Their old, familiar carols play, and wild and sweet the words repeat Of peace on earth, good-will to men. ...Then pealed the bells more loud and deep: "God is not dead, nor doth He sleep; the Wrong shall fail, the Right prevail, With peace on earth, good-will to men." Henry Wadsworth Longfellow.

CHAPTER ONE

October 1877, Wyoming

Was this really what it took to find a husband?

Amanda Geoffrey heaved a deep sigh and brushed dust from her traveling gown. She turned to one of the other mail-order brides jouncing on the buckwagon's wooden seat beside her. "Yes, from my earliest memories people esteemed me as a mind-reader. I do possess a knack for reading people's fleeting involuntary expressions." She smiled. "People immediately erase those swift reactions hoping to mask their true thoughts."

"Your ability sounds like a gift." Though they'd been riding in the wagon almost eight hours, Henrietta's eyes sparkled.

"When I concentrate, I *can* almost mind-read. But, after some awkward experiences, I've pretty much learned to keep the knowledge of my *gift* to myself. I'm trusting you not to tell a soul."

"You can be certain I'll keep your secret. I hope we can become friends. Please tell me more about your gift." Henrietta arched her back and rubbed gloved hands just below where the buckboard's backrest ended.

"Expressions truly are the window to the soul, and I knew how to peek into that window and discover whatever the owner wants to hide."

"That is frightening, Amanda. Can you read my thoughts now?" Henrietta turned a pretty face toward her.

"Like me you're tired, hungry, thirsty, and frightened at what

3

we shall find at the end of our long journey. These are not the fleeting expressions I'm speaking of. What I do is hard to explain. I study the emotions people try to hide. The emotion appears for less than a second and then the expression is hidden."

"I see."

But Henrietta didn't, of course. She, like most people, never glimpsed those swiftly hidden feelings. Amanda so wanted her new friend to understand. "When we reach Angel Vale I'll concentrate as if my life depends on what I see in my groom-to-be's face." Amanda gripped the tapestry purse jiggling in her lap until her knuckles whitened. Because her future *did* depend on what she identified in his expression.

Henrietta nodded and then leaned against the hard, wooden backboard and closed her eyes. "I'm so glad we'll be friends."

Amanda pulled in a deep breath. Her heart beat fast. If only she could relax. After upending her life, she faced a fork in the road. And she'd use her *gift* to discover the best path to her new life.

She straightened her shoulders, stiffened her back against the wagon's wooden seat, and planted her pointy-toed boots on the floorboard. Her gift gave her an advantage, but she needed every ounce of help she could secure. She had this one chance. So much could sour with this bridal agreement. So much could go wrong.

A headache pounded behind her eyes.

She rubbed her neck, trying to relax her rigid muscles. The wagon's hard ride scrambled her insides. She dug her hankie out of the large handbag on her lap and wiped dust from her face. "Such a long, dirty trip from Merville, Maine. I won't miss that smelly fishing village."

Without opening her eyes, Henrietta murmured, "Oh, I'm sure I will."

Amanda's pulse raced faster than the rugged western countryside moving beneath the long wagon. After the punishing eight-hour ride from the train station in Cheyenne, the other mail-order brides jammed in with her looked as fatigued as she felt. But exhaustion couldn't dull her foreboding, which grew greater the closer they rode to Angel Vale.

She so dreaded meeting the cowboy. Neither Aunt Bessie Mae, when she lived in Atlanta, nor Uncle Stephan, when she lived in Merville, had wanted her. She had never been good enough for either of them. What if she wasn't good enough for the cowboy either?

Lolled by the creak of wagon wheels and the cradle-rocking sway, a memory stabbed as if the rude awakening with uncle happened yesterday.

"You're not a burden." Uncle Stephan said.

Tears had pricked the back of Amanda's eyes. She'd wiped her flour-covered hands down the front of her over-large pink apron and picked up the cinnamon shaker to sprinkle the six dozen breakfast rolls. Uncle Stephan hadn't been able to hide the instant furrows and lines crossing his forehead, nor the impatient thinning of his lips, before he turned his back and hurried to the front of the bakery to wait on a couple who carried a whisk of early autumn air inside with them.

She forced the tears away. Uncle Stephan yearned to get rid of her.

Reading people was a gift, but that day, as it often turned out, her knowledge led to despair.

She'd been right to send the *Letter of Agreement* to Angel Vale, Wyoming. Her heart had raced, and the shaker almost slipped from her clammy hands. Wyoming sounded even more like falling off the edge of the world than Merville had before she arrived from Atlanta eleven years ago. No longer a spindly-legged, pig-tailed girl of eleven fleeing the Yankees burning her home, and with no control of her future, this time with the *letter,* she'd taken steps. She sprinkled cinnamon on the buns, set the shaker in its place near the huge ovens, and tugged the door open to a blast of heat. She slid the rolls into the hot oven and noted the time on the bakery's banjo wall clock.

Uncle Stephan had been elated when both of them thought Beau Pettigrew of *The Pettigrews,* who had been leaders in Atlanta society and also refugeed to Merville, had been about to ask for her hand in marriage. Though Uncle struggled to mask his feelings at finally getting her out of his hair, he beamed happiness. Since Beau started calling regularly, Uncle hadn't grumped about his potatoes being cold, or his lobster too hot to handle, or his coffee too weak.

But she'd experienced too much heart ache in her life to count her crabs before she trapped them in her pots. And the night Beau came huffing to the door, his handsome face red and taut and his gray eyes darting everywhere but at her, her heart dropped to her laced-up boots. Beau would never offer that engagement ring.

Of course, she'd been right. In her twenty-two years she couldn't remember a single time she'd misinterpreted even one person's expression. That day, she'd yearned to be wrong.

The wagon jerked and strained as the big six-seater crossed a wooden bridge. The Morgan horses' hooves thwacked like hammers on the wide span over the clear, rushing stream. One of the other ladies covered her ears with gloved hands.

Jake Underwood, owner of Jake's Mercantile in Angel Vale, and Matthew Thomas, the Marriage Broker, would meet them in Angel Vale.

The driver turned from the driver's seat to gaze back at the brides-to-be. The driver swayed in the seat with the jolting of the wagon and cupped his hands around his mouth to be heard over the wagon and team noise. "Angel Vale, next stop. Angel Vale, next stop. Five minutes to arrival."

Amanda's fingers trembled as she replaced her soiled hanky inside her large tapestry handbag. Her knuckles slid against the envelope. Best to refresh what the Wyoming groom wanted. She braced the letter against her knee.

Widow Sophie Webster and Miss Becky Patterson
Community Church, Merville, Maine
I enclose the price for one bride's train and wagon passage to
Angel Vale, Wyoming. If more money is needed, please let me
know. Matt Thomas, our Marriage Broker here in Angel Vale, tells
me you want a description of the type of woman I need.
    This being my first purchase of this kind, I thought long and
hard about the woman I want. So, here is the list:

1. *The lady must be a Christian.*
2. *She should be between the ages of 20 and 30.* Amanda touched the smeared ink on the thin parchment paper. Maybe he couldn't decide how old he wanted his bride. How old was he?
3. *She must love children, as I have a motherless baby.* The motherless baby spoke to her heart. When she'd first read the cowboy/miner's requirements, she'd cried for the child.
4. *She should have a little money saved in the event we are not compatible, and she wants to return to Merville, Maine.*

Amanda shook her head. No, if she left Angel Vale, she'd move back to Atlanta. She dabbed at an unruly tear. No, much as she'd loved Atlanta, she could never return to the South. The mere sound of a male voice with a southern accent sent chills spiraling her spine. She never wanted to hear a man speak with a southern drawl as long as she lived. One Beau Pettigrew was enough. As was one Uncle Stephan. No more slow-spoken twang for her. Did people speak with crisp, clipped accents in Wyoming as they had in Maine?

    5. *I am partial to blondes who don't carry too much weight. However, I will settle for a darker shade of hair if necessary, since I really need a wife.*
    Amanda smoothed a hand over her blonde French Roll and then twirled a curl falling around the side of her face.

She would at least please him with her looks. Before Beau humiliated her in front of the whole town, she'd been the belle of Merville. And as a youngster when she'd lived in Atlanta, Aunt Bessie Mae loved to scoff, with turned-up nose and disapproving tone, at how Amanda's mother had been the belle of Atlanta. Amanda touched the gold locket dangling from her neck. Mother's picture inside displayed a delicate-faced lady with Amanda's golden hair and large eyes. The familiar clutch at her heart made her pinch her lips together. Would life have been different if Mother had lived? Amanda so knew how lonely a motherless child could be. She blinked and returned to her letter.

    6.   *She should be of independent nature, but not willful.*

Amanda harrumphed. Leave it to a man to want independence and meekness in the same woman. Where did she stand on that spectrum? She shrugged. Aunt Bessie Mae declared to anyone who would listen that Amanda was a hand full. Her aunt couldn't wait to get rid of her and ship her from Atlanta to the rocky shores of Maine to Mother's only surviving brother. Uncle Stephan never had a kind word to say, but he'd provided handsomely for her trip. He'd even let her keep the lovely wedding dress and veil he'd had sewn by the seamstress in their small fishing village. Uncle had so hoped for that wedding with Beau. Amanda tried to tidy her hair by tucking in other loose strands. She should have refused the dress. The elegant fabric spoke to her of pain and loss. But the soft satin fit so beautifully, and she would need something to get married in. She shivered and clasped the letter in her icy hands.

    7.   *She will need a vocation. Our cabin is not completed, so she will have to live in the lodging house until Christmas, when I foresee the cabin will be ready for her and the baby.*

This last requirement had decided her. She'd have November and most of December to decide if she wanted to accept the man's proposal. If not, she'd give him the money Uncle Stephan insisted she take, which was more than enough to repay the man for the train and wagon fare. Money was not a problem. Nor was the vocation. She loved baking, and every town needed a baker. She would rise early as she had in Merville, bake the day's goods, and keep the baby with her while she sold her delicacies in the village or to the gold miners. How much care could an infant take? And she had plenty of love to give.

Yours sincerely, Frank Calloway

Amanda refolded the letter.

She so needed to refresh herself before she met the man. Surely, she could have a bath at the lodging house. And a good shot of Bourbon whiskey would help. Of course, she'd never tasted alcohol, but the drink always worked for Uncle Stephan.

The horses puffed and blew. The wheels creaked slower. With a screech of brakes, a lurch, and a mist of steam rising from the horses, the wagon stopped.

She drew her cloak close around her. She should be accustomed to being shipped to strangers like unwanted baggage.

But this time was different. The Wyoming gold miner wanted her.

She squared her shoulders, straightened her spine, and smoothed her well tailored brown travelling dress. She would make the best of a really awkward situation. She stood, furled her blue velvet cape around her body and clasped the pearl neck button. She'd make a new start, a new life, in a new town where no one knew of her humiliation and pain.

So here she was. Some man's personal Christmas Angel. What kind of man *was* Frank Calloway?

CHAPTER TWO

Where was the wagonload of brides driving from the Cheyenne train station? Late!

Frank Calloway lifted the collar of his sheep-skin jacket and gazed at the lowering clouds. Were they due for an unseasonable snowfall or just rain? Wind blew his dark hair into his eyes. Should have gotten a haircut, but with the mine panning richer and richer, hard to take the time away. Fortunately, he'd staked his claim close to Angel Vale or he would have missed meeting the wagon full of brides.

What would his bride think about the town? Sprung up overnight, thanks to the spill-over from the Black Hills Gold Rush. Probably the buildings and tents didn't offer much to a woman. On the corner, the new restaurant, its sign, *Angel Vale Eatery*, blew in the wind. Benjamin, who paced the wooden boardwalk not far away, said his bride would work there. Frank hoped he didn't look as nervous as Benjamin. Matthew Thomas's newspaper office bumped into the eatery. Matthew expected a printing press along with a new bride. No wonder the man paced the wooden boardwalk with impatient steps.

Frank turned and gazed up at Jake Underwood's Mercantile. Looked sturdy and inviting with the general store's central location on the boardwalk. Vaughn's jewelry store, *Mountain Gold*, nestled beside the Mercantile. He'd stopped at the small shop and picked up a simple gold wedding band. He hadn't far to go, because the lathe and plaster building that housed his sheriff's office and a sturdy jail hunkered next to the jewelry shop. Enticing view for incarcerated thieves. A small law office abutted the other side of his jail. Then the busiest place in town squatted on the corner. The *Golden Nugget Saloon,* where he'd gone many times to visit the back-room barber shop or to soak in a rare tub bath.

Across the wide oxen path that passed for a street, the blacksmith's hammer rang against his anvil. The blacksmith shop, complete with a corral and a stable, occupied most of the east side of the street with the gold assay office next to the blacksmith, and then the old mill converted to the lodging house. Both sides of the street offered a wooden boardwalk. Further down the street the buildings petered out to shanties and tents built on various miners' claims. He'd purchased his four adjoining claims closest to town. Nope, not much here to appeal to a woman.

Frank gazed up the oxen path toward the east. Where was that wagon? Would the bride he'd brought be pleasant? He couldn't abide an irksome woman. Beneath his coat, Frank's badge, on the left side of his flannel shirt, hefted a substantial weight of responsibility. Just last month, good old Jake pinned that shiny silver badge to his shirt.

He scrubbed the late afternoon bristles on his chilled face. Lately sheriff's duty had grown into a burden. Especially now. He'd not even had to shine his badge before Nellie or Winnie or Isobel or some other girl he'd met while sowing his wild oats, left a baby on the doorstep of his shanty and named him as the father. The Chinese laundryman dropping off his washed clothes saw the mysterious woman. She'd been dressed in a long black skirt and shirtwaist and wore a large black hat tied with a veil to cover her face.

Chang Fu handed him the note she'd left.

You are Frank, Jr.'s father. I can't take care of him. He is six months old and weaned from the breast. I'm leaving you a bottle,

11

some diapers, and some crawlers, sweaters, booties and blankets.
He is your responsibility now.

Chang Fu said the woman ran from Frank's shanty and caught the stage to Cheyenne just before the vehicle left Angel Vale.

So, he'd offered Chang Fu half the gold he panned if the Chinaman would take charge of Baby Frank's care. Turned out Chang Fu was the laziest Chinaman Frank ever met. But the small man with the long, braided pig tail usually had Baby Frank fed and dressed in the evenings when Frank breezed into the shanty after work in the evenings. Still, the baby needed much more attention and love.

Frank sighed at the memory. A day or two after he hired Chang Fu, he'd had to ride into the surrounding countryside and camp for several days on the trail of outlaws who'd held up the assay office at gun point. The whole time he'd been away, he'd feared Chang Fu would light out and leave Baby Frank alone.

When he returned and found the baby wet and hungry with Chang Fu fast asleep in Frank's cot, he'd had no choice. He'd hiked over to see Matt Thomas and jawed about the ad Matt placed in the newspaper. Frank knew the ad by heart.

Get Your Personal Christmas Angel. Sign up with Matthew Thomas.

Frank had discovered he preferred upholding the law to spending hours bent over ice cold water from the sluice, so he didn't want to give up his Sheriff's job to care for the baby. Plus he knew nothing about the care and feeding of a child. The little one needed a mother. So, like a fool, he'd signed up and written *The Letter.* Jake, as marriage broker, sent the letter off to some fishing village in Maine.

His claim provided adequate gold, but he'd had to add money from his sheriff's wages to give him sufficient funds to bring a bride west all the way from Merville, Maine.

Would his Angel bride take to the baby?

He jammed his Stetson further down on his head, paced the boardwalk in front of the mercantile that served as the stage and wagon depot and stuck his cold hands in his pocket. Another two months and he'd finish building the log cabin for his future wife on the town edge of his claim. He nodded to Riley, another soon-to-be-groom pacing the boardwalk.

Alex stomped over to stand beside him. "You ready for a wife?"

Frank nodded. "I got our cabin sides up about seven feet all the way around."

"I passed by your place this morning. Looks sizeable."

"I still have a long way to go, and I promised my mail-order bride a home by Christmas. I'll work like the dickens, but I'll get the job done."

"She'll love that cabin." Alex clomped away, distraction shading his face like a six-month beard.

Frank shoved his hands deeper into his coat and strode down the boardwalk. Every man pacing the boardwalk looked jumpy as a long-tailed cat near a rocking chair.

OK, so what if he didn't *like* his new bride? He jammed his Stetson on tighter. Too bad. The baby needed a mother. He didn't need a wife. Hadn't even thought about getting hitched. Sounded too much like two mules dragging a heavy wagon over a high mountain. With his experience with women, would he be jumping from the frying pan into the fire? A woman could be a load of trouble. Once he saddled himself with her, as a new Christian trying to follow Christ, he'd be bound to this stranger for life. That thought had his knees knocking and his palms sweating. What if he wasn't good husband material and made her life miserable?

But the boy, though certainly not *his* son, had grabbed a big chunk of his heart. Frank, Jr. deserved better than being wet, smelly, and hungry most of the time. Frank jerked his Stetson off and ran his fingers through his tangled hair. As a new Christian, he didn't know the ropes yet, and a wife might keep him out of trouble. He needed all the help he could get in that area. God had a big chore turning his life around.

He tromped so hard the boards beneath his boots shook. When he'd ordered himself a Christian bride, why hadn't he stipulated that she be pretty? He did like a pretty face. He stopped, swiped his Stetson off, and slapped his thigh with his hat. Why would a pretty girl need to be a mail-order bride? He'd have to take this one even if she were as prim as a preacher's wife at a prayer meeting.

He glanced at the sun dropping in the western sky. She should be here by now. His heart beat faster than when he'd faced a cavalry charge on foot. Despite the stiff wind, sweat slid between his shoulder blades. Jake and Matt promised an angel. Humph. She'd have to be a lot different from the women he knew.

He didn't have enough money to send her back if he didn't want her. Why hadn't he thought this through? What kind of woman traveled to marry a man she didn't even know? She had to be ugly. And fat. Maine was full of men. Why hadn't she married one of them? Why come all the way to this forsaken country to marry a man? He should have gone to Cheyenne and got himself a woman there. What a mad man to buy one unseen.

He paced the wooden boards. The wrong woman could hinder whatever ministry the Lord gave him. He'd promised to serve God if the Lord saved his life after that rattlesnake bite.

The circuit riding preacher who'd led him to a saving knowledge of Christ didn't stay long enough to teach him much about the Christian life, but he'd admonished Frank to read the Bible. Start with the book of Mark in the New Testament. So, he had.

He gazed down the empty trail. He'd like a pretty girl like Rosemary, but she'd have to be bigger and stronger. He'd traded his 30-30 Winchester shotgun for a milk cow, and his new wife would have to milk Daisy. And she'd have to cook and garden and wash diapers. Chang Fu boiled huge pots of water and washed diapers, then hung them on a line stretched from the shanty to the creek. The sound of diapers forever flapping in the breeze sang a southern tune as he squatted next to the icy creek with his gold pan. Often, he found himself humming My Old Kentucky Home. He sure missed Peach Tree Crossing. Now that place had some pretty southern belles.

His new wife would have to strain the peas and carrots and meat for Baby Frank. Frank rubbed the back of his neck. He couldn't remember when his muscles had been so rigid. His Christmas angel would have to cook the game he killed. Between panning gold, hunting outlaws, and building the cabin, he didn't have the time.

She'd have to be a veritable work horse.

How did Matt and Jake persuade these brides to leave their homes and come to this frontier? Did any of those twelve women have any idea what lay ahead for them?

He turned his back against the wind and gazed up the dirt road that wandered into empty countryside. Trees lined one side and rocky landscape the other. Behind him the ring of pickaxes on rock and the rush of water from the big creek played a muffled song. Only boots clumping on the wooden boardwalk broke the stillness. This was man's country. Would his bride take one gander and jump back into the wagon, his hard-earned money disappearing with her?

Horses' hooves rattled over the stone bridge.

Dust rose on the horizon.

The huge wagon lurched into view. The wooden boardwalk vibrated under many boots. His heart beat like the Morgan horses' thundering hooves.

No matter what the woman looked like, he had to marry her. He had no other choice.

He was a lunatic.

CHAPTER THREE

Amanda stepped down from the wagon, legs shaking. Angel Vale, indeed. The place looked desolate. One wide dirt street cut through a few dilapidated buildings, tapered off into shanties and tents, and ended in the countryside without amounting to much. The faint clang of pickaxes sounded above the huff of the tired teams of horses. Not what she'd been led to expect. She drew in a deep breath. The scent of fresh, wild outdoors mixed with lesser odors swirled to her senses. But no fishy odor, no roar from the sea, and no tinkle of rigging. *Thank you, Lord.*

A cold wind whipped her heavy cape. A thin layer of soot from coal-burning chimneys left a stench in the air. She huddled inside her wrap, shoving her arms together through the slits, her hand bag hanging heavy on one arm.

Behind her, other girls descended from the wagon. Henrietta stood beside her.

A large group of men stomped along the wooden sidewalk in boots with heels, many wearing Stetsons. Which one would stride over to meet her? She shivered.

The short man whose ears stuck out from a balding head beneath a wide Stetson? Cold air blew down her neck and wrestled with her French Roll. Or the muscular man whose gait rolled from side to side because of his brawn? The older man whose white beard and mustache looked exactly like her mental picture of Santa Claus? Too many men crowded the boardwalk.

Oh, dear Father, have I made the worst mistake of my life?

Two grimy men in miner's clothes ran from the direction of the shanty town toward the station. Was her expectant groom one of them? How was this better than Merville?

The driver climbed down from the driver's seat and directed the women standing on the boardwalk toward the men shuffling up to meet their mail-order bride.

A man rushed forward and claimed Henrietta.

Jake Underwood, the owner of Underwood Mercantile and one of the marriage brokers, touched her shoulder. "Miss Geoffrey, where do you want your trunks?"

"Until Frank Calloway steps forward, please leave both my trunks here by my feet."

"Glad to, Miss Geoffrey. Matthew will be sighting Frank soon, and then ole Frank'll be singling you out 'fore you know it, ma'am." Jake heaved her trunks out of the wagon bed and thunked them at her feet.

"Thank you, Jake."

He nodded, and then turned to dig out luggage from the big wagon for one of the other women who'd traveled all the way from Maine to become brides of men they hadn't met.

Would any of them find happiness in this town in the middle of nowhere?

A drop of rain landed on her nose. She glanced up at the darkening sky. Were they in for a storm?

Boots clicked on the wooden boardwalk. She turned. A tall man, several inches over six feet, strode toward her. His dark hair blew in the wind. A Stetson hung from his hand. He looked young, not yet thirty. His heavy coat couldn't conceal his excellent build. Black Levis covered muscular legs. Her heart beat fast. He fit the description he'd sent. That had to be Frank Calloway.

She must read his *first* expression. Discern his *first* reaction. She ran toward him.

****

Frank slapped his Stetson on. She was blonde all right. Almost white blonde. But small. And slender. Could she take care of Baby Frank? At six months, the boy was an armload.

She ran toward him, her blue cape streaming behind her. Whoa. That didn't happen to him. Sure, women liked him, but this?

Was she cold? Was she afraid? Automatically he held out his arms.

She ran right up to him. Close enough her ivory skin's smooth texture glowed in the gloom. But at the last second she stepped away, reached up and tipped his hat back on his forehead.

He dropped his arms and gazed down into her face. And gulped for air. Her big blue eyes bore into him with an intensity he'd never experienced. Like she could see into his soul. Blonde hair whipped around a face so beautiful, he couldn't catch his breath. Delicate and finely molded, with lips that begged to be kissed. He grabbed his wrists behind his back to keep from reaching out and drawing her into his arms. He yearned to kiss those lovely lips.

But she looked too delicate for the job he needed her to fill.

His second glance took in her clothes. Rich. Too rich for his blood. She'd probably never done a day's work in her life. What would he do with a wife like her? Oh yeah, his body knew what he'd like to do, but the old brain interfered. He needed a work horse, but she looked a thoroughbred. Life in Angel Vale would kill her. He'd have to dig up enough money to send her back.

****

Amanda laughed. A tinkling sound that wafted through the muted greetings and conversation behind them. She knew exactly what he thought. Her appearance astounded the tall cowboy. He would definitely take her as his wife. No worries on that score. Yet he didn't think she would survive the task. She tossed her head. Strong, ambitious, and capable, she could manage the baby, Frank, and still have ample time to become the premier baker in this

19

rough frontier town. He would see.

She laughed again. He would take her as his wife even if he thought she'd lie abed all day and order him around. Frank Calloway was smitten. *Thank you, Father, for my gift.* She'd have no trouble at all with this man. He was dough in her hands.

But would *she* accept him? She liked his build. His generous mouth tilted up at the corners as if he were a likeable person. No frown lines marred his brow. Faint laugh wrinkles fanned out from the corners of his eyes. His tanned skin showed an outdoor man. Quite good looking and well set up, his appealing brown eyes drank her in as if she were a well in a desert. What was not to like about him?

"Ma'am, would you be Miss Amanda Geoffrey?"

She jerked back from him so fast she almost tripped over her long cape. Her hand went to her mouth, and she gasped. "Oh, no!"

****

Wind blew the slender beauty's cape, twining blue velvet around his legs. Frank wanted to bend over her hand and kiss her fingers. He wanted to place his Stetson on her head to keep the wind from tousling her silky hair. He wanted to take her in his arms, sweep her off her feet, carry her to the unfinished cabin, and create a warm haven for her. He wanted to love, honor, and protect her for the rest of his life.

He wanted her.

But she gazed at him with a horrified expression, sea blue eyes wide, and mouth puckered into an O. A moment ago, she'd seemed to like what she saw. What changed so lightning fast? What had he done wrong?

She turned away to glance back at the man driving the empty wagon down the dirt street.

Would she run?

Instead she gazed up into his face. "You…you have a southern drawl. Are you not a Wyoming native?"

He tipped his Stetson. "No, ma'am. I'm originally from Peach Tree Crossing, near Atlanta, Georgia. After the War of Northern Aggression, I rode on out here to the west to make my fortune. I've been in Angel Vale about six months. I'm sheriff here."

"Near Atlanta?" Her face paled, and she gripped her big bag as if she'd lassoed a wild horse.

He reached out to reassure her.

She cringed away, a frown marring her rounded forehead.

"Um, would you like to get out of this wind? The lodging house is just down the street."

His Adam's apple rose in his throat and tried to choke him. He gulped. She didn't like him. She wanted to return to Maine. How could he stop her? "Are these two trunks yours? I'll bring them along."

"Yes, yes those are my trunks."

Her voice breathed music, like the rushing creek in springtime bubbling over smooth rocks. He detected a faint southern accent. He'd bet the poker pot she also hailed from Atlanta. He grinned. They had that in common. He hefted a trunk up on either shoulder, smothered a grunt, and nodded toward the lodging house. "You best get out of this wind."

Instead she gazed back over her shoulder at the receding wagon, the big wheels cranking around in faster circles as the Morgan horses sensed home and hay. Her luscious lips tightened and her whole body leaned toward Jake Underwood's empty wagon.

Balancing the heavy trunks on his shoulders, he used his elbow to nudge her down the town's wooden sidewalk. Maybe he *could* carve out time to help care for Baby Frank if the job proved too hard for her. He'd finish the cabin in record time, get her and the baby settled inside his snug new home, and spend all his free time with her. She *did* have that Atlanta drawl that couldn't be disguised. She might have ridden in from a Maine seacoast town,

21

but she was a southern belle, and he'd never wanted anything more in his life than to make her his wife.

Thank you, Lord, for this woman. God brought her, and he wouldn't let her get away. Not now. Not ever. Not if he had to hogtie her to keep her from leaving.

****

Father God, how could you do this to me?

Amanda pulled the velvet hood of her cape around her face. The man hails from near Atlanta. Atlanta! She planted her feet on the boardwalk. "I must get back on that wagon and leave."

His elbow nudged her back. He barely kept her heavy trunks from toppling to the boardwalk. "Not tonight, ma'am. The horses have to rest, so nobody's going back to Cheyenne tonight."

She peered at the disappearing wagon, then back at him, her beautiful eyes wide. "Oh, no, I've made a terrible mistake."

"No mistake. This is Angel Vale, and I'm Frank Calloway. Welcome. We'll get you settled and warm and fed inside the lodging house." He nodded toward an old mill whose paddle wheel rested in a dry bed. "Jake and his team aren't going anywhere except to the stable. Jake's got his own Angel to look after." He gazed up at the sky. A single raindrop landed on his mouth. His masculine hand brushed his lips. "So best to settle in and get acquainted. You'll find that Angel Vale is a fine, little town. Growing every day."

"If that's what you want." Wind whistled through the pines behind Underwood Mercantile. A compelling, insistent alarm.

The elbow in her back nudged her forward. Shivering, she gazed at the receding wagon, and then into his face. She didn't need her gift to recognize that this big man wanted her as his wife, and he wasn't about to let her go. His set jaw, determined brown eyes, and square shoulders lugging both her trunks shouted loud and clear that he meant to keep her here in this isolated town. She rushed forward to keep that elbow from pushing her. Was he so easily taken in by her appearance? She could be a shrew for all he knew. Or lazy. Or a spendthrift. Or could have any number of awful traits.

Somehow, she'd escape from him and leave this forlorn place. But the cold penetrated her cape, her parched throat screamed for water, and her stomach rumbled for food.

She had no choice. She'd acquiesce. For now.

CHAPTER FOUR

The heavy trunks roosted like squatter's shanties on his shoulders, almost more than he could handle. Silently he puffed for breath. He'd never let her know how carrying her trunks winded him. With all this luggage she had planned to stay. Had planned. He grunted. But now she didn't like him. Well, he paid for her, and she would have to adjust.

She didn't know him at all. How could she tell if she liked him or not? Everyone else thought him a likeable guy. Never had any trouble with women wanting to get to know him before. Why didn't she *like* him?

He panted as they reached the door of the lodging house. Just outside of town, the building had been a flour mill, but the miners had diverted the mill stream to their gold mining stakes, and the big wooden mill wheel no longer turned. He lowered the chests onto the boardwalk and opened the lodging house door for her. He'd do everything in his power to win Amanda. But by next week when the stagecoach rattled through town, if she still didn't like him, he would let her go. He followed her inside the lodging house. Maybe he'd give her two weeks before he released her. He shook his head. What was the hurry? He'd win her by Christmas. If she still didn't like him by then, he'd tear up her *Letter of Agreement* and free her.

He grunted. Not likely. He'd keep her here and let her take as long as she needed. But in the end, she would marry him.

He shook his head. Why kid himself? If she still didn't like him, he'd never force her to marry him.

He deposited her trunks inside the door, whipped off his Stetson, and ran his fingers through his hair. "Which room is yours?"

"I don't know. Matthew or Jake will assign one."

Outside, the wind howled, and the day darkened. Too early in the year for Angel Vale to get snowed in, but if a foot of snow fell, he'd welcome the stuff. Sometimes snow delayed the stage. "If we hurry we can make it to the Angel Vale Eatery in time to get a good table. By the time we finish and return here, we'll know which room is yours."

"Thanks, I am hungry."

He ushered her out the lodging house door and back onto the boardwalk. Nestling his hand into the small of her back, he soon had her inside the restaurant.

He helped her out of her cape and seated her at the best table.

After a quick look, he forbade his eyes to travel her trim figure. No excess flesh puddled beneath the brown dress. Just the exact right amount of woman. He hung his coat on the back of his chair and settled across the wooden table from her. Probably he could work in milking Daisy himself if he rose a half hour earlier than his usual five a.m. No use foisting that task on her.

She pulled off her long, elbow-length leather gloves.

Hands too delicate to dump diapers into hot water picked up the woven napkin beside her plate. If he stayed up late each evening, he could take that diaper-cleaning chore off her list. He didn't need more than five hours sleep anyway.

He sailed his Stetson across the room to land on one of the hooks along the wall where several other battered Stetsons hung.

She looked startled, then pinched her lips and gazed around the room.

Several other couples bustled in and sat, smiling at one another and at the other couples filling the empty tables. Frank ordered the evening special.

"I need to wash my hands. Do you mind?" Her beautiful lips trembled.

She didn't like him. A lump lodged inside his throat. He longed to tuck her chin in his hand, tilt her head up, kiss the tremble off those beguiling lips, and beg her to have faith in him. Instead, he cleared his throat. "I need to wash mine, too. The lady's outhouse is beyond that door around the building next to the exterior stairs. I installed a basin of fresh water on the stand outside myself." He accompanied her to the rough plank door. Wind whipped them as he placed his hand in the small of her back and navigated her to the outhouse, door engraved with a crescent moon to let in light.

"I'll only be a minute." She smiled and shut the woman's outhouse door behind her.

He rushed around the building to the men's outhouse, leaned over the pitcher on the outside stand, splashed cold water into the basin, and dunked his head. The soap was still big enough to use, and he scrubbed his hands and face. Then he peered into the cracked mirror tacked onto the side of the outhouse. Puzzled brown eyes in a rugged wind-blown face gazed back at him.

What about him made her shrink away? Other women liked his looks. Other women flocked to him. Why not her? His parents had taught him good manners. He owned a gold claim that paid and promised loads more nuggets. His sheriff's badge gleamed on his left shirt pocket. He was tall and strong. Came from good stock. What more did she want? He tried out a smile. Good teeth. Straight and white. No yellow stains from chewing or smoking. She didn't know he'd given up drinking. He didn't cuss anymore. Somehow, he'd escaped being wounded in the war. What didn't she like? What scared her off like a frightened filly?

He turned and meandered back to the dining area. Her seat remained empty. He plopped down in the chair and drummed his fingers on the table. She still hadn't returned when Brenda carried in trays of steaming dishes filled with their dinners.

"You got yourself one of those mail-order brides." Brenda frowned and stomped her foot. "You could a saved yourself a passel of money. I'd take care of that kid of yours." She lifted a homespun-clad shoulder and winked. "And I know how to take care of a brawny man like you." Her lips turned down at the corners. "All you had to do was ask."

"I'm sorry, Brenda. I didn't figure you'd want to settle down to just one man. I mean, to a man who is a Christian." Nope, Brenda was not the kind of woman he wanted raising his boy.

"You're not much of a Christian, yet, Frank. I don't think you changed that much. A man with a checkered past like yours."

"Past is the right word, Brenda. What's past is past. Since the Lord found me, I've become a new creation in Christ. It's not too late for you to do the same."

"Humph. You'd be the most perfect piece of manhood I've ever met if you'd forget the Christian stuff." She leaned down to whisper in his ear. "You're making enemies."

"So, you're better off staying away from me, aren't you?"

Brenda pouted her pretty mouth and strutted back to the kitchen.

His leg jiggled and his foot tapped and he kept his gaze on the front window. Might be best to go look for Amanda. But the way she'd stayed close to her trunks, she wouldn't leave town without them, and he'd left them in the lodging house. She could hire a wagon and get any of the men hanging around the lodging house gawking at the new brides in town to carry them to the wagon and drive for her. But she'd have to pass the window to get back to the old mill.

If she didn't show in five minutes, he would get up, stalk across the room, go outside, and jerk open that outhouse door. He had to eat and get back to the shanty to check on Chang Fu and Baby Frank. The Chinaman wasn't dependable for long stretches of time, and he'd run directly from his claim to the boardwalk in front of Underwood Mercantile to meet the wagonload of Angels. He shrugged. Still, he wasn't about to embarrass Amanda and get off to an even more rotten start.

He drummed his fingers on the table. What didn't Amanda like about him?

He was about to spring from his chair and fetch her over his shoulder when she glided back into the building and over to the table, all smiles.

He stood. His heart hammered like a miner's pickaxe on gold. Maybe he'd been wrong. Maybe she *did* like him.

****

The smile Amanda painted on her face started to hurt.

Frank Calloway would never willingly let her go. His fleeting expressions betrayed him. Before he'd opened his mouth, she'd almost dreamed they had a future together.

But a Deceitful Southern Gentlemen resided inside the big cowboy with the six-shooters hanging at his sides.

Easily one of the best-looking men she'd ever met, or even seen for that matter, he eagerly waited for her to become his bride. But as a girl back in Atlanta, Aunt Bessie Mae drilled into her mind from the moment she could remember that she should never, under any circumstances, trust a fine-looking gentleman. Aunt Bessie Mae had never been wrong.

Pain slashed her heart. No, she would not think of Beau. The duty-bound handsome hunk lived hundreds of miles east, and she would never see him again. She'd come all these long exhausting, dirty miles to marry a Wyoming cowboy. She'd talk with Jake Underwood and Matthew Thomas tomorrow. Perhaps she could trade her intended groom for one more suitable. This town buzzed with more men than flies around her Southern Pecan pies doused with Bourbon Sauce.

Amanda buttered a roll. Back when she knew no better, she'd

gone against Aunt Bessie Mae's instruction to her young charge. She'd fallen in love with a handsome man. She'd let that man charm her into thinking he would marry her. In all of Merville, Maine, she'd become infatuated with the one man, from the one family, who'd also fled Atlanta during the war. Beau Pettigrew, the Southern Aristocrat, compromised her reputation. Never again. Now she was older and wiser. She'd been lured to this lonely town by the promise of a Wyoming cowboy. A miner. A transplanted Southern male definitely did not measure up to her needs.

No one in *this* one-horse town must ever discover how Beau had fallen in love with her. He really had. Beau's love blossomed all over his face each time they were together. He'd brought her gifts. He'd taken her to all the parties and lobster fests. He'd declared his love. She believed him.

Everyone, absolutely everyone in that fishing village she called home, knew she and Beau would soon marry. Then he'd married another.

Oh, she knew about Southern men and their Sense of Duty and their values. About how their families raised them to do the right thing no matter the sacrifice. About how charming they could be. About how they could fall in love and lack the backbone to marry the one they loved. About how they were bred to esteem money, prestige and duty more than love.

The pain and humiliation still shredded her insides like broken glass. She would never trust her future to a Southern man again. In forlorn Angel Vale, she would stand on her own two feet. Her intended groom had written under false pretenses. He was supposed to be a Wyoming native. A cowboy. A miner.

Not a Southern Gentleman from Atlanta.

Because of that, she owed him nothing. He was another Beau Pettigrew, and she'd never trust him. She'd never marry him. She'd care for his baby until she found someone dependable and loving to take over that responsibility. Probably one of the other mail-order brides would like the chance. Then, if Matthew Thomas didn't have a different groom for her, she'd move on. Perhaps back to Cheyenne. Though wild and not yet civilized, the larger town promised respectability. She'd counted three churches and some real clapboard houses as she and the other brides in the wagon rattled through Cheyenne's streets. She'd keep tight hold of her money and when the time came, she'd open a bakery in Cheyenne. But first she'd ask Matthew if he had a genuine Wyoming man who needed an Angel.

Until then, she'd settle in and take care of the baby. And Mr. False Pretenses, Frank Calloway, would have to keep his distance. Cowboy, indeed!

CHAPTER FIVE

After dinner Frank settled Amanda in the best room the lodging house offered, which was quite small. He heaved the second trunk on the floor of her room and stood hands on his hips, pulling in big lungs-full of air.

"You can live here until I complete the cabin. Then you can move into the cabin. At Christmastime when the circuit riding preacher comes, we'll marry."

He gazed around the tiny room. *No place here for a baby.*

"Oh."

"I'll stay in my shanty until we get married." Place would get cold. Wind could whistle through the cracks in the plaster between the laths. "I'll convert the shanty into a stable after we get married." Stabling Diablo got too expensive with a new wife to think of.

"You have a horse?"

"Have to own a horse to be a sheriff."

She nodded. "I'd like to meet your son now, if you don't mind." Amanda's emerald eyes seemed too busy checking out the room to rest on him.

He stood a moment to admire her beauty. Pink blushed on her cheeks. Probably she'd never been alone in a bedroom with a man before.

"I'll bring Baby Frank here and you can meet him."

"Since it never actually rained, I'd rather go to your place and meet the baby, if you don't mind. I'd like to see the environment to which he's accustomed." She perched on the edge of the one straight-backed chair in the room and smoothed her brown dress around her. Tiny pointed boot toes peered out from beneath her hem.

Brown suited her blonde coloring. He'd often been with pretty girls, but Amanda truly had classic beauty. Alone in this room with her, how long could his heart beat so fast without causing an attack? Yet he couldn't keep his gaze off her. She wouldn't look at him. Why did she not like him? "It's dark now. My place is a good two miles from here. Why not wait until morning?"

"I'm not too tired for a brisk walk." She rose, gracefully removed her cape from the coat rack, and blew out the candles on the bureau. The room darkened. He stood like an oaf in the middle, hands hanging at his sides.

Her dress rustled as she walked past him to the door. Then she was outside in the large main room. "Are you coming?"

What could he do but follow? Outside in the big room still smelling of flour, he draped her cape over her shoulders. Her aroma smelled so sweet he drew in a long breath. He almost tasted her loveliness. Was he drooling? He wiped a rough hand over his mouth.

At the lodging house's exterior door, he fitted her hand into the crook of his arm. With her beside him, marriage sounded like climbing the golden stairway to heaven. Nothing could be better than having this one woman walk with him through life's long journey. Cold wind blustered in from the north, all but lifting his Stetson from his head. He raised his sheepskin collar around his ears. She pulled a velvet hood over her head and bent against the wind.

"Are you sure you want to do this?"

"Very."

He led her across the dark street and down the wooden sidewalk past the Mercantile. "This is my office and in back is the jail. Would you like a tour?"

32

"Another time perhaps." Her words swirled away on the wind.

"My claim is another mile and a half down the road. My stake's the second closest to Angel Vale. I've got our cabin three-quarters built." He squeezed the hand tucked into his arm. "We'll pass our home on the way to my shanty." When had *the cabin* become *our home* in his thinking? He laid his other hand over the gloved fingers, warm around his arm.

She nodded. Darkness kept him from seeing her face.

Her tiny boots kept pace with his long steps. The wind whipped her cloak, so he used the flapping material as an excuse to take her fingers in his hand and wrap his other arm around her shoulders to keep the flying garment snug against her. She fit into his arm as if God designed her purely for him. Tucked in so close, he found it hard to breathe.

She walked beside him, faster than he'd have thought possible with her smaller stride. Graceful, too. If there'd been anybody about, they'd have stepped aside to admire his beautiful bride.

"Here's our cabin." The logs of the cabin he'd been so proud of reached out like a ghost in the darkness. She didn't even slow, just hurried her steps as they passed. "I'll have our home finished by Christmas. You'll be mistress of the finest cabin in Angel Vale. I'm an expert builder. Been at the job twelve years now. I know how to build a mighty fine log cabin."

"I thought you mined gold."

"Right. Back in Cheyenne my buddy talked me into riding to the wide-open spaces of Angel Vale to make my fortune panning gold. I've been working my claim for the past six months." He puffed out his chest. "It's paying gold every day. The work slows in the winter because the creek's so cold. It'll ice over soon, and I'll spend all my time building that cabin."

"I thought you were sheriff?"

"I am. I can hear any gunshots from town out on my stake. Any commotion I miss, and Jake sends word for me to come pronto. I keep my horse saddled up, keep my guns strapped on, hop on my horse, and hightail it into town."

"Is there much law-breaking in Angel Vale?"

"Seems as more and more miners and ranchers arrive, more bandits blow in with them. I've had some nasty run-ins lately, but nothing I couldn't handle."

"What if you get shot? Or killed?"

Seemed a good time for more persuasion. "Well, that's where you come in, isn't it? If I'm killed, as my wife, you'll be solely responsible for Baby Frank. You'll also gain full ownership of my claim, the cabin, and receive partial pay from my sheriff's job. You'll survive just fine. I've taken care of the financial business already."

"Oh."

The news didn't seem to please her. Maybe she worried about his getting hurt. "We don't have to wait for Christmas. We could get married this week, and then you'd be covered if anything happened to me."

"Oh."

She hadn't jumped at his excellent idea. Before she arrived, he'd thought Christmas soon enough to tie the knot. But why wait? She was exactly what he hadn't even known he wanted. The marriage broker had done him proud. The future spread out before him like the glorious view from Saddleback Mountain of the whole valley. Even if he'd never laid eyes on Baby Frank and was foot-loose and fancy free, he'd have courted Amanda. She was a Southern Belle through and through. The perfect woman for him. He wanted Miss Amanda Geoffrey as his wife.

"There's the shanty. It's not much." He pointed to a small shack built of clapboards with smoke from a stove-pipe chimney puffing white against the black sky. "I enclosed the open side of a lean-to when the baby arrived."

"You're quite handy."

34

He gazed down into the pale oval of her upturned face, luminous in a fleeting shaft of moonlight. Were his skills a mark in his favor? "Necessity." He wrenched open the door. She'd made the cold trek, and her chest didn't even lift and fall with her breathing. Maybe she wasn't as delicate as he'd thought.

She stepped inside.

Chang Fu, face wreathed in smiles, jumped up from the rocker Frank had made. "This the woman who mothers you baby. She very, very pretty. You like she. She like you. Chang Fu leave now." He grabbed his long coat, pulled a round knitted cap over his balding head, flipped his long pigtail over his shoulder, and rushed to the door. "You pay me tomorrow. Chang Fu no return. Has laundry business to take care of." The small Chinaman slammed the door and disappeared into the darkness.

Frank dropped his hands to his sides. "That was unexpected. Um. Looks as if you start taking care of Baby Frank tomorrow. I'd hoped to give you time to settle in first." Blasted Chinaman.

"That's no problem." She tiptoed over to the cradle he'd made and peered inside. "Oh my goodness, Baby Frank looks like he's soaked, and the blanket is wet as well. Do you have any clean cloths you use as diapers?" She swept out of her cloak and picked up the dripping baby.

He rushed to the sideboard where one clean cloth rectangle lay.

Baby Frank woke, gazed into Amanda's face, and opened his blue eyes wide. He seemed mesmerized. His small mouth gaped, and he smiled.

Frank grinned. "The kid has good taste. He likes you." He tipped his hat.

Amanda swiveled to impale him with that intense gaze of hers. "Why, this baby doesn't resemble you at all. He's blonde and blue-eyed." She smiled down at the baby. "I suppose he favors his mother."

Not long ago he would have lied. Taken the easy way out. He

unbuttoned his coat. "Probably."

"What happened to his mother?" She laid Baby Frank on the sagging cot and unpinned his wet diaper.

He dampened a soft cloth with the last water from the pitcher on the sideboard and handed the rag to her. He'd have to make a run to the well for more water tonight after he walked her back to the lodging house.

She gazed into his face with that intense expression he was growing to love. "You don't know who the baby's mother is, do you?"

He gulped.

She dried and worked at diapering the baby.

"What are you, a mind reader?" How had she figured the problem out so quickly?

"You're not even sure if Baby Frank is yours?"

Could she see right into his brain? He'd never felt so naked.

"And, of course, because of your inflated Southern sense of Duty, you undertook raising this child even though you're positive he's not yours."

He stepped back. She seemed utterly against what was clearly his Christian duty. *Could* she read his mind?

"And now, you've staked you're entire future on bringing me out here to marry you and take care of Baby Frank."

Now that she put the situation that way, what he'd done did sound crazy. He frowned and pinched the bridge of his nose. That meant eleven other men in town were just as crazy. More like desperate.

"So that's that." She plopped into the rocker, Baby Frank on her lap. "Do you have a bottle for him?"

"I've got milk." He turned, opened the hut's door, and reached down on the doorstep for the milk bucket. He pulled off the lid and went about the complicated business of filling the baby bottle.

She hummed a lullaby, rocked, fed the baby, and gazed around the small hut. "What's Frank's middle name?"

"James."

"Do you mind if I call him Jamie rather than Baby Frank?"

CHAPTER SIX

Amanda bit her lip. She placed the sleeping, contented-looking Jamie down into the lovely hand-made pine cradle, pulled a worn quilt from the sagging cot, and arranged the covering over the baby. She settled into the comfortable wooden rocker.

Frank straddled a straight-backed, reed-seated chair on the other side of the nicely roaring fire. The shanty was small but comfortable with well-crafted furniture. Frank seemed a man of many abilities. She listened to Jamie's measured breathing.

"Quite gallant of you to take responsibility for Jamie. You have many admirable traits."

Frank sat rigid as a gatepost, both large hands on his thighs, staring into the dancing flames. His face flushed. "Thanks."

The stone fireplace, beautifully built, breathed expertise. With the one in the shanty so nice, the one inside the cabin must be breath-taking. The man had skilled hands. Outside the wind howled. When Frank wasn't gazing at her like she'd become a delicious Christmas Plum Pudding, she could actually gather her scattered thoughts. Strange and incredibly exciting being alone with him. She clasped her arms around her waist. His presence caused butterflies to flutter in her stomach and blushes to heat her face. Now that Jamie slept, the silence seemed intolerable. Goosebumps bubbled on her arms.

"Do you always wear two guns?"

Dark, wavy hair fell over his forehead when he nodded. "Part of my job. If a desperado caught me without my weapons, he'd shoot me dead. I have enemies, and I uphold the law." He smiled. "I hope my revolvers don't bother you. I only take them off when I sleep." He spread a well-formed, muscular hand over his face as if to wipe away difficult thoughts. "Then I keep both guns close where I can reach them fast."

"I see." Rather than disliking his revolvers, the walnut grips stuck into the holsters gave her a sense of his invincibility. Not many men would dare pick a fight with Frank. "I believe it's time I took my leave." She smiled and stood.

Frank pushed back from his chair, unfolded his athletic frame, strode to the window, pulled aside what looked like a flour-sack curtain, and gazed into the darkness. "Normally I'd be outside with the lanterns lit, adding on to our cabin. But I can't leave with Chang Fu gone." He turned and tipped his head down towards her. "Do you think you might come over early tomorrow and stay with Bab—Jamie while I finish our cabin?"

"Oh." She *had* promised to care for Frank's baby. "Well, yes, I could drop by for a time if you like."

"Thank you. I'm in a hurry to build that cabin before winter sets in."

That fleeting look. The man wanted to marry her immediately. He feared she would leave. Delightful shivers slipped down her spine. She was *wanted*. Plus, the big man had a nice presence about him. An air of gentleness, yet one of command. Perhaps he *was* a man she could trust.

A new expression flickered across his face to be immediately erased with a look she christened his Unreadable Sheriff Face. A firmer mouth, eyes slightly narrowed, and a noticeable hardening of the jaw. His stern countenance broadcast his intent to face any situation, pleasant or not.

But she'd read that fleeting expression. Goodness, Frank yearned for her to *stay tonight*. He desired to get acquainted with the woman he expected to become his wife.

"I don't think my staying longer is a good idea. Perhaps tomorrow after breakfast we could discuss our situation."

His Unreadable Sheriff Face dissolved. Eyebrows raised and mouth slackened. "How do you…can you…?"

"No. I'm not a mind reader."

Frank shook his head and meandered across the small room to squat on the edge of the cot. "One hundred years ago people in Salem would have hung you as a witch."

She laughed. "But, really, Frank, I *am* uncomfortable just you and me together here. I hate to leave you alone with Jamie, but surely you're accustomed to caring for him."

He leaped up. "I've survived caring for Bab—Jamie before. But this is the first time I've been about to marry, and I'd like to get to know my bride."

She shifted on the comfortable rocker. "We have three months until Christmas."

"I have very little free time." He stood at her feet, arms locked behind his back, brow furrowed. "But I don't want you to be uncomfortable."

"Tomorrow morning at daybreak, I'll return to care for Jamie."

He nodded. "You would do that? I thought Chang Fu would stay on until we got married." Ruddiness tinged his cheeks. "I hate to put you out, but my day starts early." He dragged his hand through his dark hair. "My cow's in the stable across from my office."

"You have a cow?"

"Right. I bring a bucket of milk here each morning and another in the evening for the baby. I'll leave the milk on the front steps to stay cool."

"I saw the ingenious way you filled the baby bottle. I think I can handle that as well."

"Good. Whenever you need anything, I'll be working on the cabin, working my claim, or facing down desperadoes. Except when I'm chasing crooks, I'll just be a hail away." He paced the small room. "You stick your head out that door and call. I'll drop everything and come running."

"I'll try not to call."

"I have the shanty set up for straining the meat and vegetables I bring home. You'll have to prepare Jamie's food. I'd be pleased if you'd stop by next door when I'm working on our cabin and talk with me. That way I can keep in touch with Jamie."

Ha, he wants to keep an eye on me. "I would be happy to do so."

"And, un, if you don't mind..."

That fleeting expression showed whatever was on the man's mind totally concerned him. He paced so close he trod on the tip of her toe.

She scooted her foot back between the rockers. "Yes?"

He raised his brows and widened his eyes.

"It is quite easy to see something else bothers you."

His mouth tilted up at the corners, giving him an almost impish expression. "Got to watch what I think around you. I don't believe in clairvoyance, but you're scary."

Her laugh tinkled out, full and free. The man had a sense of humor.

"But I'd like you to be careful where you go and who you talk with. Angel Vale swarms with hordes of single men who haven't laid eyes on a woman for weeks. When they discover you, a heap of them could make inappropriate advances or even offer marriage." He dug in the pocket of his Levis, and then knelt on the wooden floor in front of her. "I'd be so honored if you'd wear this ring. The gold band's not fancy, and I'll buy you a diamond ring as soon as I have the opportunity. But I'd like for you to wear this one now."

She tried not to shrink away. *Please, Lord, don't let him notice my hesitancy.*

He reached for her hand.

She let him take her cold fingers in his large, warm, callused hand. He slipped a gold ring on the fourth finger of her left hand.

"But this is a wedding band." She tried to slip the ring off.

"Please wear my ring. For now, this will show our promise to one another."

Oh dear Lord. Someone else's baby and a wedding band. I know I signed the Letter of Agreement for this, but I'm not sure I can keep my pledge with this particular Southern man. Please help me.

"If you think it's necessary, I'll wear this ring when I go out."

Without his moving a muscle, his face or was it his soul, cried out in pain?

Oh no, she held this poor man's heart in the palm of her hand. She averted her gaze to the room's single window, unable to witness the torment he tried to hide. "I'll gladly wear your ring and care for your child." What was she saying? She couldn't put her life in this man's hands simply to ease his suffering. She must think of herself as well. "But, Frank, I'll—"

He tapped a gentle finger to her lips. "I'll escort you back to the lodging house. I'll see you tomorrow. I'm usually working on our cabin before sunrise, but you'll find coffee warming on the stove." He touched the curl on her cheek. "We'll breakfast later at the Eatery."

She nodded and glanced at the modern wood-burning stove, which along with a dry sink, occupied half the side of the small room. He'd made the shanty quite comfortable. And sufficient for cooking. So why breakfast at the restaurant? Because being alone with him distressed her and he knew it?

He sprang up from his knees, and his big boots clomped across the thin rug on the wooden floor. With gentle hands, he lifted Jamie from the baby bed, cuddled him to his chest for a moment, then wrapped the baby in a blanket, and cradled him in one arm.

Obvious love for the child spilled from his expression.

He helped her with her cape. With his free hand snugged in the small of her back, he escorted her back through the darkness to the lodging house. Other couples milled around the door amid sounds of chatter and soft laughter.

He took her gloved hand, bent over it, and kissed her fingers. Then he was gone, boots thudding on the boardwalk.

She watched his commanding figure disappear into the darkness, her uneven breath visible in the chill air, trying to stop her heart from racing as she twisted the wedding band beneath the glove on her finger.

Tomorrow, she would ask Matthew if he had a more suitable groom. A Wyoming man.

Only Gallant Southern Gentlemen from the Deep South kissed a lady's hand. Frank displayed an enormous sense of duty. Triple duty now, to the child, to his calling as sheriff, and to her.

The man's middle name was Duty. His eyes glowed and his chest heaved when he spoke of his work as sheriff. He loved that job. She read the papers. Sheriffs didn't live long in the West. A man had to be fast on the draw to survive. And if he was, outlaws desiring to make a name for themselves drew down on a sheriff with a reputation as a fast draw. From what she'd seen of Frank, her intended groom had great reflexes. He knew how to clear leather fast. The man was good at everything he did.

But Frank had not written that he was a Southerner. He had not written that he'd been made Sheriff of Angel Vale. He'd brought her here under false pretenses.

She didn't like danger. She longed for peace and security.

And Frank had danger, duty, and devotion inscribed all over his face.

How could he so easily fall in love? She hated the role of heartbreaker.

CHAPTER SEVEN

Frank had seen enough outlaws with that *I'll escape the first time the Sheriff's not alert* expression on their faces not to know what Amanda thought. The Circuit Riding Preacher wasn't due again until Christmas day or he'd drag the pastor over tomorrow and tie the knot.

Didn't seem to make any difference to her that he'd gone out on a limb financially and practically sold his soul to pay her transportation to Angel Vale. But having her care for Jamie did take a load off. He'd still have to milk Daisy twice a day, but he'd have more time to finish that cabin knowing Jamie was safe and cared for. He shifted Jamie to his other arm.

At first sight, the baby loved Amanda. And she seemed to take to Jamie. No problem there. Like him, she seemed certain the boy wasn't his son, else she wouldn't have wanted to change Baby Frank's name.

He was the problem. For whatever reason, his bride didn't like him. He had to find out why.

Whatever he did, he'd keep a keen eye on Amanda. No way would he let her escape.

Scary how she seemed to read his mind. He'd have to watch out for that too.

She'd been nervous with him in the shanty. Did she think he would force her to do something against her will? If she really didn't want to marry him, no matter how much doing so hurt, he would let her go. She roused feelings inside his chest he'd never imagined possible. If another man so much as looked as her with lewd intent…. His fingers twitched above the handle of his revolver.

What kind of experience had Amanda had with men? Was he too big and tall for her? She was so petite. Smaller than any of the other women he knew. Just looking at her made his throat close and his heart thud loud enough for her to hear. He'd never been clumsy, but around her his hands and feet got tangled. He dare not let himself move too close to her when they were alone. Who knew what his strange, new emotions would cause him to do?

He held the sleeping child next to his chest and raced back toward the shanty. Still time tonight to work on the cabin. He grunted. Maybe he should talk with Jake and Matthew. Ask them how to go about getting acquainted with his bride. Maybe they could tell him what about his person repelled her.

No. He'd never been one to ask for advice. Wasn't about to start. He could handle one small woman.

As he sped pass the jail, Brenda all but ran into his chest. He lurched to a stop. "Hey, Brenda."

"Yeah, Frankie." She gasped and craned her neck to look up at him. "I just wanted to remind you that anything you need, I'm your woman."

He spoke low so as not to wake Jamie. "Can't stop to talk. I'm on my way back to the shanty to put Jamie to bed."

"Jamie?"

"Baby Frank. Amanda and I decided to call him by his middle name."

She gave him a saucy smile. "You mean your high-faluting lady decided to call Baby Frank, Jamie."

"She's going to be my wife. So you can call her Amanda. Maybe you two could become friends. She—"

"You got to be joshing me, Frank. How can we be friends when she's stealin' my man?"

45

"I've never been your man. And I never would be, even if Amanda hadn't arrived." He gave her arm a tap. "Why don't you get to know her? Tell her why you like living in Angel Vale. Show her—"

"No." Brenda's eyes filled with tears, and she pushed closer, all but waking Jamie. "We can never be friends. She took you away from me."

He swiped his Stetson off and slapped the big hat against his leg. "I've never been yours. You know that. Come on, do this one thing for me." Brenda wouldn't be his first choice for a friend for Amanda, but she was the best the town offered. Sal was too busy. And the Indian women didn't speak much English.

Jamie opened one eye and yawned.

"You been leading me on all this time, Frankie? A girl has dreams."

"Stow the dramatics. There are a hundred other men in this town who'll let you wind them around your little finger." He stepped away from the tall redhead. "Tell you what. You make yourself a friend to Amanda, and I'll give you the next gold nugget I dig up."

Brenda put a finger to her chin. Her hazel eyes took on a new gleam. "Give me your next five gold nuggets and you got yourself a deal."

Frank gulped. He resettled the blanket around Jamie. Take him months to dig up that many nuggets. Wasn't like they pushed themselves to the top of the rocks in the icy creek water. "Two."

"Done. Just don't you forget to pay me, or I'll tell your little mail-order angel."

"I won't forget. If you tattle, the deal's off. Understood?" He held out a hand to shake.

She stood on tiptoes and, mashing Jamie between them, grabbed him around the neck. Before he could break loose, she slapped a kiss right on his lips. And wouldn't let go.

He held Jamie with one arm, grabbed Brenda around the waist, and deposited her on the boardwalk a few feet away. "Enough. Deal's sealed."

"You sure got it bad for that little piece of fluff."

"And you promised to make yourself her friend." He turned and stomped on into the darkness.

He blew on his hands, stiff in the chill air. Cold or no, he'd get out to the cabin and work on getting that home done. He could add one more log all the way around before midnight. Maybe when she saw how big and cozy her home would be when he finished construction, she would want to stay. He'd get a haircut tomorrow and buy a new shirt. Somehow, he'd have to fit in working the claim.

Women needed friends. Having Brenda for a friend might tip the balance in his favor. Worth a try. Brenda would befriend a grizzly to earn those two gold nuggets.

He'd stop at nothing to keep his little Christmas Belle.

CHAPTER EIGHT

The sun hadn't risen above the hills. The brightening at the horizon gave only the promise of dawn when Amanda knocked on Frank's shanty door.

No answer.

Should she open the door and walk inside?

She glanced down the single street toward where Frank had said his jail was located.

There he was, striding toward her, a full milk pail swinging from one hand and a pickaxe draped over his other shoulder. The rising sun silhouetted his tall figure, his long legs devouring the distance between them. With his six-guns strapped to his lean hips, he looked every inch the Wyoming cowboy.

She caught her breath. Her heart thudded. If she'd worn a tight corset, she would have swooned.

"Morning." A charming grin lit his face. "Thanks for arriving so early. Jamie was still sleeping when I left. He's only been alone a few minutes."

"Beautiful day." Was it? She hadn't noticed until he came into sight.

"It is now that you're here." He opened the shanty door for her.

She all but skipped inside. "Perhaps if I came to the shanty before you milked Daisy, we wouldn't have to leave Jamie alone."

"I would sure appreciate that."

She leaned over the crib. Jamie's tiny hand twitched and his eyes opened. He greeted her with a wide toothless smile and coos.

Together she and Frank managed to funnel some of the milk from the pail into the baby bottle. The two of them all but overwhelmed the small space. She had to edge around him to reach the rocker. Until the day before, she'd never been alone with a man. His vibrancy permeated the shanty, making her tingle from head to toe.

"Coffee's on the stove. I've got to run. Heard tell some of the fellas at the creek found some nuggets. I've got to pan some gold before they get any nuggets that might wash on downstream from my stake." He bent, and his lips touched her cheek in a feather-soft caress.

His touch left a warm, sweet spot on her cheek.

The door opened letting in the promise of a lovely autumn day. Then he was gone.

Amanda lifted Jamie from the cradle. His wide, blue eyes smiled up at her. She settled in the rocker, and the baby soon emptied the bottle.

She laid Jamie on the sideboard and changed and dressed the contented child. How could a mother leave such a sweet baby on a danger-loving man's doorstep? The woman must have been desperate. Why else would she choose such a man to care for her child?

Ha. Easy answer to that one. The big man engraved duty on his forehead.

With Jamie in her arms, she moved to the dying fire and stooped to poke the embers into life. She threw on another log from the new heap by the stone fireplace. For a shanty, the place was cozy and warm. The little boy grew heavy, so she shifted him to one hip. He was a good child. Seldom cried. Looked at her with a big grin as if she were the best sight in the world to him. He shared that with his adopted father. Both males expected her to fill a large void in their lives.

Could she do it? Did she want to?

She'd paced the room. Jamie snuggled to her shoulder as she rubbed his sturdy back to burp him. She'd thought she might miss the breezy two-story Saltbox home in Maine, but she didn't. Not a whit. Nor did she miss Uncle Stephan's grumbling and complaining. But she did miss the feel of dough in her hands and the scents of good things baking.

She touched the sideboard Frank must have hammered together. A bit small, but perhaps she could set up a small bakery and sell her delicacies. She had no wish to burden Frank, although he seemed to have enough money to take care of her needs without undue stress.

She threw the quilt on the wooden floor and laid Jamie on his stomach on the soft covering. He gurgled, laughed and waved his arms and legs like a turtle caught on his shell. She glanced at the cot where Frank must have slept. The single, thin blanket had been tucked in neatly. She poured steaming coffee into the cup he set out for her on the home-made table.

She tried a sip. Umm. Strong, but flavorful. What would she do all day while she cared for Jamie? She sipped her coffee. How long since Frank had eaten a piece of home-made pie?

Rummaging through the food on the shelves built into the side of the shanty, she pulled out some flour, cinnamon, and a bag of apples. She had plenty of milk. Frank would milk Daisy twice a day, and the cow had already given almost a full bucket. Behind a burlap bag of beans, she discovered a large bag of sugar. After she found a big pie tin and a wooden bowl and spatula, she began to sing. Did Frank have a rolling pin? No matter. She'd shape this first crust with her hands.

She peeled the apples, stirred in the sugar and cinnamon, and spooned the filling into the lovely crust she'd made. She cleaned the sideboard and set the pie on the wooden surface.

Nice to have baby chuckles and cooing to cheer her rather than Uncle's frowns and grumbles. She could so fall in love with the cuddly baby. Someone had to love the child. She knew too well how not being loved felt and what lack of love did to a person's soul.

If she let herself, she could bask in the love that radiated from Frank. She'd not been adored for too, too long, and the love that poured from him warmed her soul.

But the man had so little time for her. He'd been in such a rush this morning, that he'd barely taken time to tip his hat. With three jobs vying for his time, where would she fit in? Just as mother to his adopted child?

And what if she allowed her starved heart to fall in love with Frank? He'd chase after outlaws and be gone for days.

He might return draped over a saddle. Dead.

She shivered.

During the wagon ride, either Jake or Matthew had mentioned the Cheyenne and Black Hills Stage. Would it arrive today? She could take the stage as far as the Cheyenne stop of the Union Pacific railroad, and then take the train southeast to any place she desired.

Jamie laughed his gurgling little laugh as if the whole world delighted him. She knelt, lifted him to her chest, hugged him, and joined her laugh with his. What a sweet little boy. His little legs tucked around her and his little arms hugged her.

He would be difficult to leave.

A knock on the door, and Frank burst into the room.

She caught her breath.

Mud clung to his cowboy boots. His ruddy wind-blown face broke into a grin when he saw them. He hung his jacket and Stetson on the pegs by the door. Rays of morning sun through the window caught the silver on his sheriff's star, making the badge sparkle on the brown store-bought shirt he wore. His guns hung low over his lean hips. He'd had a haircut, a shave, and smelled manly.

Amanda pressed her lips together.

How often had Aunt Bessie May shaken a finger at her? She could hear her voice now. *Don't you ever trust a handsome man. If a man's got a good-looking face, you can bet your life, he can't be trusted.*

But Aunt Bessie Mae *hadn't always* been right. She'd refused to leave her big home in Atlanta when the soldiers ordered them all out. Instead she'd sent Amanda to live with her older brother in Maine. And neither Uncle Stephan nor she heard from Aunt Bessie Mae again. Stephan said she probably was too stubborn to leave her home and died in the fire that burnt Atlanta to the ground.

So if Aunt Bessie Mae had been wrong about not leaving Atlanta, why couldn't she be wrong about not trusting handsome men? Yet logic couldn't dredge Aunt Bessie Mae's warning out of her mind.

Frank hurried to her side. "Here let me carry Jamie. He's a heavy lad." He held out his strong arms.

Daylight didn't dim the man's fine looks. His brown eyes romped with life, dark chocolate like fine candy.

"Thank you. He is a bit heavy." She smiled. "Did you find any nuggets?"

"Just this one." He held a small nugget that seemed lost in the palm of his big, calloused hand.

"That looks like a good morning's work."

"Not so good as I'd hoped." He glanced at the sideboard. "Is that a pie sitting there? *That* looks like a good morning's work."

As slow warmth at his praise oozed through her, she nodded.

"Shall we head on over to the Angel Vale Eatery for breakfast?" He shifted Jamie to one arm and cocked his elbow for her to take. "I want to show off my soon-to-be-wife."

A shudder blew over the warmth. "Thank you." How could she hurt this man? He was so eager to marry her. The longer she stayed in town, the harder he would take her loss.

They strolled together into the restaurant, and he seated her at the same table they'd used last night. He dropped into the seat across from her, Jamie snug in his lap.

The pretty red head rushed out. "You want breakfast?"

"None for me, thanks, Brenda. I'll just have coffee." Frank glanced at Amanda. "Are you hungry? Order whatever you want."

"Yes, please. I'll have breakfast."

"Right away, Miss." The girl Frank called Brenda slid him a funny glance, then she smiled at Amanda. "It'll be a pleasure to serve you."

Well, that was a complete change from last night. Brenda had been as hostile as a hen protecting her chickens when she'd served them dinner. Now she beamed as if she and Amanda were best of friends. But that dead-giveaway-glance that passed between Frank and Brenda meant the two of them had an agreement about something. And judging from Brenda's new conduct, that agreement had something to do with Amanda and Brenda becoming friends.

As soon as Brenda sashayed to the kitchen, Amanda touched Frank's forearm. "You and Brenda are up to something. Mind sharing?"

Red flooded Frank's face. He looked like a kid caught with his hand in the cookie jar.

CHAPTER NINE

Amanda caught the truth in his fleeting expression before Frank smacked on his Unreadable Sheriff Face.

"Um...Brenda said she'd like to be your friend." He kept his dark eyes on Jamie.

Truth, but not exactly. Hm.

"So, tell me." His white teeth glinted in a charming grin. "Why did you decide to leave everything you know and travel all this way west to marry a stranger?"

Her heart kicked like a new-born colt. Nice. She liked communication straight to the point. Get the embarrassment over immediately. "My Uncle Stephan found me a burden. I refuse to be a burden to anyone."

His brown eyes turned darker chocolate. He rubbed a gentle hand over the soft blonde curls on Jamie's head. "But I'm certain there were countless fishermen in Maine, even in a small village, who'd have given their right eye and arm, with a leg thrown in, to marry you."

Ah, there it was. Time to confess the unpleasant truth. She picked up her napkin and tucked the cloth in her lap.

Brenda arrived with a coffee pot and two cups and placed them properly on the white tablecloth. She gave Amanda a friendly smile. "Perhaps sometime today I could walk you around Angel Vale, show you the town, and introduce you to the locals."

"I'd love that. But the baby."

"Oh, my Granny has a pushchair we can borrow. Some moms

call them prams. Granny will lend you hers as long as you need one. Baby F—Jamie won't be taking steps for six to eight months yet. You can use Granny's pram until Jamie learns to walk."

Amanda stiffened. So, Brenda had talked earlier with Frank. Else she'd not have known Baby Frank as Jamie. Interesting. Had Frank persuaded Brenda to show her around? What a thoughtful man.

"That would be so very helpful. Thank you. I'd like to thank your Granny in person."

"Oh, no need for that." Brenda glanced at Frank, gave him the eye, rattled her tray and turned. "I'll bring your breakfast now."

Interesting. What scheme had the two of them hatched?

Before Brenda reached the kitchen door, Frank repeated, "Why didn't you marry any of the men in Maine?"

Amanda lifted her water glass and sipped, watching him over the rim. He tried to conceal his concern, but he worried about her reason. He thought she had some dark secret to hide. She must set his mind at ease.

"I never enjoyed living in Merville. A fishy smell hung over the town all the time. During the day Merville rivaled a ghost town when all the fishermen sailed away. They'd return in the evening, smelly and cranky. Then I hated the tedious task of cleaning all those fish and boiling those lobsters and crabs the men brought home in their nets. Plus, I discovered I have an allergy to sea food, so my food choices were limited."

That fleeting look on his face proved he didn't believe her.

"That's it? That's why you left?"

She glanced at the door. Where was Brenda with the food? "I did have a particular suitor. He loved me. My Uncle encouraged him in every way, saying the match between us was the best in Maine. But…" She smoothed her French Roll and curled a free ringlet around her finger. "The night Uncle was certain Beau would propose, instead the Southern Gentleman"—she couldn't keep the scorn from her voice— "slunk to Uncle's porch with downcast eyes and face as gloomy as a wet weekend. He fell to his knees before me and informed me his family insisted he marry a more suitable woman. He'd asked for the hand of the banker's daughter rather than the hand of a mere baker's daughter."

Surprise flashed over his face. He quickly masked his expression. She had to admire him. He erased his expression faster than anyone else she'd ever tried to read.

"This man chose another woman over you? Hard to accept."

"Yes. Well, her family had wealth on their side. He was the only son and heir. They threatened to cut him out of their lives if he married me." She smoothed her wry tone. "God bless him, he was a Southern Gentlemen who chose duty over love."

"Idiot I would say. Did he love you?"

"Yes, Beau truly loved me."

"Double idiot! Sounds like your Beau had the backbone of an octopus."

"So, you would have responded differently?"

"Absolutely." He touched the wedding band on her finger. "But I'm certain another man would have stepped in and claimed you."

She gently moved his hand away, but not before her cheeks heated. "I was humiliated. I didn't fare well with all the *poor Amanda* people from that town. They had pitched in to help me plan the wedding. Uncle Stephan ordered my gown, and they assisted me with my trousseau."

He winced.

He may as well know the whole awful story. "I gathered linens and dishes and articles I'd need as a married woman even in the rustic fishing village where Uncle fled during the war to keep from serving a cause he didn't believe in."

"And those things are in the trunks I carried to your room at the lodging house?"

56

She nodded.

"So heartbroken, you came here to me?"

She smiled and shook her head. "No. Looking back, I don't think I ever loved Beau. He swept me off my feet with his Southern charm. I never grew accustomed to the clipped speech and laconic ways of the men of Maine. He was fresh air in the fish market."

"So why did you decide to come to me?"

"The ladies from the church showed me your letter and asked if I was interested. You sounded as if you needed a good, practical, woman, and I needed a new start and a new life in a new town where no one knew me."

He took both her hands and gazed deep into her eyes. "This is a new town. You will definitely have a new life. With a new husband. Jamie and I and Angel Vale are exactly what you hoped for." His Adam's apple rose and fell in his throat. He rubbed his thumbs over the backs of her hands. "And, as a Southern Gentlemen myself, I choose *love* over duty.

Amanda gasped. Would he really?

Brenda rattled over with breakfast and Frank slowly released her hands. The pretty redhead took care setting the food out, smiling, and chatting. After she pranced back to the kitchen, Frank laid a warm, strong hand on Amanda's arm. "And you will have new friends."

She took her time to butter her biscuit. "Are these friends you arranged for?"

Coffee half-way to his lips, Frank's hand jerked, and coffee spilled over the cuff of his new shirt. Jamie squealed with delight and wriggled on Frank's lap.

"I arranged for?"

"I noticed your silent communication with Brenda." She sampled a bite of scrambled egg. Good to get the conversation off herself.

"You do practice mentalism. Or is your gift called telepathy?"

"Neither. I'm simply alert to people's expressions."

"And you're darned smart. I like both in a woman." He leaned forward and folded her hand in his. "In fact, there is nothing I don't like about you. I couldn't have received a more perfect Christmas Angel." Red darkened his ruddy cheeks. His brown eyes melted with admiration.

Her back stiffened. "Yes, well, Beau said almost the same words." She jabbed at the large slab of meat on her plate. "What is this?"

"Elk meat." He leaned back in his wooden chair and juggled Jamie on his knee. "So…because one man…" he hesitated as if searching for the right word.

Dumped her. Left her at the altar. Trampled her heart with his horse and carriage.

"disappointed you, you're leery of all men." He moved Jamie to his arms, pulled him to his chest, and patted his bottom. Jamie laid his blonde fuzzy head on Frank's broad shoulder and closed his blonde lashes.

She nodded and attacked the eggs again.

"Look at me."

She raised her head.

"You read expressions. Do I have the same expression as that fool who disappointed you?"

His gaze was steady. His entire countenance appeared as open and honest as any she'd gazed into.

"I'm a Christian man." He blinked. "A new Christian. I do not lie, cheat, or steal. When you become my wife, I will never fancy another woman. I will not deceive you. I will be faithful to you until the day I die." He leaned so close his warm breath stirred her hair. "I will do my best never to disappoint you."

"And if I disappoint you?"

His jaw dropped. "I truly believe you could never disappoint

58

me."

"Why? Because you like my appearance? What if I neglect Jamie? What if I discover a man I prefer to you? What if I don't like this town and want to move away? Will I disappoint you then?"

He blinked.

He'd not gotten beyond her beauty. Just as Beau had never gotten beyond her lack of money. Did southern men only view women in a superficial way? One has money, one has not. One has beauty, one has not. One is chaste, one is not. She was fairly sure Brenda was not chaste, and for that reason Frank didn't want to marry her. Last night Brenda made herself pretty clear that she adored Frank.

"Look, Amanda, let's not delve into things that will never happen. You are a Christian woman. You obviously have a sense of honor. You would not do such things."

No, she wouldn't, but she *was* human. She laid down her fork and dabbed her mouth with her napkin.

"We have three months to get to know one another." He grunted beneath his breath. Then, slowly, reluctantly, like a water pump working a dry well, he spoke through gritted teeth. "If you don't like me well enough to marry me by then, I'll scrape up enough money to send you back home."

"Would you mind putting that in writing?" She dug into her tapestry bag and drew out the paper, ink well, and pen she'd hoped to use to send a letter to Uncle Stephan this morning.

CHAPTER TEN

Frank pushed the paper away. "I'd never force you."

"You're a stranger to me."

"Read my face."

Slowly she retrieved the ink, pen, and paper. "You're an honorable man. I shall accept your word." She deposited her writing items back inside her bag.

"Thank you." He settled Jamie in his lap. The baby's hand started exploring one of Frank's plain leather holsters. He took the little hand and began a game of pat-a-cake with the baby. "So, you found the coffee?"

"Yes, it was quite good."

He laughed. "Strong, you mean."

She nodded.

"What else will you need to take care of Jamie?"

"Nothing." She bobbed her head prettily. "I was about to put a pie in the oven when you came for me."

"I saw that pie. Will we have it for supper?"

"Yes. I hoped to open a bakery here in Angel Vale."

Frank jiggled Jamie's bootie. "I'm not sure about a bakery. We don't have any empty buildings, but I know the owner here at the Eatery, and he'll buy your pies." He rubbed his burning eyes. Long hours must be getting to him. "And, if you want, you could go into the tent camp and sell your pies to the miners. They'd love to get their hands on home-baked pies. But I'll need to accompany you when you make that trek."

Her smile coaxed out tiny dimples. He loved to invite them to venture out of their hiding places and play in her cheeks. She brimmed with surprises, and each one delighted him more. She had such a sunny disposition even after the hard trip, taking care of Jamie, and rising so early this morning. She had a beautiful soul.

And she could bake. He swallowed more coffee. After eating nothing since last night, his mouth watered. He'd no money to waste on food for himself, even though the morning started out so badly. Daisy had been irritable, side-stepping his hands, tromping his feet, and hadn't wanted to give up her milk. Plus, the log he felled for their home had been stubborn enough to fall in the wrong spot. He'd almost crashed the tree into his sluice box.

He took a swig of his coffee and held his cup up for Brenda to refill. His stomach growled. "I love biscuits and gravy."

"Then you shall have them for breakfast tomorrow. I'll have hot biscuits and cream gravy ready for you tomorrow about this time. No sense in eating out when you can have a nourishing breakfast in your own shanty."

He nodded, not even trying to keep his intense pleasure out of his expression. How like God to send him a woman both frugal and capable. She was not the china doll he'd feared. "Um, I hope you're staying alone in the shanty during the day won't prove too difficult." She hadn't liked being alone with him. He leaned the chair back on two legs and stretched his long legs in front.

"It is a bit awkward. But I'm certain I'll adjust." Those dimples flashed again. "There just doesn't seem to be any other place available where I can care for Jamie." She leaned closer, and he caught her sweet scent like an April day in the country after a refreshing shower. "You've made the place cozy."

He slammed his chair back to the floor, leaned across the table, and grabbed her hands. "Wait until you see our cabin. The house will have everything. You and Jamie will have room to entertain."

Her sky-blue eyes sparkled.

"And I'll make the kitchen especially large so you can bake all you want."

"Oh, well, yes."

Suddenly she seemed to draw up into herself, and her manner cooled. He didn't need to be a mind-reader to realize he'd said something wrong. What had he said?

"Excuse me. I must use the facilities."

He rose and balancing Jamie in one arm, plucked out her chair.

"Please, I can find the outhouse on my own. You and Jamie stay here."

****

Amanda wiped a bit of spilt milk from her bodice and waited for the tears spiking behind her eyes to abate. She so hated to see how badly Frank wanted to please her. He wanted so much to touch her. He wanted so much to marry her. She smoothed her hair. No, she wouldn't ask the Marriage Broker for a more suitable groom. She could never live in Angel Vale after she jilted the handsome sheriff. She couldn't stand detecting his pain and the awful blow to his pride. Frank Calloway would be devastated.

She'd just have to catch the stage out of town like the mysterious woman who left her baby in Frank's care. But who could she get to take care of Jamie? The little man had entwined himself around her lonely heart with his unconditional love and happy cooing. None of the brides she'd taken the long wagon ride with would do. They all had plans of their own. And some were taking on other men's children, and others brought their own children with them. No, none of them had the ability to include Jamie in their plans.

Perhaps she could take Jamie with her. She leaned against the outside wall of the restaurant. No. Frank loved Jamie. Anyone with two eyes could see the tenderness he used with the boy. Besides the only danger worse than a woman traveling alone was a woman traveling alone with a baby. Neither of them would be safe.

62

What could she do? She'd find herself so easily falling in love with Frank. Did she dare risk her heart? She washed her hands in the basin outside the outhouse. Frank was safe. He was a haven in a world that hadn't provided a safe place for her. Winter was sneaking in. Never a good time to travel. The cabin he worked on sounded so wonderful. And Frank didn't mind her desire to set up shop and bake. He even offered to share the work with her.

The man was too unbelievably wonderful.

He'd said he would chose love over duty. Perhaps he would. And Aunty had been wrong about handsome men. At least Frank could be trusted. Perhaps she *would* stay and marry him.

Loud explosions jolted her. Seemed the nerve-wracking noises came from Main Street.

Were those gunshots? She flicked water off her hands and raced into the back door of the eatery. All the customers crowded together gazing out the front window. Frank's overturned chair lay on the floor. Brenda stood at the window, Jamie on her hip.

Amanda lifted her long skirts and sped to the window, but too many people congested the space. Even on tiptoe, she couldn't see over their heads. She dashed to the front door. A string of new shots blasted outside.

She opened the door and peeped out.

Four horses thundered down the street toward the wilderness. One man lay in the packed dirt, arms flung wide.

CHAPTER ELEVEN

Frank, a six-shooter in each hand, executed a flying leap, straddled Diablo, and kneed his horse into a gallop. He'd not had time to strap on an extra bandolier of bullets. He had only those left in his two guns and in his gun belt. He shoved the weapon he'd almost emptied into its holster. The gang robbing the gold assay office thundered down the street.

An escaping thief fired over his shoulder targeting Frank.

Frank lay low over Diablo's withers. Diablo laid back his ears and stretched out into his fastest gallop.

Already in rough country, one criminal's horse stumbled and fell. The rider pitched head-first over the horse's head, hit rocks, splayed on the ground, and didn't move.

Frank galloped past, intent on the two escaping riders. They separated, one bolting into the hills, the other speeding over the stagecoach trail. He followed the trail.

Easy to let the man go. Now he had a fiancée, a baby, and a cabin to think of. A bullet zinged past his ear. But his duty lay in catching these robbers and transporting them to justice. If he didn't, Angel Vale would evolve into a goal for masses of thieves and gain a reputation for lawlessness.

He aimed and took a careful shot. The bullet hit home, and the man slumped from the saddle.

Frank pulled Diablo to a standstill, his gun on the thief. The man rolled over and raised an arm in the air. The other arm hung useless, blood flooding his shirt.

Just a kid.

Frank threw a lasso over the kid's horse, leaped down from Diablo, and hoisted the wounded lad onto his horse. He tied the bandit's good wrist to the pommel of his saddle, turned both horses and headed back toward Angel Vale.

He'd have to track the other man. Might take him a day or two. Amanda would need to take full charge of Jamie and building the cabin would have to wait.

Hard to court his angel when he camped in the wilds. But he had to catch that other thief. Love would have to wait.

****

Amanda learned the thief in the street was dead, his stiff hand clutching a bag of nuggets. The assayer took charge of the stolen gold. Townspeople melted back to their own daily tasks.

Several men she didn't know carted off the body. Perhaps they were undertakers.

She alone stood in the middle of the street gazing after the out-of-sight riders. Nothing to see but empty, rough countryside.

Oh Father, please keep Frank safe.

She pulled her shawl closer around her shoulders and returned to the eatery to claim Jamie from Brenda.

****

Midnight snuck in before Frank knocked on the shanty door and strode inside. She'd fallen asleep in the rocker, her heavy shawl as a covering, and listened, still half-asleep, to the tiptoeing of his boots on the wooden floor. The smell of outdoors and manhood permeated his clothes.

Mm, no fishy odor clung to him. She drowsed with her eyes half-open. Nothing of Maine. He was all clean outdoors.

He lit a candle and crouched by her side. "I've got to track down the other robber. I locked his partner in jail. Brenda will see to the prisoner's feeding and other needs." He ran a caressing finger down her cheek.

Now wide awake, she smiled at his warm touch. All her senses tingled with delight. Her cheek heated where his calloused finger caressed her.

"Would you mind moving some of your things in here and caring for Jamie while I'm gone?"

"Of course, I will." Her voice still sounded thick with sleep.

"I shouldn't be gone more than a day or two." He braced both hands on the rocker's arms, leaned in, and kissed her lightly on the lips.

Oh my! Beau had kissed her a number of times, but he'd never left her with the thrilling desire to have more that Frank's kiss did. The man's lips felt soft, and firm, and warm. And like everything else about him, absolutely masculine.

Then he was gone.

****

Amanda endured the endless wait, staying day and night in Frank's shanty. She snuggled Jamie to her chest and grew more attached to his sweet baby ways by the hour.

Frank had said more robbers blew into Angel Vale every day. Could she be more frightened for his safety if she loved him? Could her heart ache more? After he admitted he'd choose love over duty, she'd begun to dream that maybe God actually brought her to Angel Vale to be Frank's wife and Jamie's mother.

But this awful pain, this spine-chilling waiting weren't to be endured. She watched Brenda and several other ladies of somewhat dubious reputation meander around town with tear-streaked faces. Women she knew Frank had no thought for. Women he didn't want Jamie to grow up around.

She'd only known Frank two days. Perhaps what she felt for him was love. If it was, then love hurt. Hurt more than humiliation. Hurt more than loneliness. Hurt more than rejection. Hurt so much she didn't want any part of love.

Frank tore her heart out riding out into the wilderness alone chasing dangerous criminals. They carried rifles to his revolvers. His big black horse was swift. He'd catch the last thief, unless the outlaw ambushed him first and shot Frank.

Oh, Father God, I'm so frightened for him.

She couldn't let herself love him. She couldn't stand the agony if he were killed. Just when she'd grown to trust and believe in him, she must make a clean break and leave both Frank and Jamie. He could send for another angel.

She could not marry a sheriff.

CHAPTER TWELVE

Amanda bit her nails to the quick. Three weeks he'd been gone, and still no Frank. What if he were dead? What if she hadn't arrived from Merville in time to love and care for Jamie? What would have happened to him? She snuggled the boy to her chest so fiercely he almost woke. Gently she toed the rocker into motion and hummed a lullaby. How long could she wait for Frank without going crazy?

Where is he, Father?

She and Jamie lived cozy and comfortable inside the shanty. She had everything she needed, thanks to Frank's foresight and generosity.

While he chased outlaws, she'd started selling her pies, home-baked breads, and cobblers—anything the folk of Angel Vale asked for. The money she earned put food on the table. She nourished Jamie and stood on her own two feet. Daily, she and Brenda toured the town pushing Jamie in the buggy. She made other friends. She carved out a new way of life in a new town.

But what if Frank never returned? What if his body lay somewhere unburied out in the hills? She'd be devastated.

On the other hand, if Frank did return...her heart beat in her throat, she'd have to live through this grueling, dreadful fear each time he tracked outlaws. But, oh she so wanted to see his dear, rugged face.

His kiss sweetened her dreams, day and night. How she longed to feel those warm, tender lips on hers again. He loved her. No doubt of that. His last fleeting expression told her that he would die for her.

But could she live with the terrifying knowledge that Frank could be murdered anytime—during a routine day or while tracking outlaws—

A knock at the door, then cold air blew in with a sprinkling of snowflakes.

She leapt to her feet, almost dumping Jamie to the raw wooden floor. "Frank!"

The wind slammed the door behind him.

Alive. In one piece. Vivid with life and energy.

She couldn't help herself. She slid Jamie into his cradle and darted into Frank's arms.

He tilted her head back and cold lips melded onto hers sending fire through her body. When he stopped too soon, she thrust her arms around his neck and kissed him again. Her hands unbuttoned his heavy coat, and she pressed against the flannel shirt covering his muscular chest.

"I wanted to make my way home before Thanksgiving."

"Oh, thank God, you did!" She raised her face. "Kiss me again."

He did. She melted.

"So, you missed me? You're glad to see me?"

"Yes. Promise me you won't ever leave like that again."

He dropped his arms, then slowly removed his sheep-skin coat. He plodded over to the fire, bent and rubbed his red hands near the flames. "I can't promise that. Slapping outlaws behind bars is my job." He hid his face, so she couldn't read that quick emotion so readily masked by his Unreadable Sheriff's Face. His square jaw stiffened, and his lips thinned.

Heat flooded her body. Her hands trembled. So *this* was the point at which his Southern-Gentlemen-Duty *overcame* his love for her. She'd thought that conflict solved. Heat burned her face.

He knelt in front of the crackling fire, prodded the logs with the iron poker, and mumbled, "Anything to eat?"

She raced about scrambling up a hearty dinner. Let him eat. Then they'd talk about where his duty lay.

His chocolate eyes in a gaunt, whiskered face showed exhaustion. He yawned.

Very masculine. Very touching but turning him into a stranger.

Night closed in as she set corn bread and beans on the little table. A peach cobbler she'd just baked waited on the warming rack.

The room grew rosy from the glow in the fireplace. She lit some candles.

"Really nice to return home to a beautiful fiancée, a hot meal, and a happy baby. What more could a man want?"

"I'm so glad you're pleased." After her first thrill at seeing him alive, heart-heaviness suffocated her. In Maine, she'd promised herself she would leave if Frank didn't suit. But he did. Oh, he more than satisfied. He delighted her. She loved his sweet grin. Loved his protective ways. Loved his working so hard so they could share a home together. But there was this one thing. This one huge situation. This one obsession she couldn't endure.

"Is something wrong?"

"I'm fine." Of course, she wasn't.

Was there always one abomination that tore couples apart? Frank was willing to work himself to death for her. Which she never had wanted. But the one action she desired above all else, he would not offer.

Could she be strong enough to support him in his role as sheriff of Angel Vale?

While he'd chased the lawbreaker, she'd discovered she was a strong woman, capable of living life on her own. Not beholden to any man. But everything inside her cried out to live life with Frank, as his wife, as the mother of his children, as his helper.

70

She'd tried so hard not to, but she'd fallen in love.

She hadn't counted on the awful dread of his not returning. And by the obstinate expression on his face, Frank told her he loved his job with every fiber of his being. So, Frank wouldn't give up his dangerous job.

And she couldn't live with his putting his life on the line.

****

Thanksgiving came and went. Frank didn't know how to mend their strained relationship. Amanda returned to the shanty each morning, and he walked her to the lodging house each night. He lived in confusion. Did she love him? She'd seemed so happy to see him that night he brought in the outlaw. Why was she so distant now?

He escorted the two outlaws from his jail to Cheyenne, where the judge condemned them to long prison terms. Took him a week. Lots of red tape, and he had to testify at their trial.

His life in Angel Vale settled down to work. On sunny days, he panned gold. But most days he labored day and night on the cabin he'd promised Amanda by Christmas. He planned to move her in Christmas morning after the circuit riding preacher pronounced them man and wife.

But would she marry him?

He'd asked her about the problem that separated them. His job stood directly in the way. She thought of it as duty. Maybe it was?

Why did women worry so?

He would die for Amanda, but give up his job? Could he? If he didn't, would she forsake him? When he thought of her leaving, his heart stopped. His throat closed. His hands grew icy and he dropped the roof logs onto the wrong spot and had to pry the heavy logs up and start over.

Would panning gold and building log cabins for other families bring in enough income to support them? Probably, but his heart hungered to keep the law-abiding citizens of Angel Vale safe. Men tipped their hats and gave respect to the man behind the badge. He needed the excitement of facing down law breakers and setting things right in his town. He was born to be sheriff. Upholding the law was his God-given calling. If he quit, he would surrender a big piece of who he was.

Should he choose duty or love? He'd told Amanda he'd choose love, but the doing was far more difficult than the saying.

If he chose duty, would she marry him anyway?

On Christmas morning he would carry her over the threshold of their new cabin. Then, Lord willing, she would say yes, and they would stand before the preacher and he would marry her.

He had to make a choice.

CHAPTER THIRTEEN

Amanda bundled into her warmest clothes. Outside white, sparkling snow drifted on the boughs of the Christmas tree the townfolk had decorated at the end of Main Street. She'd never seen anything so lovely as the moon shining on the snow-covered streets and surrounding countryside this Christmas Eve.

Frank escorted her and carried Jamie to the Mercantile to sing carols along with most of the other Angel Vale residents. Her heart lifted. She loved singing carols. And Frank's twinkling brown eyes, easy grin, and elated expression revealed that he loved to sing too, and that Christmas was a special time for him as well.

Frank appeared relaxed for the first time since Thanksgiving when he'd chased the outlaw. They sat close together as the traveling preacher delivered an inspiring sermon. Frank folded her hand inside his.

She smiled and squeezed his strong hand. Christmas truly was a blessed time. A time of giving. She so loved remembering how Jesus, though he was God of the universe, had come to earth in the form of a baby and been born in a lowly manger. Jesus offered Himself to every person who chose to receive His gift of eternal life. She loved giving gifts.

With Frank sitting by her side, this Christmas Eve had been more than meaningful. She would store the wondrous time of this very special Christmas in her memory box.

After the service, Frank, Jamie in his arms, tucked her hand in the crook of his arm, and they slogged through the snow to eat dinner at the Angel Vale Eatery. All the while her heart beat unbearably fast. Tomorrow morning, they were to be married. And she had not yet given her answer to Frank.

Inside, seated at their favorite table, Jamie sang da da, the only words he knew, as he tapped a spoon on the wooden tray of his highchair. He'd loved the carol singing and didn't want to stop. Obviously one of his parents had been musical. Not Frank. Though he sang with gusto, the man couldn't carry a tune.

"This is our anniversary." Frank's caramel eyes gazed tenderly into hers. "I met you at dusk just three months ago, and I fell in love with you the moment you ran from Jake's wagon and stared up into my face." He reached across the table and cradled her hands in his. Candlelight glinted on mahogany highlights in his dark, wavy hair. His full lips turned up at the corners as if the two of them had not experienced the last, long difficult month of strained relationship.

"My love, I'm resigning as sheriff of Angel Vale. I'll build log cabins for the people who'll flock into our town come spring. And you'll make me the happiest man in the world if you'll consent to be my wife."

How she'd longed to hear those words. She squeezed his hands.

"Oh, Frank. I've always known you loved me, but I thought you loved duty more." She shook her head. "But, no, I can't ask you to give up your job. You love that job. Every man in town respects you. You don't need to preach about Christ with your lips. You preach about Christ and the Christian life every day with your integrity and steadfastness. No, you cannot relinquish your job. Yours is a God-given calling."

"But—"

She touched a finger to his lips. How she loved the tiny, terrified expression that flashed across his features to be immediately melded into his Unreadable Sheriff Face.

He still feared she would not marry him. The only fear she'd ever seen from the man.

"Just as you're a *True Southern Gentlemen*, I'm a *True Southern Belle*. A Southern belle will do anything for the man of her heart." She smiled and nodded. "When you are in danger, God will give me the grace to trust Him and accept His protection."

Frank almost fell out of his chair. His mouth opened like a fish out of water.

Her laugh tinkled out over the room. "I love you. Merry Christmas."

Frank closed his mouth and nodded, making his dark hair fall over his forehead. He lifted each of her fingers and kissed the tips.

She almost purred. "You've not been sheriff long. Tell me how you got the job?"

"Funny how that happened." He settled back in his chair.

"That day was as crisp and beautiful an autumn day as I can remember. I'd trudged past the Golden Nugget Saloon on my way to the gold assayer's office with my bag of newly mined gold." He grinned. "A fist-fight inside the saloon burst out the swinging doors and landed in the middle of the street. Two of the few women in town happened to be crossing the road and shrieked, or I would have stood to the side like the other men and watched the brawl's outcome." He made a wry mouth. "But I've never been able to ignore a frightened woman. So I stuck my nose in. I'd trained in bayonets and hand-to-hand combat during the war. Even then, at age thirteen, I'd been a tall, muscular lad. So breaking up a fight between drunks had been as easy as throwing a two-day old calf. I was struck dumb when Jake pinned that badge on my chest. I'd not wanted to take on the additional duty, but Jake Underwood was mighty persuasive.

Jake offered money, plus the office and the jail. Other than drunks and claim-jumpers, the town seemed peaceful enough. So, at first, I spent most of my time panning my claim. I'd taken over the duties of sheriff with a light heart." His face tightened. "But lawlessness sprang up like mushrooms after a heavy rain." He leaned his chair back on two legs and pulled in a deep breath. "Take Levi Harper's younger brother, Seth. Got into mischief faster than a sack full of rattlesnakes. The kid badgered me like a weasel in a hen house. I had to handle Seth with kid gloves because Levi owns the richest mine in town and he's a friend. Kid's only eleven and with a new Mom seems to be straightening out. So that's the long and short of it."

He cuddled her hand inside his. "More importantly, what made you change your mind?"

"Some of the other Mail Order Angels told me that before Matt Thomas advertised for brides, Jake Underwood had one requirement for procuring brides. He took his demand from Genesis Chapters 24 and 25."

"Abraham insisted his son Isaac's bride must not be a daughter of Canaan but must come from his own home country and family. So, Abraham's servant traveled to Mesopotamia, to the city of Nahor, to find a bride for Isaac." She smiled.

"I remember." Frank caressed her fingers. His eyes twinkled. Crinkles appeared in the corners of his eyes.

"Because of that, Jake Underwood stipulated that we twelve brides must come from his hometown, Merville, Maine. Jake echoed Abraham's instruction to his servant to find a bride for his son, Isaac, in his hometown." She pulled in a long breath. "So, God had His Hand in all of this Mail Order Bride business. When I agreed to come, I echoed Rebekah's agreement to come, sight unseen, to marry Isaac."

Frank nodded. "Yes, I knew about Jake's provision. And like Abraham and his servant, I prayed the woman God selected for me would answer, *yes.*" He grinned. "And you finally did."

She smiled and twisted the wedding band on her finger. "Yes, I did. But neither my journey nor my decision was easy." She gazed down at their entwined hands. "Rebekah's task wasn't easy either." She peeked under her lashes at Frank. "When Rebekah met Abraham's servant, that servant prayed she would perform a difficult task to prove she was God's choice for Isaac. Rebekah had to *offer* to water the servant's ten camels. She had only the pitcher she carried on her shoulder to fill the water trough. And camels drink tremendous amounts of water."

Amanda lifted her index finger and traced Frank's lips. His Adam's apple traveled up and down the tanned expanse of his throat.

"That job probably took Rebekah hours of extra work. What if Rebekah had been unwilling to answer the still, small voice of God nudging her to rise above the necessities of hospitality and water those ten camels?" She touched the cleft in his chin. "Rebekah would have missed the love of her life."

Frank ran a caressing finger up and down her cheek. "But she didn't. And neither did you."

Delightful shivers scurried from her scalp to her fingertips. "Think of this, Rebekah had to leave her family, her familiar circumstances, her home, and ride off on a camel into the unknown." Amanda pulled in a deep breath. "Frank, darling, you've made my journey to Angel Vale end so very beautifully with the lovely cabin, the beautiful child, and all the caring things you've done for me. You've shown me great devotion."

Frank leaned over and kissed her on the lips. "And Isaac loved Rebekah the first moment he saw her from afar. You read in my expression how I loved you the moment I saw your gorgeous blue eyes gazing into mine. You had such intensity, as if you could look into my soul."

"And don't you see God's hand in the fact that Jake looked for brides from Maine, but he found you, an Atlanta girl, for me an Atlanta man? Sort of like the servant who brought Abraham's own niece for his son. Though we couldn't see it, God handled the whole situation."

An explosion of joy jolted through her. "I'm so thankful God showed me that I need to go above and beyond what I have a heart to do. I must accept your difficult job as sheriff. I suspect I'll need to renew that commitment each time you face danger. I'll have to remind myself that Rebekah didn't change Isaac. She went to him in blind trust and accepted him where he was, as he was, for what he was."

She touched the stubble on Frank's lean cheek. "And that's what I will do with you, my love. I'll trust God for your safety as you face down all the outlaws that infect this town with their evil. I'll support you in every way. Together we'll make Angle Vale a safe and wonderful place in which to live."

His grin grew larger, white teeth gleaming. "You are the love of my life. A fine Christian woman."

Her cheeks heated. "What better time to get married than on Christmas Day? The day when God came down from heaven and changed the world."

Yesterday, she'd ironed her beautiful wedding dress, and at last she would wear her white gown to marry the love of her life. She'd have no more bad memories to associate with the lovely, silky gown. She hummed a bit of *I Heard The Bells On Christmas Day.*

"After we wed, I'll save my elegant gown for our daughter who absolutely, without question, will be yours." She kissed Jamie's plump jam-smeared cheek. "And our Jamie will grow and thrive and be accepted as if he were our first born. I couldn't love him more."

Outside a Christmas bell chimed. Inside Frank's delightful lips met hers.

A joyous shiver warmed her whole body. The Lord gave her everything she ever wanted.

The Beginning

AVOIDING THE MISTLETOE
BY
ANNE GREENE

SCRIPTURE: *Therefore if any man be in Christ, he is a new creature: old things are passed away; behold, all things are become new. II Corinthians 5:17.*

Tradition: A man is allowed to kiss any woman standing beneath the mistletoe, and bad luck befalls any woman who refuses the kiss. With each kiss a berry is plucked from the mistletoe. The kissing must stop after all the berries have been removed.

DEDICATION

This book is dedicated to all my readers who believe in falling in love and living happily ever after.
I also dedicate this book to my fellow Mistletoe, Jingle Belles, and Second Chances authors: Lana Kruse, James Yarbrough, and Linda Baten Johnson
As always, my books are dedicated to my supportive husband, Larry.
And above all, I dedicate this book to my Lord and Savior, Jesus Christ.

Chapter 1

1865 – Lowell, Massachusetts

Olivia Rose Baker glanced up from the headlines in the *Massachusetts Matrimonial Gazette*. With an explosive smack, she slapped the newspaper on top of the breakfast table. "No! I refuse. I absolutely, unconditionally reject this lame-brained scheme!" She set her mouth in a hard line to keep her lips from trembling.

"You've been a widow for six months, dear sister, and take a look around you. The war wrecked our town. The men are dead, never to return. The economy is ruined. With the South destroyed they can't send us any cotton for our textile mills. And without slaves, the South may never recover. Lowell is a ghost town of devastated women, alone with no men to provide for us or offer us protection. No men to give us children." Darcy strode around the kitchen, her red hair flying, her green eyes ablaze. "No men to love."

"Please don't speak to me of love." Olivia gazed down at the slice of bread and the cup of weak coffee that would have to satisfy her empty stomach throughout the long day until dinner tonight.

"Pshaw! So, Howard Baker didn't have enough love in his heart to share with you. Not every man is so self-centered and abusive." Darcy settled into a chair at the table, wet her fingertips, smooshed up the few remaining breadcrumbs from her plate, and licked them into her mouth.

"Darcy Davenport, I never told you Howard mistreated me." Olivia glared daggers at her sister, then nibbled her bread, her stomach rumbling.

"I saw the bruises you tried to hide. I'm no Simple Simon." Darcy snatched the newspaper and shoved the sheets over. "This

Asa Mercer already successfully shipped a boatload of women to Seattle, Washington Territory. He states the ladies all celebrated excellent marriages." Darcy pointed to some lines of print. "The paper says right here that Mr. Mercer isn't searching for just any women as mail-order brides. He's *seeking high-minded women who can exert an elevating influence in Seattle, where there are ten men for every woman. Mail-order brides, yes, but of a certain caliber.*"

"A mail-order bride is a mail-order bride. You meet a man and if he looks at all decent—that is if he's not too old, not too rotund, not too bald, and not too poor, then you decide to marry him." Olivia shoved back her empty plate. "I will never rush into a marriage with a tall, good-looking, and supposedly prosperous male again." She sipped her tepid coffee. If only she had a smidgen of cream or sugar. "A war bride is not dissimilar to a mail-order bride. Besides, look at me." She gestured from her face to her toes. "No man wants to marry a widow without means."

Darcy stamped her button-down shoed foot. "But *I* want to become one of Mr. Mercer's mail-order brides. And I won't move to Seattle without you!"

Olivia gazed past Darcy's bouncy curls, out the window at the back yard draped in an overcast day that promised even more rain. The overgrown weeds and mud-coated garden with a few wilted stalks of corn poking through the unworked soil attested to the fact that no man had inhabited their salt box style home for over four years. The rumpled tool shed appeared to be held up by their weeping willow tree. If one leaned too hard on the other, both would fall. Their back porch had already collapsed.

"Mr. Mercer wants to populate Seattle with women who will bring culture, education and domesticity to that uncivilized city with thousands...of...single...men." Darcy's emerald eyes transformed from flashing to pleading. "Face facts, Olivia Rose, this might be our one chance to marry."

"I repeat. I don't want to wed. I didn't find marriage at all agreeable. I am so happy Howard didn't leave me with child when he marched away with Captain Joshua Chamberlain's Union Regiment." Olivia tried to keep the anger from her voice. No amount of prayer had erased her animosity toward her late husband.

"So, you prefer, at your young age, to remain a widow for the rest of your life? You don't want children?" Darcy leaned across the table. Her warm fingers grasped Olivia's wrist, her heart-shaped face intent. "Olivia Rose, I'm pouring my heart out here."

Olivia sighed and pushed her chair back from the table. So very difficult to deny her younger sister. And until she married Howard, she'd badly wanted children too.

"You prefer to remain here, despite Lowell's bleak prospects? You expect to remain here in our house that is falling down around our heads? A house we can't even sell because no one has money enough to buy it, even if they wanted this old wreck." Tears rose in Darcy's minty-green eyes. "You choose to remain in Massachusetts even though you know I won't ever find a husband here. You want me to remain a spinster my entire life!"

A black curtain strangled Olivia's heart. She rose and wrapped her arms around her sister's rigid shoulders. "Darling, you know I would do anything for you. Except I refuse to become a mail-order bride."

Darcy gazed up, her pearl-fresh complexion wet with tears. "Mr. Mercer promised some of the women would garner positions as schoolteachers. I know you would like that."

Olivia's heartbeat quickened. Yes, she would enjoy a position as a teacher. She could influence, teach, and love children without needing to have any of her own. She would have a job, be self-sufficient, and not rely on any man. And Darcy would gain her chance at happiness.

She bowed her head. Truly Lowell offered nothing for either of them except hunger, need, and loneliness. "Are you certain Mr. Mercer advertised for teachers as well as mail-order brides?"

Darcy pointed to the last sentence in the newspaper clipping.

There are many teaching positions available for prospective brides.

A tad cryptic, but she couldn't jeopardize Darcy's future by refusing to accept this possibly only opportunity to leave her dying town. A vision of herself and Darcy popped up. Bent with age, hobbling around their tumbled-down home, hair white. Both of them as ramshackle as the house, with nothing to show for the lives they spent. Olivia's heart bled.

She forced a smile. "Consider this my Christmas present to you, Darcy. We shall travel to Seattle, though we know nothing about the place. And you shall select a suitable husband, and I shall accept a teaching position. And may God bless us and keep us."

"Oh, Olivia Rose, I knew you would agree to go! Thank you so much for the best Christmas present I've ever received!" Her sister's eyes turned mossy green and sparkled. "I've already written Mr. Mercer." Darcy pulled a rumpled envelope from her day dress pocket. "His reply arrived yesterday. He declared we must meet him in New York City on January 16th. Then we shall travel from there to Seattle aboard the *S.S. Continental*." Darcy leaped from her chair and danced around the kitchen.

"January 16th! We've only a few days to get ready."

"Mr. Mercer sent train tickets to New York. We leave January 7th."

Olivia dropped her forehead into her hands. "How much do we owe for the train tickets and the ship passage?"

"Nothing. The men in Seattle coughed up three hundred dollars per man to transport us."

"Oh." Olivia rose from her chair and gazed around the kitchen that she'd known for the last twenty-five years. The coziest room in the home where she'd been born. Did she really want to leave? No. She'd buried Mother in the cemetery that abutted the church and set up a monument over Daddy's empty grave. He lay somewhere in a Union burial grave at a place called Gettysburg, killed in the same battle that freed her from Howard. No. She'd thought never to leave home again after she returned from the tiny rented room Howard had provided for her as his new wife. The only goods Howard bequeathed her were her new last name…and a head filled with bad memories. And the title *widow*.

Certainly, no man in Seattle desired to wed a widow, much less pay for one. The purchasers hoped to spend their money on young, beautiful girls…like Darcy.

Olivia closed her eyes. Bitter to leave her home and all she knew.

But sweet to think of a new beginning, a new life, a new adventure, and a new job. If that actually happened.

Yes, God's peace spread in her heart. This might be the right decision—certainly for Darcy...and perhaps for herself as well. She straightened her shoulders. Under the circumstances this was the *only* decision available.

Olivia glanced at a beam of sunlight struggling through the gloomy clouds. She gathered up the long skirts of her day dress, motioned to her sister, and started toward the stairway. "Let's pack."

She'd leave the home place to fall into decay. But she and Darcy would grab this chance for a new life. And unlike Lot's wife, she would *not* look back.

And she and Darcy would not make horrible choices like Lot's daughters.

She would proudly wear her title *widow.*

Or was she hiding behind her widowhood, afraid to venture again into the distasteful realm of marriage?

No matter. She would be the schoolmarm. The beloved teacher. The nurturer. The protector.

What could go wrong?

Oh, so many things.

Chapter 2

Stark Macaulay rode his long-legged powerful horse down Main Street, Seattle. Mud splattered from each of Rebel's four hooves at each step. Stark settled his broad-brimmed Confederate hat squarely on his head. Though the jaunty black plume wilted from his hat band, he'd seen too much mud, dark skies, and death to let this misty day affect his outlook.

So, this motley array of one and two-story wooden buildings was Seattle. He'd expected more. You'd think a city of seven hundred souls situated in the most remote outpost from the battles of the war would look more prosperous. But he liked what he saw of the crinkled hills surrounding and interwoven into the town. The terrain was different from the home he'd left behind. That was good.

Here he would find men who had not fought in the war but had remained safely garrisoned, guarding the post at San Juan Island. Here he expected no hatred for the gray he wore. The men of Seattle had been too engrossed fighting the British and the Indians. They had been too isolated. The lumberjacks and fishermen had thought little if anything about the War of Yankee Aggression.

His stomach rumbled.

No problem with discrimination, but would he find employment?

He'd take most any job that didn't require killing. He'd had his fill of men he'd sent into eternity haunting his dreams. He'd ripped off all emblems from his gray uniform jacket and hat with the exception of the black plume. In the same way, he would forget the war and what the conquerors did to his country.

Seattle promised a new beginning. A place to heal and to grow and to plant roots deep in the hilly soil. He twisted in the saddle and gazed out over the wind-whipped waves of Puget Sound, inhaling the pungent salt air. Maybe a teaching position at the new university. Or perhaps work at Yesler's Lumber Mill. Or sliding felled trees down Skid Row. Quite a downfall from the plantation in Georgia…but all that was gone. Best forgotten. Along with those loved-one's graves that had multiplied in the four long, hard years he'd been absent.

Burying Julia, whom he'd known since she wore short skirts with her dark hair flowing down her back to her waist, still caused his set jaw to jump. Their baby had been a boy. He'd never seen their child, but on the eve of battles he'd toasted by the campfire, tin coffee cup in hand, and dreamed of chubby cheeks and brown eyes like his own. He'd dreamed of teaching Jackson Stark Macaulay how to ride, and hunt, and look after the plantation. He'd dreamed of sweeping Julia in his arms, carrying her up the wide, curving staircase into their bedroom and giving Jackson a baby sister. His dreams had kept him alive.

Until news of their deaths arrived…just before Gettysburg. He'd fought like a demon that day—fought and killed. Not cared if he died. But the sharp agony, the lost-in-the universe loneliness, and the passage of two years and four months had dulled the pain. But not the emptiness. From the day of his birth he'd been bred to responsibility. To care for family. Losing a piece of himself year by year as each died. First his parents, then his sisters, and finally Julia and Jackson. The odd, aimless feeling took hold until he realized he had only himself to steer through the pitfalls of life. Though he knew why, the wandering, pointless, emptiness of life grew with the years rather than lessening.

Perhaps that had made him such a good officer.

But all the past was behind him. Over.

So, since the gold rush to Alaska had petered out, he'd ridden to the farthest north and west he could. He'd travelled to the end of the trail. Time to stop.

He turned Rebel's head toward Mill Street. At the bottom of the steep hill Yesler constructed his mill. He'd built a real steam-powered sawmill smack dab on the waterfront of Elliott Bay.

Newly hewn logs from the ever-receding timber line at the top of the hill skidded down the slick greased log road to the sawmill, and were milled into various shapes and sizes, then loaded on boats at the docks. Grand set-up.

Stark walked Rebel down the slippery, muddy Mill Street past five two-story wooden buildings. Smoke spewed from two chimneys of the last three buildings. The penetrating odor of fresh-cut timber and swirls of sawdust scented the air. Not unpleasant.

But the confines of spending his working hours inside a suffocating building made him click to Rebel and knee him into a trot past the sawmill. Perhaps he'd find work felling the tall timber instead. He gazed up the steep hill at the tall forest, liking the idea of danger.

Rebel threw up his head and snorted. Stark tugged on the reins, and when Rebel halted, he patted his neck.

"Well, old pal, you think you have a better idea?"

Perhaps he'd be better to seek out the university and find employment as a teacher. His saddlebag carried his certification. Father had insisted on a classical education which resulted in several certifications. But again, teaching confined him to the inside of a building.

He'd slept by an open campfire too many years for that work to appeal.

Or, he could break into a new field and join one of the hordes of fishing boats riding the waves at the docks near the downtown center. But the overwhelming odor of dead fish did little to encourage him to apply for work at one of the larger boats. That work seemed too tame and predictable. Riding cavalry with James Ewell Brown Stuart, known as J.E.B. Stuart, had left him with a taste for more adventure.

He headed Rebel toward the public stables. He had enough money left in his almost empty pockets for a night inside with a straw bed and oats and hay for Rebel. He'd camp at his horse's hooves.

And pray for guidance.

For good or ill, he was in Seattle to stay.

Tomorrow would bring answers.

Chapter 3

May 28, 1866 – Seattle, Washington Territory

Olivia gazed over the bow of the brig, *Sheet Anchor*, at the fast approaching land. "Seattle doesn't look like much from here."

"No, perhaps the town will be more appealing as we sail closer." Darcy smiled over her shoulder at the young Captain Pike. "Captain, thank you so much for a far more pleasant voyage than we experienced aboard the *Continental*. This ship is a good bit more accommodating. I'm so pleased we changed boats in San Francisco."

Olivia nudged her sister's shoulder. "Stop flirting with the Captain, Darcy," she whispered.

"My pleasure, Miss Davenport. Thirty-four young, attractive, single ladies made this voyage one I won't readily forget." Captain Pike grinned like a boy attending his first dance.

Darcy tipped her head and peeked under her eyelashes at the Captain. "Do you think Olivia Rose and I made the right choice to journey on to Seattle rather than disembark in San Francisco as so many of our Mercer Girls did?"

Captain Pike touched the black bill of his white hat with a respectful finger. "I don't know about San Francisco, but Seattle is home. And you will find a warm welcome here. We have ten men to every woman, and you Mercer Maidens will have your choice of rich, upstanding men to wed." The Captain's tanned face flushed beet-red. "I'm not a wealthy man, but I'd be honored Miss Darcy if you would consent to be *my* bride."

"Oh, Captain. Thank you so much. I shall have to consider your offer, but I must encourage you. I think quite highly of you.

Will we meet on shore or must you sail off immediately?"

I'm scheduled to dock, disembark my passengers, and sail back to San Francisco on the morning tide. If you honor me with a yes, my First Mate can marry us before you leave my vessel. He is also a Justice of the Peace."

"Oh, dear, Captain Pike. I'm so very sorry, but I must have more time to ponder your offer. Perhaps when you return?" Darcy fluttered her eyelashes.

"I will steam back in two weeks, but I fear you will already be wed by then."

Olivia scooted between the two. "Surely not, Captain. My sister shall not rush into anything so lasting as marriage. She will want to acquaint herself with any man who seeks her hand."

"But, Ma'am, the men of Seattle expect to greet seven hundred women as prospective brides. They will be unhappy to discover there are only thirty-four of you ladies."

"Yes, I can see that might present a problem, Sir. Nevertheless, my sister *will* become acquainted with any prospective suitor before she marries." Olivia spoke with conviction. Heavens, if only the men didn't tear them into pieces and pass the portions around.

"Look, Olivia Rose. Look!" Darcy pointed to the sea still separating them from shore.

Olivia turned from the Captain to gaze out over the bow. Twenty or thirty canoes rowed toward them, manned by Indians. Not the first she'd seen, but the most wildly dressed, with bare chests and feathers drooping from long black braids. Bright colors painted their chests and arms.

The Captain stepped beside her, resting his hand on the bow. "They're from Cape Flattery. They're harmless. Just their way to welcome us."

"Do other Indians war with us here?" Darcy's wide eyes stared at the Captain. Her lips had fallen open to a pouty O.

Olivia gazed at her younger sister. No wonder Captain Pike asked for Darcy's hand. She was such a beautiful young girl. As innocent as a babe and ever so much more attractive. But she would see that Darcy gained a husband more suited for her. A wealthy man who would protect and care for Darcy and provide for her every need. A sea captain, gone for months at a time simply wouldn't do. No matter how handsome.

"No, Miss Davenport, we've not had an Indian problem for over four years. We live together peacefully now." The Captain gazed at Darcy with eyes as hungry as the wolves Olivia had scared from the chicken coop back in Lowell.

As the steamship plowed through the water, the Indian canoes surrounded the ship and accompanied them into the harbor at Admiralty Head.

Captain Pike left them with a shrug and a rueful expression and rushed to the bridge to supervise the docking.

The boat bumped against the pier, and Captain Pike ordered the lowering of the gangplank.

Sailors heaved luggage piled in the center of the deck onto their shoulders and rushed down the gangplank. Olivia's eyes widened. The great crowd of men surrounding the bottom of the gangplank waved and cheered. "Why there must be hundreds of men down there."

Darcy turned a bright face to Olivia. "We shall have our choice!"

"Ah, yes. But look at most of them. By their dress they are working men, loggers and mill hands." Olivia grasped both of Darcy's hands. "Promise me, dear, you won't marry any man I do not approve of. You have the opportunity of a lifetime. You can marry a rich man. A successful man. A man of means." She squeezed her sister's hands. "Promise!"

"Of course. I wouldn't dream of marrying without your approval. But what of love, dear Olivia? I shall not be happy unless I marry for love!"

"Love!" Olivia frowned. Oh, how she prayed her sister's sparkling green eyes would never be awash with tears because of a cruel husband. "A woman in love cannot always see past a handsome face into a deceitful heart." She tied her bonnet strings against the strong breeze, gathered up her long skirts and her hand bag, tilted her chin high, and strode toward the gangplank. "You must trust *me*, Darcy, not your heart."

Darcy's gay laugh rode on the wind. "How fortunate we are

Olivia Rose, to have so many males to select from!" She tripped with happy steps down the gangplank.

Olivia followed more slowly. A gloved hand grasping the railing as she descended. She hesitated at the bottom, losing sight of Darcy swallowed in the sea of masculine heads.

A strong hand reached out from the crowd squeezing forward so tight around her, she thought she might not be able to set her foot on land. "Welcome, Miss. I'll carry your luggage to the Occidental Hotel."

"The Occidental?"

"Yes, the only hotel in Seattle."

The tall, broad-shouldered man certainly looked strong enough to carry her trunk. "My sister is here with me."

"I'll return for her trunk after I see you both safely through this mob to the hotel. They were expecting four hundred brides and could turn surly when they see only you few ladies."

"But—"

"I'm sheriff here, Ma'am. If anyone can get you safely through this mob, it's me. Grab your sister's hand and the back of my shirt and hang on." Somehow, he magically had his other hand around Darcy's upper arm.

He propelled Darcy toward her. She clasped Darcy's hand. He dropped her arm and heaved Olivia's trunk onto his broad shoulder. As he stepped away from the gangplank, she grasped the back of his gray wool shirt. Seemed expedient to do as he ordered...or be trampled.

He didn't even breathe hard from the trunk balanced on his shoulder, or from towing the two of them through the crowd. The mob of shouting men stretched out hands to touch them as they passed, but opened in front of the sheriff.

She'd expected a warm greeting from the men of Seattle, but this crush was ridiculous. What kind of man-frenzy had she and Darcy fallen into?

Shouts and heavy footsteps followed them all the way to the two-story wooden building with the lopsided sign, *Occidental Hotel,* dangling from the second story.

The large-framed sheriff turned to the gang of men who had

followed Darcy and her all the way to the hotel. "Back down, fellas. You're wound up tighter than a four-hundred-day clock. Let the ladies get settled in the hotel. You can meet them tonight at the Mayor's Reception. Remember your manners. You're in the presence of ladies."

With mutiny on their faces, grumbling, shuffling of feet, and lowering of heads, the horde turned and stumbled back toward the waterfront, sneaking peeks back at her and Darcy.

Olivia gazed up past the shining silver star on the wide gray-shirted chest to the dark inscrutable eyes. "Thank you, Sheriff. I don't know that we could have made our own way safely through that mass of men."

"Yes, Sheriff, you have our undying appreciation. I'd love to knit a scarf for you to show our gratitude," Darcy cooed.

Darcy's breathy speech sent slivers of warning through Olivia. Was her sister so ready to jump into marriage that she would throw herself at any man who approached? Oh, she had her work cut out for her!

She grasped Darcy by her shoulders and turned her toward the hotel desk. "Yes, thank you, Sheriff."

Of course, Darcy planted her button-boots on the wide wooden floorboards and refused to move.

The sheriff swept off his wide-brimmed gray hat. "No trouble, ladies. Name's Stark Macaulay. I'll be happy to return later this evening and escort you to the Mayor's Reception."

"Why thank you. That would be appre—" Olivia gasped, and smacked a hand over her mouth. She took a step back and stared.

The sheriff wore gray from head to foot. Gray...a uniform. A Confederate uniform!

The uniform of the men who had killed Father...and sent Mother to an early grave. She recognized the officer's hat decorated with the black plume. Oh, she knew all about J.E.B. Stuart's cavalry. Far more than she'd ever wanted to learn.

"No, thank you, Sheriff Macaulay. We can find our own way to the Mayor's Reception." Her words left icicles hanging in the air. She turned a stiff back to him, grasped Darcy, wide-eyed and mouth agape, by the arm and shoved her sister toward the hotel's desk.

How could there be a cursed gray-back here in Seattle?

Chapter 4

Stark scanned the four tiers of ladies seated on the stage at University Hall. Behind the seated ladies, a huge banner sported the words, *Welcome Asa Mercer and Your Beautiful Bevy of Brides-to-be.* Yes, there she was square in the center of the fourth row. Looked as if she tried hard not to be noticed.

Impossible. The abundant auburn hair piled high on her head shone like burnished copper in some new-fangled style. Her porcelain skin glowed, tinted at the cheeks with peach. Her slender form was clad in practical dark green but could not hide her beauty. Her expressive jade eyes gazed at the crowd of excited men, looking as serene as Loch Ness, but far lovelier.

Oh, he was smitten. He must stake his claim before far richer admirers than he trampled her.

She'd been friendly and grateful when he'd toted her trunk and led the two ladies to the hotel. A shard of ice snagged his heart. Then for some reason, when they stood together at the hotel desk, she'd turned to stone.

What didn't she like about him?

Mayor Denny spouted words Stark barely registered. "We tender a vote of thanks to the young ladies here for the self-sacrificing spirit you manifest in leaving the loved firesides of happy homes to plod life's weary way to this North-Western coast." The mayor cleared his throat and nodded to Asa. "Thank you, Mr. Mercer, for your efforts on behalf of the Washington Territory. We appreciate this group of fair maidens." He turned from Asa to the ladies who perched like princesses waiting to be crowned, smiling, nodding, and gazing out at the audience as if assessing which man would make the best mate.

Stark combed a hand through his long, wavy hair. Maybe she preferred shorter hair. He'd visit the barber tomorrow. Certainly, a woman so lovely possessed a personality as sweet. She appeared to believe she could handle herself in this riotous mob without his help. She didn't realize how desperate these men were for the company of a woman. He'd have to keep a close eye on her and protect her.

Mayor Denny babbled on. "The bachelors of Seattle welcome you to our youthful country. We expect you to become model teachers, wives, and mothers in our esteemed city. We expect you ladies to each make an important contribution to Seattle. We know you will become pillars of Seattle society." He smiled his I-am-the-most-important-male-in-this-city smile. "You ladies are all so very welcome. Each one of you is a young maiden of good report and most attractive to look upon."

Stark shifted on the hard, wooden chair. Good thing the mayor was married. Not that any of the young ladies would find his bald head attractive. But who knew what drew women to a particular male? He sure didn't. But he had better learn fast.

The mayor turned back to Mr. Mercer. "Our incorrigible old bachelor, Asa Mercer, whom you know as our first President of the Territorial University of Washington and a member of the Washington Territory State Senate, has snagged one of these lovely young ladies as a wife for himself." Mayor Denny shook a playful finger at Asa Mercer. "Miss Annie Stephens, please stand and show yourself as no longer available as a mail-order bride."

The lady blushed beet red and stood. Men in the hall stamped their feet and clapped, along with some boos and calls of "It's not fair! Why does he get first choice?"

Stark swallowed. The little lady he'd chosen from the bustling barrage of women standing at the bow of Captain Pike's vessel hadn't given her name. Nor had she risen when Mayor Denny called out that name.

So, she was still available. But if the woman of his dreams had stood, he would have fought the black-whiskered scoundrel who'd claimed her. Asa was good in the short run, but the man jumped from one project and line of business to another. And he seemed to leave a bunch of debt behind him wherever he ventured. Asa was a visionary without the endurance to guide a business out to a profitable end. Stark rubbed the bristles that would sprout on his cheeks every evening no matter how close he shaved in the morning. Asa wasn't the kind of man a woman could depend on.

Mayor Denny nodded to the engaged couple. "Best wishes to the two of you." He raised his voice to his usual loud haranguing pitch. "Now folks, let's all adjourn to the grounds where you'll find refreshments. And we can eat as we all enjoy a beautiful western sunset."

A rush of male feet and a press of hard bodies moved like a tsunami toward the stage where the ladies sat, anticipation on every delicate face except one.

Why was she not eager? Had she already chosen a husband?

Stark's insides quivered.

"Easy men. Remember these are ladies and are to be treated as such. Please give them precedence and ample room to make their way to the garden." Mayor Denny stood by the stage stairs and held a hand to each lady descending. As the lady's shoe hit the wooden floor of the hall, the lady was immediately surrounded by a mass of men who shoved each other for the honor of escorting the lady to the garden.

Stark kept his eye on the tall, slender, auburn-haired lady grasping the arm of a younger version of herself as if the younger lady would rush into the swarm of men and choose one on the spot.

From the expression of the younger sister, perhaps she had that idea in mind. The girl resembled a foal loosened in a spring pasture for the first time, gamboling from flower to flower and tree to tree to discover the most enjoyable.

The older of the two walked with the majesty of a queen who cared not one whit for the throng clustering about her. She gave the appearance of not being interested in any of the men seeking her attention. Assuredly, when the lady had taken her first good look at him, she'd blasted him with icy air.

While his heart had burst open like a broken caisson the first time she brought those emerald eyes up to gaze into his. Before that, he'd never thought to marry again. Not until those eyes as grassy green as the hills Ma spoke so longingly of back in Inverness lingered in his mind. Beautiful eyes fringed with dark lashes.

He followed the gaggle of men grouped around the woman he loved and her sister. Nope, he'd never expected to love again. But here he was hurling his beating heart into her small hands.

Losing Julia had about broken him. He'd never expected to risk his heart again. Never wanted to leave the one he loved in someone else's care while he marched away. Never wanted to return to a desolate, empty, burned-out home and two lonely graves.

But the pain had lessened to a gnawing loneliness he hadn't even realized gripped a tight hand around his heart. The sight of that one woman, the tilt of her head, the graceful lift of her hand, the sweep of her eyelash on her rounded cheek, the upward curve of her lips...and he was lost.

The river of men flowed in front of him out the garden door following the thirty-four women like a flood after a dam break.

He followed. Stepped out the garden door into the cool, lilac-scented air. The women had advanced to the shoreline. A phalanx of men separated him from her. Considering the testosterone each man standing there exuded, each was choosing the woman he hoped to marry.

There she was, standing at the edge of the water. She was smiling. Amiable. Chatting easily to the circle of men surrounding her. She looked relaxed and free of aggression.

Something about him had turned her good humor into hostility. What had upset her?

He had his work cut out.

But he would win her.

He'd lost one war and one woman. He wouldn't lose another.

Chapter 5

Olivia sighed, unbuttoned her shoes, placed them on the floor, swung her legs up and settled on the double bed. "How can a woman decide upon one man when three hundred men tear at one another to scramble for a moment of her time?"

"Oh, isn't it just lovely!" Darcy whirled around the small hotel room, head tilted back in ecstasy, and a grin on her face.

"No, it's not!" Olivia fluffed the hotel's skimpy pillow behind her head. "I would love some peace and quiet. We haven't had a minute to ourselves in the last two weeks. We cannot dine, shop or explore Seattle without being besieged by men."

"Oh but isn't it marvelous!" Darcy shook the ribbons from her hair, flipped a shoe across the room to land in the vicinity of the window, and backed up to her sister's side of the bed. "Loosen my corset will you, please? We are dining tonight with Doc Maynard, and I need to take a few deep breaths before then. Doc promised he'd bring along the young physician who assists him, so I'll fasten these good and tight before we go down to dinner."

Olivia twisted, sat up, and used both hands to help Darcy with her ties.

As soon as her stays released, Darcy twirled around the room on stockinged feet. "Do you think a doctor or an attorney would make the best husband?"

"I believe Henry and Sarah Yesler's nephew, Jason, might prove your best catch. The lumber mill runs the economy here. And I believe I have seen Jason fighting to gain your attention more than a few times."

"Oh, which one is he?" Darcy flounced to the window, threw it open, and stuck her head and shoulders out into the falling dusk.

"You should take more notice of him. Several of the other girls have, so I expect he will soon decide which lady he wants to marry." Olivia flopped back against the pillow and stared at the low ceiling so different from the higher, pitched ceilings in Massachusetts. She'd never admit to Darcy how she missed their cozy home. How she missed summer sunshine and crisp air. Seemed misty rain fell here almost daily. No, she must not complain. The Puget Sound was lovely, and she enjoyed the cry of seagulls and the sparkle of waves when the sun did shine. But the hotel nestled close to the dock where the fishing boats rocked, and the odor of fish permeated the piers and floated through the air for blocks.

Darcy pulled her torso back inside through the open window. "So, is Jason the rotund one who always wears a three-piece suit that crunches him as if the material was cut two sizes too small? Or is he the tall, lanky one who resembles a scarecrow?"

"Neither, dear, Jason's quite presentable. Just a tad on the quiet, bookish side. He—"

"Oh, him! He won't suit me at all. Olivia Rose, don't you even know me by now? I need a man with life in him. One who is good to gaze upon. A man other men respect." Darcy closed her eyes and smiled. "A tall man with broad shoulders and a good head of hair. Bright blue eyes would be nice." She grunted. "And I'd prefer a man who doesn't have a doting mother butting into his affairs. Even if he is rich. I don't want an interfering mother-in-law."

Olivia rubbed her aching temples with her fingertips. "Darcy, ten of the women we travelled with from Lowell are already engaged and will soon be married. I really didn't expect to push you into marriage, but women are seizing the best men. You don't want to be left with only a mill worker or a smelly fisherman, do you?"

Darcy plunked down on the double bed causing the thin mattress to tilt. Olivia adjusted by scooting to the far edge of her side. "But, I'm having too much fun, dancing with one and then another, dining with one and then another, and walking with one and then another. I don't see how those other ladies decided so quickly."

Darcy bounced the bed so hard, Olivia had to laugh.

"And what of you, Olivia Rose, what of you." Darcy made a little song, "What of you, Olivia Rose, what of you."

Olivia levered up and smiled. "I'm to talk with Mr. Mercer tonight after we dine with the Yeslers. He promised me a teaching position, and I will sign a contract tonight or my name isn't Olivia Rose Baker." She frowned. "Mr. Mercer already enrolled quite a number of ladies to be teachers. I don't think it a coincidence every one of those promised teaching positions have already selected a husband. Mr. Mercer's dangling the teaching posts as a reward for those ladies who marry quickly."

"And you think if I select a husband that Mr. Mercer will offer you one of the few teaching positions left." Darcy flounced out of bed. "You're using me to get what you want." She slammed her hands on her hips. "I thought better of you. I thought you had my welfare in mind moving here. Now you force me to choose a husband when I prefer to take my time and have a rousing good time choosing."

"No, dear Darcy, really. I'm sincere when I say the richest men are being snatched off the market. I really want my little sister to enjoy a marriage made in heaven."

"We've prayed enough. Surely God is saving each of us a splendid husband." Darcy danced to the mirror and glanced at her reflection. She designed her hair into various styles. "I do enjoy Thomas Johnson. He's well-spoken, lives in one of the nicest homes, drives a carriage and four, and his father owns the newspaper. But he still lives with his mother." Darcy pinched her cheeks and stepped back to admire the pink blooming there. "Thomas begged me several times to make him the happiest man alive by marrying him."

"Do you like him well enough?"

"Not so much as I have a fondness for Captain Pike."

"Oh, Darcy, do you realize how lonely a life the wife of a sea captain has? He steams into port, stays a few days, and then steams out again. Is that what you want?"

"No. But the Captain is so handsome."

"Looks fade, dear. And yes, Captain Pike seems a grand

person. But surely one of the young men here in Seattle would make a more brilliant match."

Darcy stuck her bottom lip out. "And, what of you, Olivia Rose? Men swarm to you like bees to honey. You've enjoyed as many proposals of marriage as I have. When will you choose a husband?"

"I came to teach, not marry. I have no interest in chaining myself to a man who has complete control over me." Olivia pushed herself up on her elbows. "It's so important you know what lies within a man and choose him for his good qualities rather than for his looks." She raised up to a sitting position, leaned down for her shoes, and slipped her foot into one. "I'm not asking you to set a date. Just to choose a good man and get to know him."

"How long will that take? You knew Howard a full month before you two married."

"Yes, dear, but Howard was riding back and forth to his training post. I saw him only four days of that month. We hurried into marriage because he had to leave for the war." Olivia stood and straightened her long skirts. "Looking back, I can see I was seduced by Howard's handsome looks and fine physique." She smiled gently. "I don't want you to make that same mistake."

"So, you wish me to marry an ugly man?"

No, dear. My desire is that you…" Oh, could a woman trust any man? She rose and strolled to the wash basin. She shifted toward her sister. "… not make the same mistake I did." She grabbed her sister's hands. "You should know him so well before marriage that you can predict his behavior after marriage."

"So, no surprises then. That doesn't sound like any fun at all."

Olivia squeezed her sister's hand for emphasis. "Marriage isn't fun. It's a contract between two people. And you should know exactly what you expect from a husband…and what he expects from you. Perhaps you should accept a teaching position and forget about the mail-order-bride business altogether."

Darcy pulled her hands away. "What if I settle on three men and take my time deciding which I want? Unlike you, I don't have a whit of desire to teach." She danced to the armoire and peeked inside. "Would that please Mr. Mercer enough to sign you up for a teaching position?"

"That would surely help."

"But Olivia Rose, I think it's only fair for you to choose a man. So many men want a wife. I think you are being selfish! Just because you got stuck with a bad apple, doesn't mean the whole bushel is rotten."

Was she? She'd never thought of herself as selfish. Was she using her little sister? She really wanted only the best for Darcy.

But, was marriage a good thing for any woman? Certainly Mrs. Yesler appeared happy. And Mrs. Johnson. She poured water into the wash basin. Actually, all the married ladies she'd met in Seattle seemed happy. And the ten Mercer Girls who'd said yes to a husband struck her as being ecstatic.

Was she being a sour apple?

Then there was the problem of money. The men from Seattle had paid for their passage and one night's stay at the hotel. They'd expected the women to disembark the ship, rest a night, choose a husband the next day, and go directly to the Justice of the Peace to be married. And some of the ladies had done just that. But Darcy must select wisely and that took time. Yet, too fast their finances dwindled. The hotel bill alone drained her funds.

And school didn't begin until September. *If* she won that contract.

Then there was the problem of numbers. Each time a Mercer Girl agreed to marry a Seattle man, the number of men yammering for her attention grew.

No wonder Darcy found it hard to select one man out of the crowd.

Olivia finished with the wash basin and opened the armoire door and chose a dress for dinner. If only she could drape a veil over her face and never interact with a man again.

She shivered. Especially that scoundrel who sported the Confederate uniform. Didn't he realize the war was over? And he had lost.

The man lived in the past.

She buttoned her dinner frock. Perhaps he wasn't the only one. Perhaps she did as well. Had she dragged her past with her into her new future?

Then there was the other problem. With Darcy safely married, she would be alone.

Even with her teaching, even with her students to love, would she be happy?

Could she live alone?

Was a lone woman safe in this raw, new town filled with desperate men?

Chapter 6

Stark ran a hand through his fresh haircut. From a barbershop, not his own shears. He'd polished his boots, shined Reb's tack, taken a bath, and shaved. He'd had his uniform cleaned at the Chinese laundry. He'd not been so spruced up since the day he'd left *Macaulay Oaks*. Almost forgotten what a man had to do before he went to pay suit to a lady.

He hadn't courted Julia. The two of them mostly wandered into marriage. He'd loved her, of course. What was not to love about sweet Julia? Everyone loved her. Just as everyone had expected them to marry from the time he wore short pants and she plaited her hair into pigtails. Both were from old Southern families with side-by-side plantations.

Both were Presbyterians. But the war sharpened and honed his faith. No right-thinking man faced battle before confessing his sin and making certain he had a right relationship with his Lord. His walk with God was the only good thing he'd found in the war. And after. How did a person who didn't know the Lord ever live through the agony of a wife and son's death? How did anyone keep living? Without the peace Jesus gave, he would have gone off half-cocked and murdered the Yankees who'd taken over his land.

All that was past. All except his faith. Still fresh and new and living.

What he felt for Olivia was so different from what he'd experienced with Julia. Hard to compare. Julia had been comfort, warmth, and familiarity while Olivia was lightning, excitement, and extreme attraction. And not a little fear.

He tucked his dog-eared Bible into his bureau drawer and rubbed his chin. Should he wear his weapons out in the open or conceal them? He slipped his bowie knife into his ankle sheath. With the lumberjacks, mill workers, and fishermen stirred up to fever pitch by the few ladies in town, trouble burst out on street corners, in shops, and gambling houses. Since the ladies arrived, men fought each other everywhere, not just the usual saloon brawls. He pulled on his cavalry trousers and tunic.

He pinned his silver star below his left shoulder. As sheriff, he had no choice about the guns. He strapped on his double holsters. His holsters fit over his tunic jacket in place of the wide Confederate belt that carried his sword sheath. Sword wasn't much use in a gun fight. But the tunic was still serviceable, made of good gray wool, and the rough men in town recognized him by the color from a distance, where most chose not to engage with him. He spun the gun cylinders, checking for bullets, and then slipped the special-made Colt revolvers into his holsters.

Uniform would serve him well for another five years or more. By then the new women in town would have civilized the place, and he could retire. The wad of bills buried in the toe of his old boot was building to a sizeable pile, and he could buy that buggy shop he saved for.

That enterprise would bring in a good income. Enough to make him a financial leader in the community for the special woman he planned to make his wife.

Found out her name. Olivia Rose Baker. He, as well as every other red-blooded man in Seattle, knew each woman's name, that she hailed from Lowell, Massachusetts, her age, and a good bit of her history.

As sheriff, he'd been privy to that information, but it appeared that Asa Mercer handed each lady's information to any man who asked him.

Unlike the other Mercer Girls, Olivia Rose Baker, was a widow. So much the better, he was a widower. They had common ground. He'd never been convinced of love at first sight, but one glance at Olivia, and he'd become a believer.

He dropped on his cot and pulled on his shining boots. Had Olivia been in love with her deceased husband? Did she believe in a second chance at love?

Or was she like many of the ladies already spoken for, only interested in securing a wealthy husband for themselves?

With a face that sweet, she must believe in love.

Who'd guess a seasoned soldier like him, a fast-draw sheriff, a no-nonsense law enforcer, deep down inside where it counted, was a die-hard romantic?

Best to keep his secret hidden.

He'd maintained a close eye on her for the past two weeks. Heard second-hand that she'd turned down a good number of proposals. Done recon on her habits. What she enjoyed. Where she went. Who she went with. But hadn't learned much except she kept a restraining hand on her younger sister. He'd guarded the peace. Intercepted many men from vying for her attention at once. Broken up squabbles between men intent on capturing her attention as she walked from place to place. Kept her safe.

He knew her well enough to think she would take her time and evaluate who might make a suitable husband. She had a level-head, wasn't a chatterbox, and worshipped in church rather than scanning the crowd for a handsome man. Strange, she seemed in no hurry at all to select a mate.

That set her apart from the other Mercer Girls.

The more he saw of her, the more certain his heart grew that she was the woman for him.

Now, he had only to overcome some hundred or so other suitors.

Continue to keep the peace.

Protect Olivia and Darcy from harm.

Figure the best way to present his case.

And win her love.

Not as hard as searching among the hundreds of dead bodies for some he could help after the battle of Gettysburg…and not so hard as realizing that the South had lost the war, though they continued to fight.

But frightening.

He had no idea how to start.

And she didn't seem to like him.

His spurs jangled as his boots thudded on the old wooden floor.

His heart thudded like it had each time the trumpet sounded for battle.

Chapter 7

Olivia drew in a sweet breath. The cool evening air felt delicious. And the fresh breeze from Puget Sound brought the scent of salt and a mixture of roses and lilacs. Perhaps after the long, difficult journey she had indeed found a new home. Moonlight sparkled diamonds on the huge body of water slushing to the rocky shore. In the distance loomed the dark shadows of the Cascade Mountains.

The star-spangled sky seemed to promise a better future.

Certainly, the men were eager to claim wives. Though they kept a discreet distance this evening. Even with her back to the throng, she sensed their pressing forward to gain a better view. Yes, musk of masculinity mingled with the sweeter odors.

"Say you haven't chosen a husband yet, Darcy. You need to make absolutely certain the husband you choose is a man of integrity as well as a wealthy man. Or at least he should be able to support you."

Moonlight bathed her sister's oval face in incandescence. "Olivia Rose, this is so exciting! What other women ever had this grand banquet of men!"

"More reason to take your time." She'd love to dip her foot in the dark water. If only she could be alone for an hour or even fifteen minutes.

"Just think, Olivia, I've had over thirty marriage proposals!"

"And, Mr. Mercer refuses to give me a contract to teach! What shall we do?"

"I believe I've made my choice." Darcy raised her hands together as if in prayer. "Please give me your blessing."

Olivia's heart slid to her stomach. Oh, she so hoped she was wrong!

"Captain Pike arrived yesterday, just at dusk."

Olivia blew out a tired breath. "I know. I saw the *Sheet Anchor* steam into port. But you told me you were walking with Jason Yesler, the eldest son."

Darcy blushed. On her, the color looked becoming. Oh, Darcy could have married the Yesler heir. He was so smitten with her. She could have been happy with him.

"I did walk with Jason. But Peter—"

"Peter? I don't understand."

"Peter Pike. Oh, Olivia Rose, he's such a handsome man. And so delightful. Why, he could have chosen any of the forty Mercer Girls. Well, thirty-four by the time we changed to his vessel. Nevertheless, you need not worry. Peter earns an excellent income. And the *Sheet Anchor* belongs to him. He also owns part-interest in another vessel and even though he lives with his mother on Whidby Island, the mansion is his."

Olivia's knees went weak. She leaned against the nearby maple tree, the rough bark poking through her silk gown. "Slow down, Darcy. I can scarce keep up with your chatter."

"I'm trying to tell you that I'm head-over-heels in love. Peter asked me to marry him again, and I said 'yes'."

"Are you certain you want to live the rest of your life with that man?"

"Oh, very, very sure. Absolutely. He's all I've thought of for the past two weeks. I gazed at the harbor every day with the hope he would return sooner." Darcy made a little face. "But, of course, with business, he couldn't."

"No, of course not." Olivia's mind raced. Many men had asked for Darcy's hand. Rich men, brawny lumberjacks, smelly fishermen, and Seattle's best businessmen. Yet, she continued firm that she preferred that Captain Pike. So, perhaps something inside Darcy, some intuition or knowledge, some ancient answering of woman to man, some discernment, gave Darcy wisdom to agree to this union. *Dear God, please show me if I should oppose this marriage.*

"Peter wants to marry as soon as possible. He doesn't trust all the single men in this town to keep their distance from a merely engaged lady. Especially since he'll steam out again in two days."

"I understand Captain Pike's concern and it is valid. However, I think you need to grow better acquainted with him before you enter into wedlock."

"I knew you would agree." Darcy pirouetted down the seashore's rocky slope and back, her long skirts fluttering like the sails of an old-fashioned vessel. Her joy lit the darkness.

"Please promise you won't jump into this marriage without getting to know Captain Pike better."

"Please call him Peter." Moonlight glinted on Darcy's smile. "But I think I should heed my beloved's wishes rather than my older sister's." She emphasized older.

Suddenly Olivia did feel older. So much older. So much wiser. And yet, her wisdom was based only on her experience with one man. Her brain told her that Harold wasn't every man. Perhaps Peter was a good man. A kind man. She'd prayed so for Darcy's future. Perhaps Peter *was* God's good answer.

She really hadn't prayed before she wed Harold. She'd been too overwhelmed with his handsomeness, his supposed wealth, his loving her. He'd swept her off her feet. Dazzled her.

But now her emotions trumpeted that no man could be trusted.

On her honeymoon, the minute Harold was alone with her, he'd turned ugly. Oh, she must dismiss Harold from her mind. She must cleanse herself from every thought of him.

"Excuse me, Miss Baker. I hope I'm not interrupting."

The large man had approached without her noticing. And he *was* interrupting.

Darcy erupted into a huge smile, gave a slight curtsey, and backed toward the water, leaving her with the giant.

The breeze wafted his clean scent. His broad shoulders blocked the moonlight and sent her into deep shadows. She moved away from the tree, and as far from him as politeness allowed. A shaft of starlight gleamed on the star pinned to his chest.

"Is there a problem?"

"Problem? No." He seemed confused by her question.

She smiled. Perhaps she needed an interruption. Time to digest what Darcy wanted. "You're the sheriff. Usually you arrest people." Her lips tilted up, hoping he caught her slight humor.

He laughed. A deep bass, pleasing laugh that made her want to laugh with him. "Certainly, I'd like to arrest such a beauty—. Uh, no. I didn't come to throw you in the clinker." He shifted his feet.

Odd, he seemed awkward. Uneasy. Oh, he was no doubt single. Another suitor. She sighed and lifted her long blue gingham skirts. How could she get rid of this one nicely?

"Do you mind walking with me? Or would you prefer to sit on the bench over yonder by the water?"

He had a lovely drawl. Never heard any quite like it. Sounded deep, smooth, but with the words drawn out like taffy from a New England pull. Very pleasant. "I was just returning to the hotel with my sister." That sounded too impolite. She didn't want to be known as uppity, especially since as yet she had no job. "Perhaps you'd like to accompany us?"

He stepped close to her side and extended his arm.

He did have excellent manners.

With a giggle, Darcy fell in behind them.

"I've been making inquiries and have located a family who are more than willing to take you into their home until you ...." His voice trailed off.

"Choose a husband?" She laughed. No need to offend the man.

"Yes." He cleared his throat. "Many of the Seattle families are taking in ladies who don't have the funds to continue living at the hotel." He coughed. "What I mean to say is we Seattle folks are happy to extend our hospitality until you ladies are settled on your own."

Oh, Father God. You know my money is almost gone. You are using this man to answer my prayer. Thank you so much. "Are you married, Sheriff?"

"No!" He grunted deep in his throat. "I'm sorry, Miss Baker. I'm not going about this very well. I'm not inviting you into my home. The Barlows are an established, respected family. They have opened their home to you."

Oh, thank you, God! "And, as sheriff you vouch for these people?"

"Yes, Miss Baker. I do. You will be quite comfortable with

them."

"It's Mrs. Baker. And thank you, Sheriff. When can we move in with them?"

"I'd be glad to help you tomorrow morning. If that time pleases you."

"That would please me well. And, of course, the Barlows promised to take in Darcy as well?"

"Yes, *Mrs.* Baker. Although, I understand that Miss Davenport has agreed to become Captain Pike's wife."

She jerked her hand in his arm and almost stumbled on the boardwalk. Heavenly Days! Did the whole town know about Darcy before she did? "You are correct, but perhaps not for a while yet."

The sheriff gazed down at her, and something in his expression verbalized that Darcy would not be living with the Barlows very long. Her stomach curled.

She was to be taken in by strangers and live on their hospitality. Very charitable. But extremely humbling. Her livelihood depended on strangers.

She must obtain that teaching position. But she'd done everything except beg Mr. Mercer.

What else could she do?

Oh, the sheriff was talking. What had he said? "I'm sorry, will you repeat that?"

The sheriff swallowed so hard that she heard the sound over their footsteps. Was he unwell?

"Umm, I asked if I might take you to dinner tomorrow after I help you and your sister move to the Barlow home."

Bother! Would every man in town turn into a suitor? This man was quite pleasant. And he was the sheriff. Perhaps if she was seen around town with him, the other men would leave her alone. And he had helped with her financial dilemma.

A shaft of moonlight washed over him.

"A gray uniform! The Confederate!" Olivia smashed a hand against her mouth to silence her startled words. How could she have forgotten?

Goosebumps popped out from head to foot. She sucked in air to silence her rapidly beating heart. "No thank you, sir. I appreciate your help, but I shall not dine with you." She withdrew her arm, stalked up to the hotel entrance, shoved open the door, and rushed through.

Darcy shuffled in after her.

The sheriff stood motionless on the boardwalk as if frozen in place.

"What?" Darcy motioned to the man, her eyes wide. "Why?"

"Nothing. I just developed a headache."

Chapter 8

Stark smacked his forehead. He should have known.

Okay, so the uniform spooked Olivia. He stared at the closed wooden door of the hotel, propped up his drooping head with stiffened shoulders, and ambled back toward his small, rented room, his boots clomping and spurs jangling a lonely cadence on the boardwalk.

Olivia's husband must have died in the war. Being from Massachusetts he'd have been a Union man. Stark stopped to gaze over the sloshing waters of Puget South. The washing of the waves onto the rocky shore soothed his shocked nerves. Cold, distant stars twinkled in the heavens. A cool breeze ruffled his hair.

He set his jaw. Forget the blow to his pride. He had his work cut out.

Devastating to discover that in this rowdy, male-dominated society, he, the lawman, scared her the most.

Lord, why didn't you tell me?

He gazed up the boardwalk at the main street. Not much to the town. Nothing fancy or even comfortable. Pure utilitarian. Mercer had brought these women here to inspire the townsmen to build churches, schools, libraries, and homes. True, men had a profound need of the gentler sex to bring civilization. But Mercer probably had a monetary motive. Nevertheless, Olivia's arrival awakened a soul-stirring need. One that threatened to tear him apart. And distract him from keeping the peace in this boiling pot of a town.

With the arrival of the Mercer Girls, the pot boiled over far more often. Yet, eventually the ladies would encourage civilization. But Olivia prompted more than progress and taming of the town. She inspired emotions he hadn't wanted to allow or even acknowledge. She brought chaos to his soul.

She had a strange accent. Crisp and to the point. But sweet like a juicy apple. And there could not be a more lovely lady anywhere either south or north of the Mason Dixon line.

The last several weeks while patrolling the town he'd been called in numerous times to act as witness to the many marriages. The Justice of the Peace had been working double-duty with all the weddings. Seemed every man in Seattle was more than willing to thrust his neck in the matrimonial noose with the ladies they'd paid Mercer to provide. Men who had already staked out farms and ranches along the coast and toward the Cascade foothills. Men who had made fortunes in timber, fishing, and farming while he'd been fighting the lost battle and watching so many of his fine, intrepid men die in battle. The flower of the South who now lay beneath the scorched soil upon which they had so gallantly fought. He shook his head. No, he must force those memories from his mind. He had to focus on life after death. Surviving.

And Olivia Rose Davenport Baker was the bright spot of that focus. Not only must he forget the past, he would separate from it. For her sake. For his.

He strode toward the undulating water and gazed out over the bay. He unbuckled his holsters, dangled the weapons in one hand and unbuttoned his gray tunic with the other. He shrugged out of the clinging wool, wound the big mass into a ball and threw the bundle into the water where it landed with a splash. Soon his gray tunic became water-logged and bit by bit submerged.

He prayed aloud, "That's my past, Lord. All the memories, pain, and loss are sinking to the bottom of the sea tied to my tunic." He lifted his hands to the sky. "The past is in Your hands. Cleanse me from my sins, pain, regret, and loss. Let me walk with You anew, as I did when I first received Christ into my life." He tilted his face to the sky, eyes closed. "Let me walk with You fresh, clean and new." He bowed his head. "Thank you, Lord."

A load lifted from his shoulders. His chest felt light and free. He holstered his guns around his undershirt. God was the God of new beginnings. New life. New hope.

Renewed faith. Like the Bible verse he learned as a child,

Therefore if any man be in Christ, he is a new creature: old things are passed away; behold, all things are become new. II Corinthians 5:17.

His words came out in a bullfrog whisper. "Tomorrow is a new day. I'll start over with Olivia."

Chapter 9

Knock. Knock.

Olivia dragged in a relieved breath. So, despite her hair-raising reaction last night, she hadn't frightened him off. He had given his word he would help.

She exchanged a glance with Darcy who sat primly on her side of the made bed, her gloved hands folded in her lap, her small hat perched atop her abundant curls.

Olivia threaded her way through the packed trunks, her new satchel, the bed, and the dresser. She fortified herself with as deep a breath as she could take given her tight corset, then opened the door.

A tall, broad-shouldered man looking dapper in a black tweed double-breasted frock coat stood, tall silk hat in hand, polished English-style laced shoes peeking out beneath tailored slacks.

She gasped. Dizzy spots peppered her vision. She'd steeled herself to face the Confederate gray. But the shining sheriff's star adorning the man's chest proclaimed she'd made no mistake. This was Sheriff Macaulay. And he was quite a handsome man. A noticeably handsome man. An over-abundantly handsome man.

She'd never quite scrutinized him before, having been stopped by the gray uniform. Mahogany eyes fringed with dark lashes stared at her with what she could only surmise as an anxious expression. His nose indicated aristocratic breeding. His pleasant lips were parted in an apologetic smile, showing even white teeth. Quite a balanced face. One an artist would love to paint.

Her hand rose to her throat where her pulse throbbed. He rather took her breath away.

He nodded. "Mrs. Baker. I'm here to help you move to the

Barlow residence. I trust you are packed and ready to leave."

"Um, yes."

"Shall I come in?"

"Oh, I'm so sorry. I've forgotten my manners. Do, please come in. Yes, by all means, come inside." So, the man wasn't *flaunting* his Southern sympathies. She'd had a mistaken view of him. Obviously, the man standing before her didn't live in the past.

Why didn't he come inside? Oh, she blocked the doorway. She moved aside.

His melted chocolate eyes glanced around her small hotel room. "These two trunks. Anything else?"

"No, this is all we have." Why didn't Darcy say something to break the awkward silence? Where was her little chatterbox mouth when she needed her to speak?

"Let's get to it. Won't take long. The Barlows only live a few blocks east of the waterfront." He heaved the nearest trunk to his shoulder. "I'll return for the other trunk."

Olivia motioned to Darcy to follow the man's back as he left the room and headed for the staircase.

Darcy shook her head. "You follow him. You're the one he's mesmerized with. He scarcely glanced in my direction. Probably doesn't even realize I'm here." Darcy's eyes sparkled. She grinned, looking very much like a fluffy cat who pounced on a particularly succulent canary.

Olivia's hands flew to check her hat. On and balanced, yellow rose spilling properly over her hair. Hatpin would hold against the sea breeze. She smoothed her gloved hands over the folds of her oldest day dress. Why had she worn this old green silk? She should have dressed to make a better impression on the Barlows. Oh, why fool herself? Sheriff Macaulay was the first man she'd cared at all about dazzling since she arrived in Seattle. More to the point. He was the first man she'd wanted to charm since before she'd married Howard. And discovered how awful a man could be.

Without realizing her power, she'd attracted Howard. Then he'd seduced her with his loving words and soldier's uniform. He'd been handsome. But Howard had never been thoughtful. Or helpful. Or even kind.

Why hadn't she noticed that lack before she married him? There hadn't been enough time.

She scurried down the stairs, nodded good-bye to the hotel manager behind his desk, and hurried out the door. Sheriff Macaulay, already halfway down the block, hiked as easily as if he had no enormous trunk weighing down his shoulder.

Darcy's footsteps pounded behind her. Then her sister caught up. "Olivia Rose, where have you been hiding that man?"

Olivia managed a smile. "He's rather an eye-full, isn't he?"

"Um, yes!" Darcy giggled. "If I weren't engaged to Peter, I might be setting my sails for yonder sheriff myself." She hurried to catch up with the sheriff and called over her shoulder so Sheriff Macaulay couldn't help but hear, "Our helpful mover is obviously only interested in you, Olivia Rose!"

Olivia's face burned. Her neck burned. Her ears burned. She slowed her steps and followed her sister at a distance. Darcy loved being a minx. Especially since her sister was engaged and thought herself to be out from under Olivia's thumb.

Darcy's dancing steps caught up with the sheriff. He turned into a gravel walk that led up to a small one-story wooden home. Not a fancy place, but a wide porch welcomed them.

The sheriff knocked at the unpretentious door.

The door flew open and a young woman smiled up at the sheriff as if they were friends. "Welcome, Stark." She leaned over to see beyond his broad frame, a pretty smile on her face. "Welcome, ladies. We have a room ready for you!"

Oh dear, perhaps they wouldn't be welcome long. The house was small. A child clung to each side of the young lady's day gown. And the gown couldn't hide that the lady of the house would soon become a mother again.

Surely the small home was already crowded. How long until the new baby was born? A month, two at the most.

Darcy ran to Mrs. Barlow and bestowed a careful hug. Darcy's unlined face was bright with unconcern. Happy with love. Mischievous with teasing.

Olivia pressed a hand against her wildly beating heart. With Darcy's engagement to a man who loved her, Darcy's future was secure. But not her own. Sheriff Macaulay had found a temporary home for her. A very temporary home. She should be grateful.

The sheriff seemed a kind man, finding them a home and interrupting his busy day helping them move.

Kind, but was he trustworthy?

She must set out at once and visit Mr. Mercer again. She would not leave the man alone until he contracted her for a teacher in one of his schools. She would beg him, pester him, and beseech him, but she must get a teaching position.

She followed the sheriff through the front door, down a short hallway, passed by a Lilliputian-sized living room and several rooms with closed doors into a diminutive back bedroom where he deposited her trunk on the floor near a miniature armoire.

"I'm sorry the room is so small. I thought the home was larger." He kept his voice low.

She couldn't answer. Just tried to swallow the lump in her throat.

"I'll bring the other trunk."

Worry creased his forehead. But the fast walk in the heat hadn't caused him to break into a sweat. Well, he didn't have a corset strangling him like she did. Or making him breathless.

She should be thinking of her future and how to care for herself.

Instead she gazed up at him. Why hadn't she noticed what a fine figure of a man he was?

Wouldn't it be lovely if she had not a care like Darcy and could fall in love with a man?

She turned and dumped her satchel on the bed. But she did have cares. And she would find it difficult to fall in love with a man again. She'd been a wide-eyed innocent once, but those days were long past. Men could be very cruel. There must be something about her that drew brutish men to seek her out. Fortunately, she had no such worries concerning Darcy's Captain Pike. The man might not be the richest catch Darcy could net, but Peter Pike obviously believed Darcy to be the moon and stars given to him to navigate with. The man adored her.

"I'll be on my way."

"Thank you for your help."

"I'm available anytime."

Olivia pretended she hadn't heard. She unclasped one lock of her trunk.

His footsteps echoed through the small house, then the front door quietly shut.

Darcy bounded into the room. "Oh, he's wonderful. You must choose him, Olivia Rose!" She giggled, "Or I might break my engagement and marry the handsome Sheriff Macaulay myself!"

Olivia whirled to face her sister.

Darcy giggled and giggled. "Oh, you should see your face! I knew you liked him."

"Nonsense. Help me unpack." She snapped open the trunk. "Actually, you unpack. I must go thank our hostess."

She tread softly out of the room.

She really must get over her shock and behave more like a lady than a shrew with Sheriff Macaulay.

But she was obligated to walk a fine line to be certain she didn't encourage the man. She had no wish to break a vulnerable man's heart. Probably best to see as little of him as possible.

Chapter 10

Stark turned his feet toward the saloon and the Justice of the Peace office. Had to show the law's presence on the street as well as accustom the unruly residents to his new identity. He flipped open the bottom buttons of his new suit jacket to reveal his double holsters. He'd left his silk hat at his rented room and exchanged the fancy top hat for his new-fangled brown Stetson.

Liked the fit. Shaded his eyes and gave him a more formidable appearance. Probably keep the rain off too.

Okay. He'd settled Olivia and Darcy on Skid Row. Not the best neighborhood in Seattle, but the small house perched on the respectable side rather than the seedy side of the street which constituted the border to the poor areas of town. But, by the look of Mrs. Barlow, the mistress of the house would need that guest room soon. Yet, he'd scouted out every house in every neighborhood and there weren't any other married couples in Seattle willing to take in a Mercer Girl. So, the small house had to do. Until he could persuade Olivia to marry him.

Only one complication. Olivia Rose Baker didn't like him.

He'd work that dilemma out like he did all problems. One step at a time.

She had seemed to be partial to how he'd spruced up in his new garb. Her eyes lit up like a Christmas tree candle. But she wasn't typical of the other Mercer Girls. Most had already chosen a husband and been bound to him by the Justice. Nope. She was different.

What else could he do to change her mind about him?

Chapter 11

July 1866

Olivia tiptoed into the kitchen. Betty Barlow startled at the slightest noise. The woman looked utterly miserable with her huge stomach poking her day dress out like a dome in front of her as she tended to the three dirty, sweaty children straggling in through the kitchen door.

Olivia had taken over cooking, cleaning, and mending to help the young mother. Darcy had married her Captain Peter Pike and Olivia had grown to love and appreciate her new brother-in-law. She'd given her blessing to Darcy's quick marriage. Her sister had moved into a stately home on Elm Street that Captain had recently purchased. His mother remained in his other home.

Darcy invited her to move into a large upstairs room and Olivia accepted, but insisted she pay rent.

However, Olivia counted out her rapidly shrinking pile of coins each day as if she were a miser hoarding gold. Darcy did not ask that she pay rent or board, but Olivia couldn't mooch from her sister. She must beg Mr. Mercer yet once again. She simply had to procure that teaching contract. Was the man a fraud? Had he lured her here with the promise of a position when there was none to be had?

Why were so many schools needed when Seattle had been settled by bachelors? Where were the children who needed to be taught? Still, she hounded Mr. Mercer with his black pointed beard and bushy-browed eyes. She had done everything but threaten the man to gain a contract. She shoved the biscuits into the oven and turned to mash the potatoes.

Soon she had dinner on the table, the three children washed and seated, Betty and Bill Barlow at each end of the table, and her standing, since there was no other place to eat in the tiny kitchen. Mr. Barlow said grace, then they all dove into mashed potatoes and fried chicken.

She'd just finished her last bite when a knock reverberated at the front door.

"Oh, no. Not another suitor. Olivia, when will you settle on a husband? I do believe every man in town has come to our humble dwelling." Betty smiled to take any sting from her words.

"You may as well answer. We know the caller is looking for you."

Olivia nodded and scurried to the door. The sooner she got rid of whoever waited on the other side, the sooner she could wash and dry the dishes, then retire to her room and kick off her shoes.

She opened the door. Oh my, the handsome sheriff with the ruddy complexion, smooth shaven but with a shadow of whiskers darkening beneath his skin.

He swept off his Stetson and his brown eyes twinkled through the growing dusk. A smile tipped his lips at the corners. "Mrs. Baker, would you consent to an evening walk to the waterfront?"

"No thank you, Sheriff Macaulay." She'd answered automatically, so accustomed to discouraging other hopeful suitors.

"I have something I'd like to show you." His smile flashed. "I think you will like what you see."

"Can you not show me here on the front porch? I'm rather tired."

"Fine." One strong hand pointed to the swing at the far end. "Shall we sit?"

Despite herself, she smiled. "We can." She led the way and settled in one end as far toward the arm of the swing as her full skirts allowed.

He lowered himself smoothly, not crowding her. A clean masculine scent wafted over. Despite herself, she breathed in his fragrance.

"Lovely evening. Not too hot." His bass voice rolled over her like the smooth ebb and flow of the waves against a pier.

"Yes. But you said you have something to show me."

He unbuttoned his coat and reached inside his vest pocket. The shine of a gun snug in a holster caught her gaze. Nice to have a lawman nearby. And he was interested. His polished boots, pressed trousers, neat suit with a trim fit over his broad shoulders, and his newly barbered and clean hair all attested to the fact that he'd spent time on his appearance before he showed up. Some of her callers didn't but rushed over straight from work as if afraid someone else would beat them to her.

The sheriff held up several, folded pages. "This is for your signature, should you decide to accept this position."

Her heart beat faster, slightly blurring her eyesight. Could it be? She unfolded the paper. Four pages. It was! Oh, heavens, she could not believe it. Was this man a magician? He'd pulled a slight-of-hand with Asa Mercer. A man she'd found immovable.

Carefully she read the four pages, scanning for some trickery or catch. There was none as far as she could tell. A year's contract for a teaching position.

Her hand shook as she gazed down at the sheets. "A recently built schoolhouse? It's called Central School and the building is located right in Seattle, not on one of the islands! Oh, this is perfect!" She almost gave into the overwhelming urge to hug the sheriff, but his large presence didn't seem embraceable. Until he twisted toward her on the swing seat and opened his arms.

But she caught herself in time. The man was too attractive. Too masculine. Too inviting. But she did take his hand. "Thank you so much, Sheriff. I know you must have somehow orchestrated this because Mr. Mercer remained adamant, he had nothing for me. Whatever you did to change his mind, I am profoundly grateful!"

The sheriff nodded. "Please call me Stark."

"Stark."

"Yes, I donated the land. And the house." He shook his head when she tried to place the contract back into his hands. "Believe me, Mrs. Baker, the Seattle district has a need for a good schoolteacher. Sign the paper. I'll be your witness, and I'll return the contract to Asa tomorrow morning."

The man was pure comfort. His bulk promised safety. And his face, kindness. "Thank you, Stark. You may call me Olivia."

She smoothed the contract over her knee, and in the growing dusk, took the pen he handed her and signed the agreement with a flourish. "How—?"

A scream raised the hair on the nape of her neck. "It's Betty. She's past term. The baby must be coming. I have to go inside. Have you ever delivered a baby, Stark?"

"Not in my line of duty, Olivia." His words caressed her name.

She jumped up and rushed across the porch to the front door, her hand on the knob. "I'm sorry to hurry off, but I have to go."

She entered the house, pressed herself against the wall. And waited for his footsteps.

Finally, the swing creaked, and his steps thudded across the porch and down the stairs.

Obviously Stark had wanted more from her. Perhaps he, like so many other far less attractive men, had wanted to ask to court her.

Stark truly had burrowed a soft place in her heart. But it was a very small place. And big as he was, and try as he might, he'd never fit inside.

LOVE AT CHRISTMAS

Chapter 12

October 1866

Asa Mercer rested a hip on Olivia's desk. He'd stalked into the classroom and up to the front as soon as her last pupil shuffled his papers and thrust them inside his desk. But the tall student didn't leave.

"It's all right, James. Mr. Mercer is an acquaintance. I'm perfectly safe with him." Her heart warmed and she gave James her most confident smile.

The eleven-year-old nodded and scooted for the door.

As soon as she was alone with Asa Mercer, Olivia raised herself from her chair to face the man. She planted her feet, with her hands braced on her desk, her eyes level with his. "I've never thought of myself as a particular woman, but no man appeals to me in the least." Olivia straightened and crossed her fingers behind her back. "The men I knew in Massachusetts were so different. And I understood their ways." How many times would Mr. Mercer seek her out to lecture on her need to marry?

"Nevertheless, you must choose one." Asa Mercer stroked his beard.

"But the men in Seattle are as unfathomable to me as is the reason why my late husband volunteered to fight a war he had no good reason to join."

"I repeat, you must choose a husband. All the other ladies have taken a husband and are well on their way to becoming pillars of society. Being a teacher is fine. Being a wife and mother is far more admirable. Look to your sister for a good example."

"True, Darcy is blissfully happy. And I'm gratified she's found such a compatible husband."

"Mrs. Baker, as a single woman, a widow, you are not safe. I cannot guarantee your safety among so many desperate-to-marry males. You must make a choice!"

"I'm quite safe living with my sister, inside her home." She bent to pick up a sheaf of test papers.

"Captain Pike is absent three weeks out of four each month. Do you not realize every single man in Seattle is aware of his schedule?"

Her throat tightened. Some of the papers slipped from her grasp. "Um, no I did not." She let the rest of the papers slide to her desk.

"Please do not force me to threaten you. Men in this town paid three hundred dollars for your passage here. I spent precious months of my time bringing you here. Your stepping foot on the steamship was overt agreement to our written contract." His frown furrowed his forehead to a deep V between his eyes. "You are the single unwed woman from the ladies I transported here. You're the topic of conversation in every building, fishery, saloon, and cabin. Not to mention the object of numerous fist-fights and heated discussions!" Mercer's beet-red face grimaced. "You have until Christmas to make your choice."

"Or what?" The tattoo of her heart almost drowned out her voice.

"Or I will choose for you. Or you will pay your three-hundred-dollar debt in cash on Christmas day. And you can be certain your teaching contract will not be renewed."

****

The next day Olivia strolled between the double row of school desks, pig-tailed girls in one row and mischievous boys in the other. She had only six students ranging in age from seven to eleven, but she loved each one of them. And hoped they loved her.

Each head bowed over her tests, pencil in hand, and the children either pulling a tuft of hair, or a tip of tongue protruding from a pursed mouth, or a cheek propped on an upraised fist. Thinking. Answering. Working out the arithmetic problems.

If only she could work out her problems as easily.

Mercer had reached the end of his patience. As she had known he would eventually. But she still had no answers. She meandered to her desk which Stark had centered in the front of the school room. Her gaze swept across the room of intent students and out the large rear window. The Cascades loomed a lovely purple shadow against a crisp, clear autumn day. Solid. Protective of the small town growing beneath the mountain's shelter. The air so pure she could see for miles.

October with its pumpkins and falling red, gold, brown leaves already painted the outdoors. Halloween and Thanksgiving would soon arrive and depart. Then Christmas would stampede in. She had so little time. What would she do? Mercer did not make threats in vain. He would pin her to the wall. And he'd chosen Christmas, her favorite time of the year, as his deadline. She loved the carols, the decorations, the good cheer, the special cookies and cakes, the parties, and the giving. But best, she loved remembering the sacred time of year they celebrated when her Lord Jesus left His home in heaven and was born in a humble manger. When God Himself became man.

All six of her students would dress-up to participate in a play for the parents. They would enact the sacred birth, the shepherds, and the angels. O Holy Night. The Barlows' new baby was not too old to play the part of the infant lying in the manger. She didn't miss living in their tiny back bedroom, but she did miss Betty and her rowdy household. She would stop in to see—.

Bang! Slam! The door flew open.

Six heads pivoted back to see who had slammed into the schoolhouse.

Olivia sprang up from behind her desk. What?

The tall, broad-shouldered man clad in a heavy flannel shirt, denims, and tall boots strode up to her desk.

The children watched, wide-eyed. James half rose from his seat.

"Mrs. Baker." The man thrust out a thick, muscled hand. "I'm Jewett Thompson." He grabbed her hand in a tight grip that almost made her cringe. He turned to the open-mouthed children. "Back to work, urchins! I'm here to talk with your teacher." He targeted them with eyes so fierce they lowered their heads and pretended to work. She nodded to James to sit. The skinny eleven-year-old would be no more match for the lumberjack than she.

"Mr. Thompson. You can't simply barge in here and interrupt—"

"Nonsense!" His waved a hand as if to dismiss any inconvenience he might have caused. "I'm here to talk business. You're a woman with a strange accent, but pretty as any picture."

"Please, Mr.—"

"Hold your horses, until I've had my say!" His voice boomed through the room like thunder. "Now, you're a widow woman. And I'm a widower. Live over on Whidbey Island. I've five children to raise and am gone from home from daylight to dusk working as a lumberjack. So, you see I have need of a wife. And you have need of a husband."

"But—"

He bent and pushed a finger to her lips to shush her. Asa sent me over and told me to put a ring on your finger or he'd put one in my nose. So, what do you say?"

****

That night as she sat around the dining table at Darcy's elegant home, Olivia threw her napkin on the table. "Oh, stop laughing Darcy, the man's breaking into my schoolroom and proposing in front of the children is not in the least funny."

Darcy giggled so hard her face turned red. She coughed and choked.

Peter set his water glass at the edge of his plate and glared. "You say Mercer's sending men to propose? What's his problem?"

"I don't know. He wants money or marriage, and I don't know why."

"Hmm. I've heard by way of scuttlebutt that Mercer's hard up for cash. Three hundred's a lot of money. I don't have that kind of greenery lying about or I would go to him and pay him off. He has no right to pressure you." His kind look and understanding stirred Olivia's heart. Darcy had married a prince.

"Oh, but I think Mr. Mercer really wants you to find a wonderful husband as I have." Darcy's smile brightened the room more than the candles flickering at the center of the table. She and Peter shared a loving look. "I understand that many men besiege him daily to put a good word in your ear for them. I think he really wants to see all his Mercer Girls happily married."

"But your sister needs time." Peter stuck his fork into a delicate piece of his sautéed trout.

"Ha, she's had almost five whole months. Why in that time you and I," Darcy blushed prettily, "are a quarter of the way to having our first little bundle of joy."

Peter's chest puffed, and a look of pride settled on his face. He popped the fish into his mouth and reached a hand across the table to take Darcy's slender fingers. "You will make a splendid mother."

Olivia couldn't keep the happy smile from her face. Dear Darcy had indeed made a fortunate marriage. Back home in Lowell she would have been shoveling snow and pining away for a life, as well as a husband, and she'd have no delightful baby on the way. Yes, moving here had been the answer for Darcy.

And she was content teaching children who swallowed learning like fishermen's nets snapped up a fresh catch.

Darcy's eyes twinkled with mischief. "Tell Peter about when Mr. Peacock, who owns the Cadillac Hotel, offered his penthouse to you if you'd consent to become his wife."

Olivia shook her head. "No. It's not kind to make fun of poor Mr. Peacock. He does need a wife."

"What about the story of when the owner of the *Seattle Gazette* promised you that he'd work for women's suffrage if you'd marry him."

"You've heard that story too? I'm ashamed I've told you about some of my proposals."

"Tell Peter what you heard after school yesterday."

"I overheard Hiram Burnett, owner of the steam-engine powered lumber mill, beg Mr. Mercer to bring another load of marriageable women to Seattle. He wants a wife, but he said I, the last unwed woman in town, was too uppity for his taste. When Mr. Mercer declined, the sawmill owner produced a huge diamond ring and asked me to marry him. I was his last resort!"

Darcy and Peter laughed. Olivia thought she'd better keep the rest of her proposals to herself. Despairing men really weren't funny.

A knock sounded at the front door.

Olivia sprang up, trotted to the front room, and opened the door. She stood and talked for a few minutes then returned to the dining table.

"What was that?"

"You'll never believe me, Darcy."

"Who? Who?"

"Doc Maynard just asked for my hand."

"Of course, you said no."

"Of course."

"That was fast. How did you get him to leave?"

"I didn't. He admitted he was a curmudgeon as well as a dedicated bachelor, and that Mercer blackmailed him into asking."

"So, he was happy you didn't agree to marry him? Why is Mr. Mercer trying to marry you off?" A pretty frown worried Darcy's forehead.

"I think the men in town are pressuring Mr. Mercer to force me to make a choice."

"Once you do, the town will settle down. But until you do, riots will break out. You're quite a commodity, Olivia!" Peter rubbed his chin and looked thoughtful.

"Olivia Rose, isn't there a single man in this town that you would wed?"

"I'm more than happy teaching my children."

"What of the money you owe Mercer?"

"Yes, there is that problem."

She had no money, nor was she likely to obtain any. Her small salary went straight from her hands to Peter's. She insisted on paying for her room and board. She didn't want to be a burden for the newlyweds.

So, money was out of the question. Was there any other way to pay off Mr. Mercer?

Chapter 13

December 1866

With the moon high in the sky, Stark shimmied up a leafless apple tree in Doc Maynard's prize orchard. The full moon lit a large growth on a lower branch, and he cut the clump from the tree with his bowie knife. His boots slipped as he climbed to a higher branch, skinned out to the end, noticed a chickadee nesting in the full-flowered mistletoe, and passed by the fragrant greenery. He climbed higher and crawled further out on limbs that bent beneath his weight. Finally, he dropped down to the grass. He opened his bag. Yep, he'd harvested seven bunches of mistletoe.

Wind ripped through his jacket as he high-tailed back to the small, rented room he deemed good enough until he married. After that he would build a fine home for his wife.

****

Stark rode Rebel to a hill above the schoolhouse and reined him in. He'd been busier than a one-armed man saddling a green bronc trying to keep all the young, red-blooded men from killing each other. The town remained in an uproar over the one remaining unwed Mercer Girl. But no more in a turmoil than his own heart. He loved her.

No, he hadn't known her since childhood like he had Julia, but she held his heart firmly in her lovely hands. He'd watched from afar as she interacted with the school children. How kind and loving her smile as she tended each one. Even those older boys who played tricks on her and on the girls.

He loved the artistic ability Olivia displayed in decorating the school room and writing stories for the children so they could act in plays. He'd noticed her sensitivity to other people's needs. Most of all, he applauded the love she showed to each child, naughty or nice.

Seemed Olivia loved everyone in Seattle…except the battalion of men vying for her hand.

Christmas was a scant twenty days away. Every man in town knew Mercer had ordered Olivia to make her spousal choice before Christmas day. Men had grown as frenzied as fish in chummed water.

But she remained distant from all of them, including every rich, powerful, influential man in Seattle.

And especially from him.

Rebel shied, ears thrust backwards, and front hooves pawing the air. He pranced in a circle.

Stark gentled him with soothing words and pats. What made his horse nervous? No predatory animal roamed this part of the woods overlooking the schoolhouse. No man dared burst into her schoolroom again or he'd face the law in the person of Stark Macaulay. No storm approached.

What?

A wisp of smoke rose from one window of the schoolhouse. Fire!

Chapter 14

Too many nights without sleep. Olivia propped her elbow on the desk and her chin on her hand and fought to keep her eyes open. She had no solution to her problem.

But she would not be forced into marrying a man to pay her debt, or to retain her teaching position. She had no money to move to another town, nor did she want to leave Darcy. She and her sister had no other family. There was only Darcy and her, and now Peter. And soon the baby. Leaving them would tear her apart. Alone at night, writhing between the sheets and the quilts, she spent endless hours trying to form a plan.

But no plan came to mind.

Last night she'd barely slept. Her head slipped off her chin, jerked and woke her. Goodness, even the children seemed sluggish and drowsy today. She would have opened a window to allow fresh air to blow inside, except the day was raw with overhanging clouds and gusty wind.

Elsa, her youngest pupil, had her head resting onto her curved arms on her desk. Even rascally Ned's eyes were lowered at half-mast. She must stir herself and encourage the children to finish their homework. But the effort seemed too great. She lifted her head. Her whole body felt sluggish.

She rubbed her eyes. The room seemed hazy. And too warm for such a cool day. Something red wavered at the point where the wall met the floor just behind James's desk. A crackling sound. Her tardy brain registered.

"Fire!" The door burst open, and a big man hurtled into the room. "Out! Everyone out! The place is on fire." A star twinkled on the man's chest. He sprinted to the back of the room and shook

James's shoulder.

The boy looked up and slowly nodded.

Every action seemed as if it occurred underwater, slow, wavering, and moving against an invisible barrier.

Stark had come. He would do the right thing. Olivia smiled and lay her head on her desk.

****

Stark grasped James by the neck of his shirt and hauled him to his feet. "Run outside!"

James nodded and plodded, one slow footfall after another toward the doorway.

Stark collared the other two boys, yanked them to their feet, and headed them toward the door. "Outside fast!"

The two boys trudged toward the door like wooden soldiers, legs and arms moving with jerks.

Stark gathered two of the younger girls, one under each arm, and carried them out the door into the yard where the boys stood, open-mouthed gazing red-eyed, water streaming down their cheeks, at the burning schoolhouse.

Stark raced back inside, flung the oldest girl over his shoulder, lugged her outside and dumped her on the grass. Then he dashed toward the building where flames licked up all sides of the wooden building like gluttonous tongues.

Inside, dark smoke obscured his view. Where was she? His lungs burned. Olivia had been sitting at her desk near the front. He bent his elbow over his nose and mouth to protect as well as he could his breathing. She was here somewhere. His searching hand felt a student desk. Further to the front. He touched the edge of the larger teacher's desk. Then collided with her soft shoulder.

He bent, hauled her into his arms, and shuffled toward the exit. She was not a large woman, maybe a hundred pounds, plus a few more. His breath scorched inside his chest. He coughed, the sound hoarse and raspy. She was limp, her head bobbing over his arm. Dead weight. But he had only a few feet more to navigate, and they would be outside in the crisp, fresh air.

He stumbled, fell to one knee. Dragged himself to his feet. Roaring filled his ears. The fire blazed fiercely, consuming the building, bellowing huge black clouds of deadly smoke. Which direction? He'd lost his way.

"Over here!"

Stark followed the faint voice. He'd gotten turned around in the heavy smoke. He dragged his heavy feet, and the doorpost bumped under his boot. Then he struggled outside to light and air. He inhaled large gulps of oxygen, then coughed and coughed.

He carried his precious burden to the tree under which all the rescued children clustered. He stumbled again. This time he let himself fall to both knees, then lay Olivia out on the winter-brown grass.

Townspeople drawn by the smoke gathered around them.

A crash reverberated as the schoolhouse collapsed into burning timbers and ashes.

Someone offered a gourd of water. He drank, then tried to see Olivia. No chance. Women surrounded her and the children.

"Hero. Stark Macaulay's a hero," people whispered.

Stark tried to speak, but his hoarse words fell uselessly to the ground. "No hero. God had me at the right place at the right time."

LOVE AT CHRISTMAS

Chapter 15

Once Olivia recovered from the fright and physical reminders of the fire, she left Darcy's new home and set out for the sheriff's office. Her boots clattered on the boardwalk past the mercantile, the grocery, the Occidental Hotel, the Milliner's, the seamstress, and the ice factory. She turned into the single wooden door with the word Sheriff printed in black paint with uneven script.

Inside a desk faced an empty jail cell. Both were small. A pot-bellied stove in the corner humming with heat sent rosy beams through the glass window to be reflected by the wood sidewalls. A coffee pot sat on the flat iron surface. Four rounded-back wooden chairs lined one wall. Despite the meager furnishings, the room seemed cozier than she'd expected. Maybe the stack of books overrunning one corner of the desk. Or the harmonica lying where a hurried hand had placed it. Or the red, white, and blue rag rug lying in front of the desk. A faint fragrance tickled her nose. She followed the direction of the sweet scent to a bowl of water, filled to the brim with fresh-looking sprigs of olive-green leaves dotted with white berries, half-hidden on an antique cabinet behind the desk. She touched a leaf. Who could believe clumps of mistletoe decorating a sheriff's office?

Oh my! The ancient tradition jangled around inside her head. *A man is allowed to kiss any woman standing beneath the mistletoe, and bad luck befalls any woman who refuses the kiss. With each kiss, a berry is plucked from the mistletoe. The kissing must stop after all the berries have been removed.*

There were so many berries on the leaf stalks. Twenty-five or thirty on each sprig and she counted, one, two, three, four, five, six, seven sprays. That was a lot of berries. A delightful shiver spiraled up her spine.

Kissing. She'd never been kissed. Howard had never taken the time to kiss her. He'd been in a great hurry to— She shook her head. No, she wouldn't think about that.

Would it be pleasant to be kissed by a man? Mama and Papa always kissed her goodnight. Darcy pecked her cheek now and then. Some people must enjoy kissing if they kissed until the last berries were removed from the bough.

Her heartrate sped and heat burned her cheeks. This was Stark's office. Those were his boughs of mistletoe. Still fresh enough to waft fragrance.

She turned toward the door, suddenly feeling like an intruder. No question who they were meant for since she was the only single woman living in Seattle. Had she peeked into a very private place inside a man's heart?

She turned the knob. Fiddlesticks!

A sudden rainstorm doused enormous buckets of rain onto the street. She gazed at the sky. Cloudy, overcast, gray. But not thick clouds. The storm should abate in a few minutes. She need only wait a short while to avoid getting drenched, and she'd worn her best dress and straw hat to thank Stark.

She'd wait out the storm.

She tiptoed over to perch on one of the wooden chairs. The bowl of mistletoe changed the whole atmosphere of the room. Now she felt sneaky. Window-peeking into a man's soul

She reached over and flipped the top book to read the title. Poetry? The brave, hard-fisted sheriff read poetry? She frowned. Now that she thought of it, he'd been southern born. She'd heard those southern men carried soft hearts beating beneath their hard-muscled chests. What a study in contrasts. Lumbermen, husky fishermen, businessmen, seemed every sort of man in Seattle respected Stark. And he kept the peace in an unpeaceful town. She bet none of the tough men he ruled knew he read books of poetry.

She smiled. His honey-smooth drawl brought to mind a slow pace of living where people took time to know one another. Living in towns filled with flowers she'd only read of, crape myrtle, hibiscus, magnolia. The man was a study in contrasts. He never walked without his weapons. Yet he never passed Darcy on the street without tipping his Stetson and asking how she fared. Even the curmudgeon Doctor liked Stark. And, he'd never missed a Sunday at Church. Perhaps that was the secret to Stark Macaulay. The man walked with God.

Howard had not. Nor had he ever opened a book in her presence, and certainly not a book of poetry.

She gazed out at the rain slanting hard with little hisses against the windowpane. She should leave before he returned and found her in his private lair. She smoothed her best silk dress. Not yet. Soon the rain would slack and then end as it did so often during these dreary winter months.

This small room with its forbidding jail cell should feel cold and uncomfortable. But it did not. Rather it provided a haven. Perhaps because of the man who spent portions of his days here. The pot-bellied stove sent out a rosy light and heat and the occasional crackle and snap of sound. No doubt kept him company when no one lolled on the cot inside the cell.

She strolled over to the desk, fingered the top volume, and unable to control her curiosity opened the book. Wordsworth. She'd memorized her favorite, *Daffodils*. She spoke the lines softly without seeking the words in the book.

"And then my heart with pleasure fills, And dances with the daffodils."

The molasses slow voice joined with hers in the final lines. Then he shut the door.

She backed against the desk. "Oh, dear! I didn't notice you come in."

"I'm happy you didn't. You know Wordworth's words by memory. He's one of my favorites."

Olivia gripped her handbag with both hands. "Well, uh, I stopped by to thank you for saving my life."

His eyelids lowered, shutting out the intense brown of his gaze. "Anyone would have done what I did." Red tinged his cheeks.

"No. No. I don't think so. And you saved all the children. I shall be forever grateful."

"No need. I was just in the right place at the right time."

"Nevertheless, I am grateful." His shirt was dry, and the hat he held in his hands did not drip. She glanced out the window. "Oh, I see the rain has stopped. I shall be leaving."

He stepped aside from the door, his boots scraping on the floor. "You brighten my lonely office. Won't you stay a while?"

A twinge of mischief tweaked her. "I think your sprigs of mistletoe lend just the right touch to make this jail a sanctuary. What do you plan to do with all those boughs?"

Red crept up from his cheeks to brighten his ears. He shifted his feet. Then he swallowed and flashed a smile. "I'm planning to hang a sprig over every doorway she might walk through until I catch my future bride beneath the mistletoe."

"And then what do you plan?" Had those saucy words slipped from her mouth?

"I plan to marry her on Christmas Day, the holiest day of the year." He moved toward her and snatched a sprig of mistletoe from the bowl. He shook off the water and held the spray over her head.

She should run. The rain had stopped. She was alone with a man. He held a sprig of mistletoe over her head. What would it feel like to be kissed by a man? She stood on tiptoe. She meant to find out.

Stark was a man of action, and he did not need a second invitation. His lips came close, then hesitated.

What was he waiting for? She opened her eyes. His lips hovered tantalizingly close. His aura so masculine. Fear slashed through her breast, almost making her back away. Yet, something about him gave her confidence to hold her ground. He was strong enough to easily overcome her, if that was his intent. But he waited. For her to decide. His eyes were closed, and his arms hung at his sides, everything about him hushed, waiting.

She stretched up her hands and cupped his angular face, feeling whiskers soften under her touch. She tugged him closer and pressed her lips to his. Ahh…lovely. She stepped away.

He reached out with one arm, encircled her as if she were a treasure to protect, and drew her close. His other hand still dangled the mistletoe above her head. He brought his lips down on hers. Warm. Sensual. Not demanding. Not asking. Taking his time.

Exploring.

When she ended the kiss, she reached up to where he continued to hold the mistletoe above her head and plucked off two of the berries. "Goodness, see how many lovely berries are left clinging to the greenery."

He kissed her again.

The world stopped. They were alone. Nothing in her past nagged fear or dragged on her soul. This was a new experience. Her heart danced, but not with daffodils, with lovely boughs of magic mistletoe. And they had more berries, many more berries on the twig. That made her heart dance and sing.

Definitely, she would not have bad luck from refusing a kiss standing beneath the mistletoe. There were still more berries. Would they pluck them all before she left his office? She hoped so.

This was a man she could trust. A man who was not demanding. A man who honored her wishes above his own. A man who would not abuse her as Howard had.

And here in the Northwest, as well as in the South, and of course back home in Massachusetts, a kiss was an implied contract between a man and a woman. Not lightly entered into.

Stark dropped to one knee. "Olivia Rose Davenport Baker will you give me the honor of becoming my wife?"

Chapter 16

With the schoolhouse building burned, Doc Maynard offered Olivia his office as a temporary replacement. The Doc seldom used his office as he did most of his doctoring on site. When someone needed him, he hopped on his horse and galloped to the injured party. With severely injured patients, Doc often spent the night at their home or at the logging camp.

Olivia noticed that the middle-aged Doc enjoyed popping in and regaling her students with some of the history of Washington Territory and how Seattle sprang into being when Arthur Denny conveyed a group of travelers from Illinois to establish a logging camp. Doc also painted a picture of how Seattle became a gateway to Alaska during the Klondike Gold Rush. He'd caught the fever but returned poorer but wiser.

The children loved the Doc's colorful stories. And so did Olivia.

She soon transformed the spacious office to a busy schoolroom with Christmas art and decorations supplied by the students. Helping the children decorate the room brightened the dreary, chilly, rainy days leading to Christmas.

And helped relieve her uncertainty. With the days speeding by until her deadline, Olivia grew more certain. She would not be forced into marriage.

When she was not teaching, she enjoyed getting together with the ladies she'd journeyed from Lowell with. The ladies, along with every other woman in town, fifty-one in number, formed a Women's Guild which met once a week at the Yesler's home. The ladies decided a Christmas play would liven the holidays.

Everyone was invited. Olivia would write the play depicting

the birth of Jesus in Bethlehem, and the children would be the actors. Because so many residents were expected, the play would be performed at the Washington Territorial College auditorium. Afterward, everyone would adjourn to the reception room for refreshments, provided, of course, by the Women's Guild.

That evening Mayor Denny would preside over a tree-lighting of the twenty-foot tall fir tree growing in front of the Mercantile. A contingent of ladies assembled in the classroom to work along with the children making decorations for the communal tree.

Every evening during the week before Christmas Olivia joined an ensemble of carolers and traipsed from house to house singing carols. Other carolers assembled on the corner of Main and Elm to serenade those people doing last-minute Christmas shopping or enjoying the Christmas festival atmosphere. The Women's Guild all agreed they wanted to make their first Christmas in Seattle memorable.

Christmas certainly would be memorial for her. A deadline.

In addition, the Women's Guild planned a dance. Since Seattle had no building large enough to hold a dance, some of the talented carpenters set to work constructing a large building on the level end of Main Street. Everyone agreed that after the dance, the building would be converted into a new Central School with two rooms, one for the younger children and one for the older. Hopefully in a few years there would be enough children to fill the schoolhouse.

Every able-bodied man not out felling trees or throwing the huge weighted nets into the sea showed up to lend a hand.

By Christmas Eve the two rooms were floored in, timbers at the corners supported a roof. Darkness fell as Olivia left the schoolroom at Doc's office and strolled by to see how the project was progressing. She pulled her shawl closer to ward off the cool wind from the ocean. The platform appeared sturdy and quite lovely, unfinished as it was. It held promise. As did the bustling town. She'd made many friends here. Her job gave her a sense of satisfaction. Darcy's baby would soon make an appearance. Contentment almost overruled the nagging in her heart. She'd made her gifts. The children were ready for the play. The platform would support a large dance including the band of Seattle men who played fiddle and flute. All preparations were ready for Christmas.

But she still had one thing to do before tomorrow.

As if she'd thought him into being, Stark materialized from behind the platform. The moon rose and showered them with beams.

Her heart sped. What a dear man. A strong man. Trustworthy and kind. A Christian, not afraid to live his faith. And the man could kiss. Oh, yes, he could kiss. She felt safe in his arms. He erased all her negative thoughts concerning marriage. Gone. Forgotten. Did all this mean she'd fallen in love? And with a Southern gentleman?

"Hello, Olivia."

His soft words caused a thrill that centered in her heart and streamed all the way to her toes. What if she had missed all this joy?

She pulled a wilted sprig from her handbag. "Come closer?" she whispered.

He stepped so close both their breaths mingled in the cool air. "Do you have an answer?"

"Bend a bit, please. I have to know one more thing."

He bent his dark head, hair waving in the breeze. She held the mistletoe above his head. "Now kiss me, please."

He didn't hesitate. His strong arms wrapped around her, sending his warmth through her chill. He lowered his lips and kissed her thoroughly.

She would never get enough. But she finally wiggled free. "Yes, I'll marry you. Tomorrow we'll visit the Justice of the Peace, and I'll become Mrs. Stark Macaulay. No more a widow." She traced his lips with her gloved finger. "Not because Mr. Mercer forces me to marry. No. Never that. I'm marrying you because I love you. Because I want to marry you."

"Thank you, God! I've loved you from the moment I set eyes on you walking down that gangplank, your pretty mouth unsmiling, your stubborn jaw set, and your lovely eyes clouded. I wanted to put a smile on your lips, and a sparkle in your eyes. Something inside my chest exploded love. I love you, Olivia. I shall never hurt you. I'm not rich, but you've made me the wealthiest, happiest man in Seattle."

"Second chances. How many people are given a second chance to love?" She didn't bother hiding the astonishment in her tone. "God has given us both a second chance. Isn't that amazing?"

"Yes and no."

"No?" She snuggled inside his she'd-found-her-home embrace.

"God is full of surprises. No. I'm not surprised. And yet I am. Surprised at the magnitude of His gift. And that He healed your wounded heart. And so grateful. He brought you all the way across this great nation of ours...to me.

"Promise me one thing."

He nodded, his brown eyes melted chocolate. "Anything and everything."

"Promise me we will have a tree in our yard that mistletoe can leech into." She smiled up into his wind-reddened face. "I'll never avoid mistletoe again, as long as I can share it with you."

"We'll have an orchard full of trees overgrown with mistletoe."

"Kiss me again."

She felt secure in his tender embrace, his lips warm, promising her safe haven, his soul twining with hers.

Was the jingle of bells real or only in her imagination? Not far away one of the choirs sang, *Silent Night, Holy Night.*

The choir would catch them embracing. But she didn't care. On this night, over two thousand years ago, her Savior had been born. How appropriate that she discover the love of her life on Jesus' special night.

A WILLIAMSBURG CHRISTMAS
BY
ANNE GREENE

DEDICATION

To my wonderful husband, Larry. Thank you for our love story.
Thank you for supporting me in this great adventure of being an author. You are a gift from heaven. To my editor, Cynthia Hickey and my beta and critique friends, thank you.

To my readers. Much of what you'll read has historical truth and
threads of truth woven into this story. May you find love in your
Christmas.

Chapter 1

December 1, 1955

"I hope this Christmas won't be a disaster like last Christmas was." Holly Belle Silver clasped her hands under her chin as if in prayer.

Shirley Matthews wrinkled her long nose. "What are the odds?"

"Nothing can top last year. Even if Christmas turns tragic, this holiday can't best last year's."

"Want to talk about it?"

"No. I don't want to dwell on how close to the edge of catastrophe I live. Or think about how one minute I was snug, secure, happy, and the next my world dissolved under my feet." Holly shook her head. "Or how easily calamity could happen again."

"Okay. Not a good topic for today. I'll take a rain check."

"Great." Holly glanced around the interior of *Ye Olde Queen's Inn* and smiled at her fellow waitress. "Change of subject. I love decorating for Christmas, don't you?"

Shirley shrugged. "You went ape with the decorations. They're bad news to me. More work and extra hours. It bugs me no end Charlie makes his help do all this extra work."

Holly giggled. "Charlie asked for volunteers. I'm just happy you let me come up with all the ideas while you painted your nails."

"I've got a bash after work tonight." Shirley pointed her index finger. "You fracture me, always missing out on the fun." She slapped her hands on her hips, her newly painted crimson nails flashing. "Sure you can't go with me tonight?" Her face crumpled into a wry expression. "Don't be a wet rag. Let your sitter take care of the rug rats this once."

Holly smiled and retied a red ribbon on a wreath in the window. "Rake and Randy expect me to rush home and roast marshmallows in the fireplace, make hot chocolate, and read them a Christmas story. I can't disappoint my sons."

Shirley pulled out one of the Inn's leather Captain's chairs and flopped down. "How old are they again? They're twins right?"

Holly slid into a warm leather chair across the white-clothed table from Shirley. She flipped off the old-fashioned brown pumps that accompanied her Colonial costume and wriggled her tired toes. "Yes, twins. They're eight." She propped her feet on an adjacent chair's padded seat. "Charlie hired them to act as elves during Christmas vacation." She clapped her hands. "He doesn't know what he let himself in for."

Shirley jerked off her mop cap and shook out her blonde ponytail. "Bet those two mischief makers jumped at the chance to earn a little money."

Holly inhaled the sweet, outdoorsy scent of fresh fir boughs. Much as she enjoyed the Christmas lights on the huge tree in the center of the room as well as the small trees placed around the restaurant, she frowned. "They did. But I have horrible reservations. My twins are a handful. If they break one of the hurricane lamps and set fire to this place with the candles, Charlie better have his insurance paid-up."

"What they gonna do, hand out candy canes?"

"Yes. Christmas cookies and eggnog are involved as well." Holly adjusted the red ribbon around the poinsettia centerpiece. "But both boys love the elf costumes and are raring to come work with their Mom."

"Will they dig into those Christmas stockings you hung on the fireplace mantle?"

"I'll instruct them to touch nothing except what Charlie gives them to hand to the customers."

"Think that will work?"

"Nope! They'll need straightjackets." Holly cupped a hand over her ear. "Listen, we can hear the outside music."

Muted tones of the Trapp Family Singers and *Little Drummer Boy* floated through the windowpane. "Oh, I love Christmas and everything the giving season stands for! I love to commemorate the time when Baby Jesus was born in the stable. Such a precious—"

Shirley slapped her hands over her ears.

Holly pressed her fingers against her lips. Oops! Shirley hated her to talk about anything connected with Holly's faith.

"Time you started to look after yourself and get cooking with men again." A frown marred Shirley's pleasant face. "You still got a classy chassis and a mug to die for." She laid a warm hand over Holly's. "Don't flip your wig, but your better half's been gone two years now. Time you let go of the past and move forward." Shirley jumped to her feet and danced around the tables, her arms outstretched to embrace an imaginary partner. "Not many dreamboats steam into this restaurant, so you're gonna have to hit the road to find Mr. Dreamy."

"Shirley, I don't have time to date!" Holly sprang from her chair and joined Shirley. Felt good to let loose and dance.

When the drums to the Christmas carol faded, she padded barefoot to refold a napkin at the adjoining table, then placed the folded cloth back into the stemmed glass. "Because I love to have fun doesn't mean I'm ready to date." She placed a hand over her heart and shook her head. "I'm not."

"Okay, okay, don't get frosted. I gotta beat feet." Shirley swiped imaginary lint from the tablecloth. She gazed at Holly with a coy expression. "I could get on the horn and wrangle up some cool cats I know who'd be jazzed to date you."

"Go on to your party and have fun. Don't worry about me. When the best time rolls around, I'll meet Mr. Right." Holly smiled. "But thanks for offering."

"Hon, that kinda stuff, waiting around for a man, only happens in the flicks. Real life's no picture show." Shirley punched her shoulder. "Meanwhile back at the ranch, *we* gotta dig up that right man ourselves."

Holly skipped to the window and gazed out at the darkening street scene. Old-fashioned globe lights gleamed over happy shoppers hurrying toward home. Most of them couples. She jerked her attention back to the restaurant. "Never mind. Christmas is coming. Don't you believe in miracles?"

"Nope. We ordinary people make our own miracles. Look at me. I've been single all my life. I'm thirty years old, same as you, and no miracle has happened in this life. I attract either nerd or nowhere man. Why is that?"

"Maybe because you *don't* believe in miracles."

"Well, party pooper, let's head on upstairs and shed these threads. This costume's not the coolest duds I've ever worn."

Holly winked. "I don't know. The blue in our gowns brings out the sky-blue in your eyes." She raised her arms and swiveled her body from side to side. "And the white head-to-toe apron covers a lot of what we like to hide."

"As if you have any bad curves. But these mop caps are an absolute drag. The ugliest head coverings I've ever seen. Hides every lock of hair." Shirley smirked. "Even worse than head scarves. And my blonde halo's my best feature."

"Truer words were never spoken." Holly whipped off her mop cap, shook out her shoulder-length brown curls, and tossed her head to loosen them. She slipped the fat inch-and-a-quarter heels back onto her aching feet. "Feels good to finish for the day. I'd not noticed how my feet ache and my back hurts." She'd been too busy placing candles, wreaths, red holly berries, and lights around the restaurant, and trying not to get miffed with Shirley's lack of help. She glanced around. The Inn always looked warm and hospitable, with its wide-planked wooden floor, nicely spaced tables and chairs and floor-to-ceiling stone fireplace. But the extra Christmas candles and fir and cinnamon-scented decorations added enchantment to the scene. "It's magical, don't you think?"

"Right-o! We did a good two hours extra work. The place looks fab." Shirley undid the buttons at the nape of her white shawl, unhooked her white apron, and slid the neck-to-ankle white covering off.

Holly took one last look at her work and then clattered after Shirley up the steep flight of wooden steps to the employees' dressing area. Inside the stark room, she removed her apron and turned to let Shirley unbutton the back of her white shawl collar and her 1776 blue ankle-length gown. "I don't mind wearing this costume while I work, do you?"

"It's not so bad. Say, your family coming to spend Christmas with you?"

"Uh, no. My parents passed when I was the same age as my twins." Holly tugged the ankle-length blue dress over her head.

"Brothers or sisters?"

"No. Just me. I have an aunt who lives in Florida." She hung the dress on a hanger and slipped it onto the clothes rack. "Someday I'd love to scrape up enough money to visit her, but I don't see that happening anytime soon. What about you? Big family?"

Shirley rolled her eyes. "And how. Four sisters and four brothers. Mom was all happy with her brood, and then I came along. The mid-life surprise. We have a blast on Christmas when we all get together. You can join us." Shirley had her dress half off but struggled to get it over her head. "I'm such a spaz. Help me, will you? I didn't unbutton this all the way."

Holly helped her untangle the dress and tug it over her head. Would she and the twins fit in at Shirley's home or would they intrude on the Holiday family gathering? "You hang eleven stockings on your fireplace mantle?" Both stood in their long Colonial petticoats.

"Yep. House gets so crammed with people and ankle biters you can't turn around without stumbling over someone."

"Sounds like fun!" No, she couldn't barge into Shirley's family over the holidays. She swallowed. Though she'd love to experience a traditional big family Christmas get-together. "Chilly up here. Sure would be nice if Charlie coaxed the owners into installing a stove."

"Won't happen. I've been working here three years, and they haven't done a thing to improve this room." Shirley glanced around. "Not much more than an attic. Nothing here but cobwebs and clothes racks."

Holly slipped out of her long petticoat and into her own half-slip. She wiggled into her long-sleeved pink angora sweater, pulled her tweed pencil skirt over her head, tucked her sweater inside her skirt, and cinched her wide black belt around her narrow waist. She bent to slip into her black ballet slippers. "Ready?"

"Sure. Let's lay a patch." Shirley turned a waggish face to her. "We're tight, right?"

"Absolutely. You're my new best friend."

"So, like it or not, I'm hunting down that dreamboat for you and sending the two of you to the submarine races."

Holly shook her head. "Please don't. I have my hands full raising my twins. When they're grown, I *might* consider dating again. But for now, I'm too busy."

"So *you* say." Shirley winked a twinkling blue eye.

Oh brother. What did Shirley have up her sleeve? Her friend was a mover and shaker. A meddler. An enterpriser. She didn't let any grass grow under her feet when she had a scheme.

Obviously, Holly had become a project.

Holly sighed. This holiday might become a disaster after all.

Chapter 2

December 7, 1955

Holly lifted her face to the crisp late afternoon air and inhaled the scent of Christmas. How she loved this holiday.

Shirley met her at the corner and matched steps. Their ballet shoes made no noise on the cobblestones as they crossed Nicholson Street with its corner Apothecary shop and the Silversmith Shop that abutted the red brick building. Both shops were decked with bright red ribbons and green wreaths. Candles would soon light the windows.

Holly wrinkled her brow and spoke about what lodged uppermost in her mind these days. "What presents can I give the twins? Between rent, groceries, and other bills, I've got precious little money set aside."

"You'll come up with something." Shirley's concerned smile lit her plain features. "If they were girls, I'd crochet or knit them an afghan. But your rough and tumble boys would throw one of those in the back of their closets and never think of them again…except as an embarrassment."

"Right. Rake's interested in astronomy and yearns for a telescope. Randy keeps dropping *hints* that he wants Santa to bring him a Schwinn Bike. I wish they wanted something easy like a football or baseball bat."

"Don't they have a grandmother?"

"Nope. Just my boys and me."

Shirley's grin plumped her rosy cheeks. "Meet their honorary aunt then. I'll help you buy those expensive toys. I'd hate to see those kids disappointed by Santa."

"Oh, Shirley, can you? I'll find a way to pay you b—"

"Aunties don't get paid back. I'm Aunt Shirley." She giggled. "I've been Aunty Shirley for almost as long as I can remember. Two more little nephews can't break my bank."

Holly stopped and hugged Shirley. "I knew God would find a way for my smart, mischievous twins to build great memories this Christmas."

"Sure. Every Christmas in Williamsburg is red-letter. But I doubt God is involved."

"I know He is. He's using you with your heart of gold even though you're totally unaware He is. Don't look like such a Doubting Thomas."

"Whoever that is." Shirley grinned and winked. "I've got a hunch this Christmas will be one *you'll* never forget!"

Holly mugged a face at her friend and grinned. "What else do you have up your sleeves? I don't need you to be Santa's helper on my behalf."

"Santa can't deliver all those toys to happy little boys and girls without lots of help." Shirley's blue eyes twinkled. "By the way, are those elves of yours coming to the restaurant after school today?"

"Not until next week. They're absolutely on cloud nine about spending time there with me." She poked Shirley's shoulder. "They like to be with you as well. Rake says you're a blast and a half and Randy declares you're a cool cookie."

"Yeah? Imagine that. Those two characters are boss!"

Tucking her money woes into her I'll-think-about-that-problem-later shelf in her mind, Holly's heart lightened so she almost skipped down the Duke of Gloucester Street. "Shirley, admit you love the swags and boughs of firs, magnolia leaves, and red berries draped over the doors and windowsills of all the shops. Admit you love how magical this place is at night with all the Christmas lights glowing."

"Sure. Who wouldn't love it here this time of year?" Shirley's plain face lit to almost pretty. "You've only lived in Williamsburg a few months. I love this place in all seasons. Spring brings mounds of flowers and new menus at the Inn. Tourists jam our streets in summers. Fall is glorious with gold, rust, and red colors. But this season is best, with carolers, piped-in music, and those decorations you love to use." Shirley grabbed Holly's hand and swung it between them. "Christmas is especially beautiful when we get that once-a-year snowfall."

They passed the Millner Shop. Almost passed. Holly stopped and peered in the decorated window. A scroll-filled antique sign *Just Imported From London* heralded above an array of gorgeous women's 1776 large brimmed hats decorated with masses of flowers and ribbons. A gorgeous red cloak, with luxurious white fur outlining the hood, held court at one end of the display while a collection of men's tri-cornered hats presided in the opposite corner.

Shirley tugged Holly's arm. "Come on, we'll be late."

They strode past the gunsmith, the basket maker, and the print shops without stopping to stare into the windows. The sun hung low in the west casting a golden gleam over the restored Colonial town. "I've only been here a couple months, but I love living here, working here, and raising my boys here."

Shirley nodded. "The longer you live here the more you'll love it. You were lucky to get that last apartment inside the park."

"Not luck. God's hand."

Shirley wrinkled her nose and walked faster.

Bing Crosby's *White Christmas* wafted through the streets from the town's audio system. Holly hummed along, nodding to the many visitors, hands gripping their children's on the crowded streets.

"When the fall color-show ends, guests pour in to enjoy the Christmas season. Population's building already. We're going to rake in a lot of tips tonight. People are generous at Christmas."

Holly nodded. She would sock away any extra money until the Christmas sales began the last week of December.

The gaily painted red trolley rattled past. Smiling faces beamed from the windows. "Yesterday I noticed the Williams Market on Main Street was in full swing with a costumed group front and center singing Christmas carols. Shirley, you sing so well, you should join the carolers."

"I might someday. Now I have way too many parties to attend. Speaking of, you look like you don't have a care in the world. But I know you do."

Holly nodded. "I do. But as long as I don't think too far in the future, I'm okay. Sometimes at night I can't sleep. I'm concerned I might not be able to send the boys to the College of William and Mary."

"Yeah, boys need to go to college. W & M only has about five thousand students. Between now and then, you'll get the bread. The tuition's a fraction of what other colleges cost."

"If I'm still living in Williamsburg, I'll not need to pay for a dorm room. But will the boys decide they want to major in Liberal Arts? I understand that's all the college offers." Holly sighed. "God's taken care of us since Vince died. He'll continue to care for us. He has a special heart for widows and orphans."

Shirley shot an unbelieving stare. "If thinking that makes you feel better, okay. Just don't spread that stuff around me." Then she grinned. "Besides, you don't know what fate has up his sleeve!" She smirked.

Bing finished his song and his mellow voice launched into *Silver Bells,* with Shirley's lovely soprano accompanying him.

The old-fashioned sign, *Ye Old Queen's Inn* swinging from the lamp post, welcomed them to work.

"Didn't we do a fab job with the wreaths in the windows and the fir boughs above the doorway?" Holly stood back to admire last week's work.

"Gangbusters!"

They scampered up the three steps and entered the double red doors.

"Thought you girls would be late." Charlie greeted. "Hurry on upstairs and change. I need you to punch in early tonight. We have special music and the customers are lined up inside waiting to be seated."

Holly twisted her long brown hair into a bun and thrust the

tresses under her mop cap. She smoothed the apron over her bust and glanced at the patrons already seated at her station. Families. Many couples with four children. She'd wanted four, but Vince thought they could afford only two. Probably best they'd not had more, but she still yearned for a daughter. She hurried to the first table and started taking orders.

Behind her, footsteps thumping on the wooden planks announced the special musicians had arrived.

Bumping of instruments and squeaking of chairs announced they would soon play. Holly hurried from table to table. Hearing the patrons' orders over musical instruments always proved a challenge. She needed to take these orders before the group began to play.

The quartet warmed up with the usual toots and blares. But one French horn sounded louder and more insistent above the other instruments. Annoying. The flute, clarinet, and bassoon faded and then stopped playing, but the French horn kept blowing—almost like saying hello. Still annoying.

Holly turned from the family whose order she'd finished jotting on her pad and gazed at the front of the huge room. The instruments were grouped in a semi-circle before the huge stone fireplace. A flute, a clarinet, a bassoon, and a French horn. The French horn blowing had become irritating. What was wrong with that musician? Why did he insist on repeating those two notes that sounded very much like hell-o? She frowned in his direction.

Then dropped the old-fashioned padded menus she held. Heavens! Could that dark-haired horn blower be Trent Conway?

The man's lank form overflowed the chair. The French horn hid the lower half of his face, but the dark hair was different from his high school crew cut. The laughing brown eyes were unmistakable under dark brows. The straight nose she'd always admired remained newsworthy. The lean cheeks hadn't put on extra weight in the last ten years. Imagine Trent Conway here!

She waved her fingers.

He nodded and stopped playing those annoying two notes. He flashed that smile she'd fallen in love with when she'd been too innocent to know better.

The clarinet player nodded, and the group dove into a mellow rendition of *It's Beginning To Look A Lot Like Christmas.*

Holly hurried toward the kitchen with her orders. Trent Conway! Why was he here?

Chapter 3

Holly and Shirley trudged down Duke of Gloucester Street toward the buildings where each of them rented an apartment.

"What's buzzin', cuzzin? Saw a ghost? You looked like something the cat dragged in this evening at work."

Holly nodded. She needed to talk to help clarify this new situation in her mind. "It's a long story. And not very pretty."

"Those are the best kinds. Hit me with it."

Holly drew a belly-up breath. Tonight, even the Christmas lights failed to cheer her. "You noticed the quartet that played this evening?"

"Sure. Their name's *Radioactive*. Bunch of cool-looking cats with their pegged jeans, their black-striped shirts, and their ducktails. Played good too." Shirley gave a thumbs-up, then winked. "Did you see that dreamy one who played that big brass horn? I could go for him in a big way."

"Feel free. His name's Trent Conway. We went steady during our senior year of high school."

"Cool beans!" Shirley gazed at Holly's face. "But no way I'd go out with one of your old flames." She tugged at Holly's red wool coat sleeve. "You saw a ghost from the past. I'm all ears."

Holly walked a short distance. Why not? They had time before they reached their apartments. "Okay, you asked for it." She forced a smile. "Start with two years after high school. My broken heart had almost healed when I met Vince. Haven't thought about these high school memories in years."

"That horn player broke your heart?"

"He did. I'd been expecting a proposal and a ring the summer I got a job and before Trent left our small town to attend Ohio State.

He promised to write." Holly tried to sound light-hearted. "But he didn't. At all. I tried to contact him, but he'd left no address. After a year of mourning and moping, I left my job in West Liberty and found work in Columbus. I rented a room at the YWCA near Ohio State." Holly gave a rueful grin. "Since we lived in the same city now, I started each day expecting to run into or hear from Trent." She shook her head. "Neither happened. Like he'd fallen off the face of the earth."

"Why would Trent do that?" Shirley's blue eyes sparkled tears.

"I don't know." Holly smiled. "Then Vince exploded into my life like a superhero with a whirlwind romance and marriage. I almost forgot Trent."

"Way to go!"

"I thought I'd forgotten him, right? Does a girl ever forget her first love?"

"You never saw Trent again—until now?"

"Right. The last time I saw him was the day he climbed into his 1941 Ford and left for college. He kissed me and said, 'I'll always love you, Christmas Girl.'"

Shirley's blue eyes opened so wide she resembled an astonished child. "He called you that? How romantic!" She took several steps then stopped. "I wish a boy would call me something sweet."

"Trent had several nicknames for me, but that's the one he used the last time we saw each other."

"Oh, Holly, you're so lucky a boyfriend cared so much for you."

The pain certainly hadn't felt lucky. Or the years of wondering. Or the shock of running into him again with him looking even more attractive than he had in high school. "Nowheresville! I never want to see Trent again. Not now. Not ever."

"Well, you're lucky. Dream Boat Trent is *not* the one I set you up with."

"Yuck!" Holly stopped dead and grabbed Shirley's arm. "No!"

Shirley's face sported a huge grin. "Yep. Mr. Clarinet Player…and all the guys…are used to girls asking them for dates after their gigs. Groupies they call us. Anyway," Shirley's bright smile dimmed for a second, "he turned me down at first...until I pointed *you* out. Then he asked, 'When and where?'"

"You didn't, please say you didn't."

"Honey, you need to get out of that apartment and see some nightlife. Santa's bringing Mr. Clarinet Player to pick you up at seven. I'm babysitting." Shirley flashed a genuine this-will-be-so-good-for-you smile. "His name's Bob Robinson."

Chapter 4

The doorbell rang.

"Rake, will you answer that? Tell Bob I'm not quite ready. You and Randy keep him company. He's early, so he shouldn't mind." Holly slapped on some make-up foundation.

The front door opened, and a male voice rumbled. Her two sons answered in their higher-pitched voices, but she couldn't distinguish any words. She dabbed powder over her face and tugged the brush rollers from her hair, fluffed the curls out, then brushed her shoulder-length hair until her locks shone.

The conversation in the other room continued, but though she pressed her ear to the wall, she couldn't understand what was said. She hurried, but Bob had arrived thirty minutes early. She swiped on mascara, dabbed a bit of pink rouge on her pinkie and blended. Then applied *Hazel Bishop's Love That Pink* lipstick. She slipped on her nylons hooked them to her garter belt, and wriggled into her half-slip, then her ballerinas.

She slipped into the pink dress with the spaghetti straps which would take her anywhere and rushed into her small living room. "You!"

Trent rose from one wedge of her two-sectional brown couch. "Sorry, your sons just told me you're expecting a date. A guy Shirley set you up with. I'll clear out before he arrives."

Holly's hand flew to her neck. "How—?"

"I wheedled your address from Charlie. Threatened to quit *Radioactive* and split if he didn't fork it over."

"But—?"

"I know. I know. You have a million questions. By the way, you look sensational!" His chocolate eyes danced.

Trent filled her small living room with masculine aura and good will. A vase of roses set on her coffee table, tied with a Christmas ribbon and smattered with shiny green holly leaves. She managed a squeaky, "Thank you."

The boys jumped up and down, then raced from the room, their feet pounding the wooden floor of her second-story apartment.

With them gone, Trent seemed bigger than life and twice as real. All the old feelings scrambled back to strangle her.

"Those are great boys you have. Full of life. I guess the red hair comes from their dad?"

"Came," she corrected without thinking. Rioting emotions blocked her thoughts. Her pulse sped. Her cheeks burned.

"You're divorced?" His lips, that she remembered so well, turned up at the corners like they always had. Kissable lips.

"No, Vince died two years ago. Plane crash."

His chocolate eyes lit like a kid about to taste an ice cream cone. "I'm sorry."

No, he wasn't. His face reminded her of the awed expression he'd had after their first kiss.

"Should have guessed since Bob's taking you out tonight. He's cranked. Haven't seen him so hopped up about a date in a long time."

"You knew Bob was coming?"

"Guilty. I wanted to talk with you first. Bob's got a winning way with the ladies. Wanted to warn you."

The kettle calling the pot black. "I'm capable of taking care of myself, thank you."

Trent's dancing eyes grew serious. His mouth tightened. "I also needed to figure out how to apologize. I blinked, and ten years had passed."

The doorbell rang.

She jumped.

"Must be Bob. Right on time. Usually he makes his dates wait. He's got it bad for you."

"How could he? I've never ever met Bob."

"Didn't have to. Holly, you're one in a million." Trent's wingtips headed toward the door. He turned in her small entry to face her. "We need to talk."

The doorbell screamed again.

Holly stepped toward the door, but Trent blocked her way. "Please leave, Trent. I really have nothing to say to you. You bowed out of my life. So, please leave. Now."

The crushed expression on his face sent a knife through her heart. She shook her head. Why did he think he could step back where he left off?

The doorbell rang as if someone leaned on the bell and didn't release it.

Still, Trent didn't move.

She brushed past him and jerked open the door. A tall, handsome Swedish-type male filled her doorway.

He stepped inside, swept off his hat, and bowed. "Hello, I'm Bob." He glared at Trent as if he'd expected him to be right where he was but planned to toss him on his tail. "I take it you're leaving." Bob balled his fists. "If not, I'll give you a knuckle-sandwich."

The two tall men glared at each other.

Holly found her voice. "Heavens! Trent will you please leave, or shall I call the police?"

Trent's red face and clenched jaw and fists made her certain he counted slowly to ten. His fists uncurled. "Okay, Christmas, I'll leave." He glared at Bob. "For now."

After Trent sauntered out the door and down the hall, Bob strode inside. Holly drew in a deep breath and shut the door.

"Mom, that was boss!" Both boys yelled, totally forgetting their quiet voices.

When did they steal back into the room? She pulled in a ragged breath. "Hello, Bob. I'm Holly. I'm sorry you were part of that."

"No problem. You look fab. Ready to paint the town?"

"These are my sons, Rake and Randy." She planted an arm around each boy's shoulder. "Please shake hands and say, 'I'm glad to meet you.'"

The boys rushed Bob. Each grabbed a hand and pumped Bob's hand and arm up and down. "Glad to meet you. Glad to meet you. Glad to meet you." They screamed.

What were they doing? "Stop it boys! Behave."

A frown flashed across Bob's face. He freed his hands, straightened his tie, and rearranged his blue suit coat.

"Didn't you bring our mom a box of candy?" Rake screamed.

"All her boyfriends bring candy." Randy's voice lowered a decibel.

She frowned at them and grabbled each by a shoulder. "Boys, where are your manners?"

Bob's helpless expression almost made her laugh. Evidently, he didn't spend much time with misbehaving boys.

Randy grabbed Bob's hat and tossed the black felt to Rake.

Rake crumpled the dress hat into a ball, then dropped it at Bob's feet.

She shook each by the shoulder. "Stop acting up. At Once! Give Bob his hat."

Rake took a long time retrieving Bob's hat. He fiddled with the tall man's shoes, then stood and handed him the hat. "Sorry."

Bob nodded, then stepped forward and fell into her arms.

She grunted with his weight, bowed under the pressure, and backstepped until she landed on the couch. Bob on top of her.

The twins laughed, patting each other on the back. One or both had tied Bob's shoelaces together.

Bob smiled, showing dimples, and buried his nose in her neck. "Mum, this is nice."

She heaved herself up but couldn't move from beneath his weight.

"This is more than I expected, but I'm game." Bob's lips moved close to hers. His breath smelled minty.

She groaned. "Please get up. You weigh a ton."

"Not quite." He pushed himself off, then held out his hand to help her up. "Thanks, boys."

She would have a major heart-to-heart with the boys when they got up tomorrow morning. They were up to something. This behavior was unacceptable.

The doorbell rang.

Holly shuddered. Not Trent again! Oh, yes. Her babysitter. She smoothed her dress, then walked as sedately as she could manage to open the door. "Come in, Shirley. You missed all the fun."

"Not *all* the fun, I hope." Bob's warm breath tickled the nape of her neck. "I'm looking forward to a lot more," he murmured.

Oh, she'd been away from the dating scene way too long.

She wasn't ready for this.

Chapter 5

Holly fluffed her hair and pinned on a fascinated expression as she and Bob reigned together in the most conspicuous booth in the most expensive restaurant in Williamsburg.

She loved the surroundings with their Christmas lights and candles. She smiled and inhaled the scents of fir, vanilla, and cinnamon. A trill of pride swirled through her. Her decorations at *Ye Olde Queen's Inn* looked just as Christmassy, if not as elaborate. She would add elf dolls and angels in unexpected spots when she went to work tomorrow. Until tonight she'd not known where to best place the miniatures.

Bob proved to be an interesting and thoughtful date. He was easy to talk with. They chatted like old friends during dinner. The candles burned low as they lingered over their dessert.

Laughing together, they rushed to make the last picture show.

Inside the darkened movie theater as they watched *Rebel Without A Cause* starring James Dean and Natalie Wood, Bob held her hand. Uncomfortable. Too fast for her, but he expected her to comply. So, she did. Perhaps first dates had changed in the past ten years.

Afterwards, as they strolled from the theater, a cool wind ruffled her hair. "Good flick, but I didn't fall in love with James Dean unlike half the females I hear talking at work have." Perhaps she was too old. Or too wise. Or feeling too chaotic inside dealing with a first date.

"I'll clue you in." He flashed a smile complete with deep dimples. "Natalie Wood's a show-stopper. But I had trouble watching her on the screen when I have you sitting next to me. You're incredible."

She laughed. "I understand why you have a reputation as a lady-killer." She let him take her hand as they walked toward her apartment building.

He grinned. "Where did you hear that rumor?"

"I can't reveal my sources."

"I dig you. Would his initials be TC? That bird dog wants to see me go down."

"My lips are sealed."

"Then why do *you* think I'm a lady-killer?" Bob squeezed her hand.

"You know what I like, and you treat me like a queen."

"You are a queen."

People smiled at them as they ambled hand in hand as if they were a permanent couple.

"Want a coffee or hot chocolate?"

She glanced at her watch. "No thanks, I need to get home to the boys. They shimmy out of bed bright and early, and I promised to take them to The Craft Shop tomorrow." Holly smiled to cover her edginess. "They want to make a special Christmas present for me." Would Bob expect a good-night kiss?

He nodded. "Family first."

He hadn't said a word about how naughty her sons had behaved. "I appreciate you not mentioning how badly my sons treated you earlier this evening. I'm so sorry about how Rake and Randy acted. They're not usually so rude. Tonight was out of character for them. I've taught them better manners."

"Must be hard for them to see you interested in me. A bit of jealousy I suspect." He winked.

"You're probably right." She shrugged. Yet they hadn't misbehaved with Trent. They seemed to like him.

Maybe Bob didn't know how to interact with children. "So, you've never married?"

"Never found the right girl who could settle me down. That might have changed tonight." His smooth baritone lowered into an insinuating whisper.

Ha, what a line! "Do you enjoy your life as a musician?" Dating different women wherever his gigs landed him? Or was he ready to settle down and begin a family? She couldn't read Bob.

Which turned her thoughts to Trent. Had *he* married? She tossed her head. But she was with Bob. She must focus on him. "How long have you been a musician?"

"All my life. I play every instrument under the sun. Clarinet best. With that I lead any quartet."

"How long have you played together?"

"*Radioactive's* been together five years." He opened the door to her apartment's atrium. "Trent's new. Only been with us a month. Plays a mean French horn, but horns in on my dates too often. Pardon the pun."

"Really? Trent does that a lot?"

Bob shook his head. "Once is too much." Bob walked her upstairs to her second-floor door. He tilted her chin up and brought his lips close.

She turned her head aside. Not ready to kiss a stranger, no matter how enjoyable the date. "Um, thanks for a great time."

He kissed her cheek. "I hope this won't be the last. Our quartet plays the Inn until after Christmas. Can I see you again? Say tomorrow night?"

"I'm sorry. I don't date much. Two evenings in a row stretches my free time. My boys need me."

"I'll phone you then for next week. May I have your number?" Bob pulled his wallet from his pants pocket and unfolded a small slip of paper. He reached into his vest pocket and slipped out an expensive-looking fountain pen.

"I prefer not to give out my number." Bob was fun. He spared no expense on their date. But when she gazed into his blue eyes, Trent's chocolate brown eyes appeared in her imagination.

Bob nodded, but he flashed a frown, then concealed it with another full-court grin. "I'll meet you at work then. We play five evenings a week. Do you always work the evening shift?"

"I rotate. Three days I work early shift and three days I work evening." She didn't want him to insist on another date, so she said, "I'll see you at work."

Bob reeled her into his arms, tried for a kiss, but with her swivel, ended with a hug. "Count on it."

Trent blew a few notes into his horn. Yep, right pitch. He hunched in the folding chair Charlie provided for each of the musicians. His B flat had sounded uncertain. Not like him. He positioned the French horn across his lap and swept his gaze across the huge dining room.

No Holly yet. Maybe she wasn't working this shift tonight. He tapped his fingers over the brass valves.

Bob swaggered to his seat beside him.

Trent raised a hand in greeting.

Bob frowned and slammed down into the chair making the wood creak. "Okay, horn man, listen up!"

Horn man? Trent had expected Bob to forget the confrontation at Holly's. She had to be just another girl in a long string of girls to him.

"Get this straight! You've seen the last of Holly Silver or you're out of the quartet!" Bob loomed over him, his frown meant to intimidate.

Trent's mouth dried. He swallowed. "What?"

"Steer clear of Holly Silver. No talking. No smiling. No dates."

The hair on his neck rose. Trent pressed his rising anger down and counted to ten. Should have expected something like this from Bob. The man was a tyrant. But the clarinetist dated so many women, Trent hadn't expected any more than joking repercussions about his being in Holly's apartment last night. Bob hopped from one woman to another like a mallet over xylophone keys.

"You got my drift, Trent?"

"If I don't?" Trent tightened his fingers around the horn's bell.

"David will play your seat. Starting tonight."

Not a hard choice. He'd lost Holly once. He wouldn't lose her again. He tugged his music case over, with careful fingers removed the horn's mouthpiece and placed it into the special compartment inside the case and dug out the polish cloth. He buffed his fingerprints off the shiny brass, placed the horn inside the case, and fastened the latches. "See you around."

"Hey!"

"*You* broke our contract, Dude, not me."

"I'll sue." Red spread over Bob's face like blood pooling on a white sheet. His fists curled. "You're leaving a great gig for a girl you don't even have! Why would she choose you over me?"

"You heard him fire off that ultimatum, guys." Trent nodded to the other two players.

Both Damon and Ralph stared, open-mouthed.

Trent strode out of the restaurant into the bright Christmas lights and piped music. He could have used the extra cash, but the price tag was too high. A quick phone call from Bob and both David or Jake, though they couldn't hold a candle to his playing, would flash in to take his place, French horn in hand. *Radioactive* would start maybe fifteen minutes late. No hair off Bob's chest.

Trent sighed. He'd have to place that sign in *The Peanut Store's* window tonight.

His plan better work. He had no Plan B.

LOVE AT CHRISTMAS

191

Chapter 6

Holly matched strides with Shirley through the chilly late-night air, every jar of the sidewalk sending throbs through her ballerinas into her aching feet. She tried to concentrate on Shirley's chatter, but depression crept in.

Trent did it again. Disappeared without a word. Some other guy played French horn all evening. She'd kept expecting Trent to show, but he never did.

Spending less than a half hour in his presence had raised her hopes to heavenly expectation. Then as quickly as he'd appeared back in her life, he was gone. Again, he left no word.

She had only herself to blame for letting him rock her world. She'd promised herself never to let anyone break her heart again.

All her own fault.

Trent shattered her poor heart for a second time.

The following morning before heading to work, Holly strolled through the atrium of her apartment building. Outside the sun shone. Though the air inside smelled heavy with evergreen, and a Christmas tree in the corner blazed bright lights, her dismal heart cried.

Brakes screeched outside.

Holly sauntered to the floor-to-ceiling windows that abutted the entrance and stared outside. With another screech of brakes, a delivery truck pulled into the driveway across the street in front of Shirley's apartment. Holly rested her hands on her hips and watched through the window. Shirley ambled from her apartment to the truck while the delivery man slid the back door open.

Because the truck obscured her view, Holly couldn't see Shirley, but her friend soon walked back toward her apartment, a huge grin creasing her face. She carried a red and green Christmas floral arrangement in both hands.

Fab. Did Shirley have an unknown admirer, or had she sent the flowers to herself?

Holly turned the key in her apartment mailbox, but no mail today. Not even advertisements. Her ballerinas slid over the smooth stones of the entry as she paced, waiting for the mail delivery.

A banging of the across-the-street apartment building's door distracted her. Shirley's neighbor, Paisley Robbins, minced outside and talked with the delivery driver. Holly only had a nod-and-hello acquaintance with the older lady, but she liked the woman. Paisley turned from the truck. Her neighbor carried an antique cage with some tiny birds fluttering inside.

Holly was about to journey across the street to talk with Paisley, when the delivery truck gunned out of Paisley's drive…and right into Holly's.

She sucked in a quick breath. What? She hadn't ordered anything. Maybe the truck was turning around.

But the truck pulled up, stopped, and a teenager with duck-tail styled hair jumped down.

Lucky neighbor. Someone else was getting a flower delivery. Which of her neighbors? Holly leaned against the wall to watch. She needed some joy in her life, even if the happiness came from a neighbor's enjoyment.

The delivery boy opened the door to her apartment entry. "Holly Silver?" He asked since she was alone in the entry. The boy carried a clipboard.

"Yes?"

He grinned. "Um, Miss. You got a delivery."

"Are you sure? I'm not expecting anything."

"Yep. Only problem is—um, we got a glitch in our orders. So, Gramps sent me out with these names on this clipboard, and I got packages, but I don't know which flowers go to which names."

Holly chuckled. "Got caught in the Christmas rush, did you?"

The kid nodded and backed out the door. Unlaced tennis shoes flopping on the drive, the young man hurried out to the rear of the delivery van.

Holly followed.

"Can you look at these orders and see which one yours is?" He opened the back door.

"Yes, but I can't imagine…" Holly let her words fade as the boy hauled out a huge box of chocolates in a gold package with a fancy red Christmas ribbon. The thought of a man sending candy made her heart race. The expectation such gifts brought tingled her stomach. "Is there no card?"

"No card, Miss. Do you think this candy is for you?"

She shook her head. "No. I wish it was, but I don't think so."

"These must be for you then." He pointed to an emerald vase filled with a dozen long-stemmed red roses sitting in the groove that usually held the spare tire.

She bent inside the van, stuck her nose close to a velvet bloom, and inhaled the rich rose scent. How many bouquets had she received and taken for granted? Strange, these gifts getting their cards and addresses tangled up. Was God sending a message? Was He nudging her not to turn her back on love? She'd been too afraid to risk her heart these past two years. The pain had cut so deep. But with that restraint she'd lost the joy and the excitement and the deep satisfaction of caring about someone else more than about herself and her boys. She inhaled the sweet, rose fragrance. And, the one man she wanted in her life had disappeared. Again. "No, I'm sure this one is not for me. I wonder if there is another Holly Silver in town."

"No Ma'am. We checked. And for sure, there's no other Holly Belle Silver." The teenager's voice cracked. "I've got this one more."

Judging by his sympathetic expression, he must have seen her regret. He handed her a bouquet of bright red flowers and a vellum envelope.

Smooth and rich in her hand, the envelope's ivory paper invited her to peek inside. She glanced at the delivery boy. "This looks as if it's been opened."

"Yes, Miss. Miss Mathews and Miss Robbins opened the letter to see if it was for them. But it wasn't. I only have two more addresses. And the two other packages. Do you think this one's for you?"

She slipped the textured paper out of the envelope. Her heart fluttered. Beautiful inked calligraphy invited: *One Christmas portrait painted Sunday afternoon at Ye Olde Portrait Studio on Beacon Street.*

Tears pricked her eyelids. This couldn't be for her either. She couldn't afford to have her portrait painted. A small note at the bottom read: *Gift from a friend.* She was about to fold the note and return it to its envelope when she glimpsed a symbol in the corner—a beautiful picture of Christmas holly painted by an artistic hand.

Holly couldn't stop smiling. "Yes, thank you, this one *is* mine. This has to be my present from Shirley. She knows I have no photographs of myself, except for a few precious black and white ones from my wedding to Vince."

The kid nodded and ran his fingers though his slicked-back hair. With a hitch of his pegged jeans, a slap of tennis shoes, a door slam, and a squeal of burning rubber, the delivery truck barreled down the street.

The beautiful embossed envelope silky smooth in her fingers she decided to accept the invite. She needed her spirits lifted. Perhaps sitting for her portrait would help her forget Trent's sudden return and abrupt departure. She smiled, her feet tapped the rhythm of the lilting notes of *Winter Wonderland.*

She had to trade shifts for this Sunday afternoon, but even extra money for the sitter wouldn't keep her from accepting this surprise. Nothing would keep her from Beacon Street on Sunday. She ran upstairs to put the flowers in a vase.

She'd have her portrait painted, even if Bob Robinson had given this gift.

Even if strings were attached.

She'd face that hurdle when she encountered it.

Chapter 7

Holly turned into *The Peanut Shop* on Beacon Street. She glanced around. Why hadn't she visited here before? The place welcomed her with warm wooden floors and colorful displays. Christmas decorations overwhelmed her with red and green happiness. She sniffed the mingled scents of fir, chocolate, peanuts and sugar and spice.

Candy, sparkling every color of the rainbow, dazzled from full-length shelves lining one wall. Her mouth watered. She'd choose some for the boys. Huh, who was she kidding...and for herself? Candy always called her name. She loved any kind.

On her right, a display in tall glass jars flaunted every kind of peanut from caramel apple to chocolate covered double dipped. She could gain weight just looking.

Fondness for this store, with every inch of the wooden walls overlaid with yummy goods to savor, could turn into addiction. She moved to a side table supporting tasting bowls filled with peanut and other exotic dips. Using pretzels as spoons, she sampled each one. Sweet, tart, and salty. She baby-stepped past baskets of other colorful goodies. If she weren't careful, she could spend her entire check here.

She inhaled a deep breath. Delightful odors teased her stomach into a rumble.

She clutched her shoulder-purse and pressed the tan leather against her body. She'd come for a different purpose. Strolling to the counter manned by a pleasant-looking white-haired lady, Holly smiled. The saleslady wore a navy colonial dress. A mop cap rode on the crown of her head, displaying her hair.

Holly made a mental note. She would try that look. Though not historically accurate, revealing hair looked far more attractive than every hair poked beneath the cap.

"What can I do for you?" The saleslady smiled, her hazel eyes crinkling her crepe skin.

"You have a sign in the window. I'm looking for the artist. Does he have a studio somewhere on the premises?"

The older lady burst into a friendly grin. "Oh yes. He's my new tenant. Just moved upstairs a few days ago." She pointed. "Head back out of the shop and enter the side door that leads to a set of stairs. His studio is upstairs." She glanced at a lollypop clock on the wall. "I'm sure he's there now. The door's not locked. Just walk on up."

Holly smiled and nodded. "Thanks. I'd like to buy a pound of this toffee peanut brittle crunch." She touched the glass above the delectable candy inside the display case. The boys would eat every smidgeon before she had a chance to taste. That worked for her figure.

As the pink-cheeked saleslady rang up her purchase, she nodded toward an intriguing display of different sized jars and bottles. "I hope you will try our variety of free samples of jams, jellies, and sauces."

"After I finish upstairs, I'm returning to taste more of your wonderful products."

The lady nodded. "Do. We have such a variety of peanuts, almonds, pecans, and cashews that you'll think you'd died and gone to squirrel heaven. Our prices are extremely reasonable." The woman smiled, then turned to one of the other customers inside her crowded store.

Holly wove through the display cases and made her way to the side door. She mounted the steep incline, her insides jiggling with anticipation. Such an adventure. She'd have to puzzle-out a unique Christmas gift for Shirley.

She walked into the studio. The scent of artist oils, terpenoid, and drying canvases filled the large, sunny room. A pleasant productive-type odor. She strolled among several completed portraits, nodding and smiling, unable to resist touching one. Beautiful skin tones. Lovely poses. Shirley had chosen well. Holly clasped her hands together. This would be the highlight of her year. How could she ever repay –?

Her knees went weak. "What? You?"

The tall form unfolded from behind a large canvas. Dark hair fell over a wide forehead. Serious chocolate eyes gazed at her from under straight black brows. An artist brush, clamped between kissable lips, held a drop of crimson paint about to drip. Blue paint smudged one lean cheek. Strong fingers disengaged the brush from his mouth. His eyes warmed. Their pupils dilated making his brown eyes resemble mahogany. He laid aside the palette in his left hand and stepped forward. "Holly. I hoped you would accept my invitation and gift."

"Trent?" Her voice trembled. "You sent the invitation?"

"I thought you might remember I dabbled in art in high school."

"Oh."

"Guess you forgot." He waved a hand. "So, this is my loft. Welcome!"

"Nope. I haven't forgotten anything about you." She made a wry face. "Except your art classes. Probably because I never took any."

His brown eyes glinted. "You were too busy with your secretarial and bookkeeping studies. Did you ever use what you learned?"

Holly nodded. "I worked for several years as a legal aid in a law office but discovered I didn't enjoy being confined to a desk."

"Understood. Not my bailiwick either." Trent wiped his hands on a paint rag. "Can I get you a cup of coffee?" He turned toward an alcove where a pot of coffee perked with soothing gurgling noises.

"Yes, thank you." She needed time to let this situation sink in. Trent was an artist! This was *his* studio. His work! "I would not have guessed our high school football star had an artistic bone in his body. That the long fingers of the star receiver could also paint beautiful likenesses of people." She gazed at his classic profile bent over the coffee machine. "Though I don't know much about art, your work looks brilliant."

His cheeks reddened. "Not brilliant." He laughed. "But pretty good for a part-time job." He handed her a white mug. "You take sugar or cream?"

"No thanks. Black."

His hand brushed hers as he passed the cup. Strong, masculine hand. Dark hair sprinkled over a wrist that extended from a faded blue shirt splashed with different types of dried oil paints, brought back memories. All exciting.

"After I finish your portrait, I'd like to paint Rake and Randy. I –"

"You've changed." Her voice sounded breathless to her ears. "Not so much physically –" He looked younger than he had at her apartment or at the restaurant. So bursting with life he took her breath away. This loft was his milieu. Where he felt at home. Where he was at ease. Where he had purpose. Doing what he loved.

Her heart thudded like a set of snare drums. "First the French horn and now oils." Holly's hand trembled as she brought the coffee cup to her lips and sipped. She wrinkled her nose. Trent might be a world-class horn player and artist, but he fell short on coffee making skills. She chuckled. "At least something you're not super good at."

"Yeah. Can't get the right mix of grounds. Coffee stinks." He rested both hands behind him and leaned against the coffee shelf. "I've done a lot of things I'm not super good at. But I'm a different guy now. In the past ten years I've learned not to be so arrogant and self-centered." His smile sent butterflies fluttering in her stomach. "I'm glad you came today. I owe you an apology."

"So, the portrait is an apology?" She lowered her gaze to her coffee.

"No. It's a gift. Let's call you being here a new beginning. I've gained some wisdom in the last ten years. I've learned what's important in life." He scooted closer beside her at the small counter, his hand next to hers. "These days I'm going all out for my dreams."

A sliver of fear shafted her heart. Had he changed? Was she ready for this discussion? She shook her head. Not yet. She turned her back and ambled among his paintings. "I love your work. I'm delighted to sit for you."

Waves of feelings radiated from his gorgeous body.

She moved further from his proximity. "But you must let me pay."

"A gift doesn't require payment. You accept a gift."

"I'm not sure I can accept this one. The price you charge your other clients must be high." She cleared her throat. "Perhaps I can make monthly payments."

"The price has been paid."

What did he mean? She'd paid a tremendous price in tears and regrets when he'd disappeared. But when she met Vince, she'd found happiness. What price had Trent paid? She shivered. Best let that can of worms remain closed.

"In that case, when do we start?" Had she just agreed? She really was silly. Asking for pain. And yet, before Trent disappeared, she'd been a risk-taker. She'd slipped caution off like an unnecessary raincoat on a sunny day. "What is it about you that makes me want to take chances?" To throw caution to the wind. To spread her wings and fly.

"Because I believe everything is possible."

"Maybe you haven't changed as much as you think." Holly sighed. "You've always been a risk-taker."

"No. Not in some very important matters." He turned toward his painting stool. "I avoided taking one risk I always regretted. I went through a dark period after I left you. My parents convinced me not to take the biggest chance of my life." Trent situated a fresh 16 x 24 canvas on his easel. He repositioned his paint table and palette, not looking at her.

Her heart faltered, then beat double-time.

He didn't say anything. Squeezed some tubes of paint in a semi-circle around a fresh palette.

"What happened?" She bit her lip. The first time they were alone together, and she had blurted her disappointment out.

"I chose to please my parents rather than follow my heart." His brown gaze caught her and held her with a mesmerizing stare. "Mom and Dad had big dreams for me. They expected great things of their only child. A high school love didn't fit into their plans. I wouldn't admit they brow-beat me…but they did. They threatened. They bribed. They begged." He sighed. "I relented." He dipped his head and heaved another huge sigh. "I'm not proud of leaving you without a word." He crushed his empty brush on the palette. I don't deserve a second chance." His dark eyes looked as serious as death. "But will you give me one?"

Chapter 8

Holly gulped. "Are you asking me to fall in love with you again?"

"I am. I never fell out of love with you. At the end of my sophomore year when I returned home for summer vacation, I planned to chuck all my parents' dreams, break their hearts, and ask you to marry me."

Holly whispered, "But you read in the newspaper that Vince and I were to be married on June 3rd."

"Exactly. I was too late." He reached out and took her hand. "If I had shown up, would you have ditched Vince and taken a second chance on me?"

Would she have? She shook her head. "No. I loved Vince. I couldn't have hurt him. I knew first-hand how much a heart can be wounded. No. Not even for you."

"That's what I figured. You're brim full of loyalty. I was short on that when I left for college." He grunted. "But don't think I didn't pay a high price when I left you behind. I left my heart with you."

"I would have waited for you."

Trent nodded. "I know." He groaned. "But my parents had a college-educated girl in mind for me. You didn't fit into their plans. I'm so sorry." His cheeks flushed. "I admit I didn't have the backbone to break with them over you. I've paid that price ever since."

"Where are your parents now?"

"Still back home. Still prodding me for a grandchild. And, I think, older and wiser. They know now that what we experienced was not *puppy love*."

"Oh."

"Do you think you can give me a second chance?"

"I don't know, Trent. I have the boys now. And…and I'm not sure I trust you."

Trent groaned. "I deserve that. But I'm walking with the Lord now. He gives me the strength I lacked when I was eighteen. Though my parents never admit their mistake, they realize they were wrong to break us up. They'd be more than happy to accept you into the family. And they'd be overjoyed with Rake and Randy."

"I'm mixed up and confused, Trent. Part of my heart does flip-flops of joy. But the other part shrivels with doubt. Even looking at you and the success you've become, my mind vacillates one way and then the other. I'm a bundle of uncertainty."

"We'll take things slow. Give you time to fall in love with me again." He winked a sparkling eye. "At least I pray you will."

"That's the easy part, Trent. You're so easy to love." Holly picked at the green silk in her dress and mumbled, "Trust is the hard part. And hurt that you never explained things to me."

Trent hung his head. "Yeah. I was a definite heel. I don't deserve your love." He raised his head and the old risk-taking, come high-water or hurricane he'd-do-what-he-needed-to-do look transformed his expression. "But miracles happen at Christmas!"

Holly nodded. "Christmas is a special time when God came down to live among us. But—"

Trent nodded. "Let's get down to business. You probably have to work today. You're wearing the perfect outfit. That green makes your eyes look like emeralds."

She glanced down at her silk dress. "This is one of my favorites."

"I need to take a couple photographs first. Then we can start." He reached for a camera on a cluttered side table.

Exactly what was she starting? A scary shiver slid down her spine.

Chapter 9

December 15ᵗʰ

Holly shifted on the antique white-cushioned posing couch. Though she found holding her back straight and trying to appear relaxed fatiguing, she never tired of gazing at the artist. His mahogany eyes seemed to look right into her soul and enjoy what they found. And the way his dark hair fell over his forehead each time he bent to dip his brush into his palette made her toes tingle. She wanted to spring up and run her fingers through that well-remembered wavy hair, then smooth the unruly strands out of his eyes. The urge grew stronger each day he painted her portrait.

His gaze concentrated on the canvas. "If I remember correctly, and I'm sure I do, you were active in Christian organizations during your junior and senior years."

"Yes. And if *you* remember correctly, we met at Young Life." This was a safe subject. "I'd been a silent Christian after I received the Lord into my life when I was a freshman. But Young Life taught me to read my Bible every day and to take all my cares to God in prayer."

"Me as well. The group was good for both of us. And?" He changed brushes and colors.

"As I learned more and more about God and the Christian life, being with other Christians grew extremely important. And talking about God came naturally."

"That's one of the many facets of your personality that attracts me. And did back then."

Holly shook her head. "No conversations about our previous attraction yet, please." Best to take this new development in her

206

life with slow steps. Let her heart catch up with her mind. "Perhaps some other time. I'm not ready for depth yet."

His face tightened. "Okay, whatever you say."

She glanced around the studio. "You said painting's your part-time job. Is playing the horn your full-time job?"

Trent snorted. "No. Tooting's a hobby. Gets me out of the studio."

She tilted her head. "Then what's your real job?"

"I'm a detective with the Williamsburg Police Department."

She almost fell off the posing couch. "What?"

"Yep. That old risk-taking gene needed an outlet. I discovered early on after I graduated college with a business degree that I wasn't cut out for riding a desk. Or for trading stocks. Or for surgery." He held up a brush and measured something about her face. "Nope. Disappointed my folks all around."

"A detective." Holly nodded. "That sounds like you." She grinned. "I bet you're a good one."

"The best!"

"No bragging there." She smiled. "Is your job dangerous?"

"Hah. I've got stories to tell."

She nodded, tossed her head, and waved a hand. "I have the time."

"You asked for it. This is a funny one." He lifted a brush and pointed it at her. "I'll tell you about the day Santa Claus robbed a bank." Trent's brown eyes twinkled. He painted as he talked. "First case I ran that I worked undercover."

"You work undercover? In disguise?"

"Yeah. I'm on leave now. Plus vacation."

"Heavens! So much I don't know about you. You're a law enforcement officer! And a French horn player. And an artist." She frowned. "How long is your vacation?"

He squirmed and cleared his throat. "Six weeks while the department investigates me for shooting a perp. He didn't die." He grinned. "Add three more weeks for vacation." He winked, but his eyes remained serious. "Since I discovered you had moved to Williamsburg, I negotiated a vacation-with-a-purpose."

"I won't ask." Holly smoothed the concern from her face. But not from her heart. Trent had always thrived on danger. Apparently, he hadn't outgrown that quirk.

"As I was saying. My first case undercover I wore my new Resistol cowboy hat. I was assigned on a different case to this little town in Texas called Christmas. While I was there, the police discovered Helms Hillman and his four-man gang planned to rob a bank in Christmas."

"Is there really a Christmas, Texas?"

"Texas is full of cutesy town names – Surprise, Cut and Shoot, Loco, Gun Barrel City, Ding Dong, Dime Box, Jot Em Down, Turkey…"

"Okay. Sounds like fun places to visit. But how did Santa rob a bank at Christmas?"

"Our department discovered later that Helms hid behind a plastic Santa mask because his mother worked at a diner in town, and he didn't want to be recognized."

"Good reason. Not many mothers want their babies to grow up to be bank robbers."

"Or detectives. As I was saying, December twenty-third two years ago, the Hillman Gang rolled into Christmas about midday driving a stolen Buick." Trent painted furiously as he talked. "Helms hid on the floorboard until his men parked the car in the alley behind the bank. A group of kids caught sight of him and followed *Santa* into the bank as if he was the pied piper. The children kept asking for candy and presents." Trent changed brushes and squinted at his work.

"Inside the busy bank all eyes turned to Santa. The banker smiled and said, 'Hello, Santa Claus.' Then he saw the drawn guns. He froze."

"Scary."

Trent nodded, his gaze focused on his work. "One mother, standing at a teller's window cashing a check, took one look at the guns and shoved her daughter all the way through the lobby, past the tellers, and scrammed out the back door. She grabbed her daughter by the hand, dashed to the police station, and raised the alarm."

Holly clapped her hands. "Good for her."

"Typical Texan." Trent blended two colors of paint on his palette, then dabbed his brush into the paint mixture. "Inside the bank the Hillman gang held the bankers and the customers at gunpoint. The little kids watched wide-eyed while Santa ordered the bankers and tellers to fill some potato sacks with money."

"Those poor children."

"The rest of this story could only happen in Texas." Trent lifted his brush from the canvas and flashed a grin, his mocha eyes twinkling. "As the gang headed toward the exit, Santa fired at a man peering from outside in through the front window. A hail of gunfire blasted in from the street. The Police Chief and half the town had converged on the bank. The owner of the local hardware store had emptied his shelves of guns and ammunition and passed the weapons out to the town folk. They all surrounded the bank."

"Hooray for Texas!"

"Bullets rained on the robbers like a sudden hailstorm. The four robbers herded all the customers, including the ten or so kids, to the bookkeeping room in the back, returning fire as they went. Outside, townsfolk shot hundreds of bullets through the bank's front windows. Some people staked out the back alley."

"It's a miracle none of the bank customers were hurt."

Trent nodded and waved his brush. "Santa and the robbers wrangled a hostage into the alley, and onto the Buick's back seat. Two robbers piled into the stolen car. The hostage, a young college student, slid all the way across the back seat, leaped out of the getaway car, and raced for cover."

Holly giggled. "Amazing."

"Another robber shoved two crying middle-school girls into the back seat. Running to the car, Santa shot the police chief and his deputy. A shotgun blast hit the remaining Santa's man, who collapsed into the Buick. The four robbers took off with the two girls as hostages. When they drove away, the postmaster shot out one of the rear tires. The car swerved all over the road."

"Oh. Those poor girls."

"About a minute later the car stopped in the middle of the road. Hillman discovered the gang had failed to fill the Buick with gasoline."

"You're kidding!" Holly laughed.

"There's more. Santa hopped out and waved down a passing car. The kid driving pulled his Oldsmobile over, cool as a cucumber jumped out, and sped to safety. Santa's robbers transferred all the potato sacks of money, the sobbing girls, and the bleeding robber into the stolen Oldsmobile. Once they were all finally inside, Santa discovered the fourteen-year-old driver had fled from the car carrying the keys."

Holly laughed so hard tears formed in her eyes. "A comedy of errors. Really funny." She wiped her cheeks. "Smart kid. Dumb robbers."

"With their car stranded, Santa and the uninjured robbers ran off and hid in the brush. We arrested the bleeding bank robber lying inside the car. The girls escaped to their mamas. We fine-combed the brush and the forest but couldn't track down the gang."

"So, they got away?"

"The story's not over." Trent leaned back on the stool, his eyes laughing. "We discovered later that Santa crept back into town, stole a Ford, and slipped out of the county."

"Why is that funny?"

"Can you believe he wrecked the Ford?"

Holly shook her head. "Sounds like Santa didn't know how to drive."

"Maybe not. But wrecking the car didn't stop him. He hijacked a Dodge. The driver's father stood outside on the sidewalk feeding a parking meter and chased the fleeing car. Trying to stop Santa and get his car back, the driver's father accidentally shot his son in the arm."

"What happened to the son?"

"Santa kicked him out just before he ran the next red light."

"What did you do?"

"After that fiasco we called in the Texas Rangers. They captured the robbers at a roadblock. So, the Rangers arrested Santa on Christmas Eve."

Tears and laughter doubled Holly on the posing bench. "You're making that story up, Trent. You always could tell a tall tale."

"No. I swear. Those slapstick events happened. And the whole town did go after Santa."

"I always loved your stories. Are you sure you're not a writer in your spare time?"

"Nope. I tell stories. Love to make people laugh. But, yeah. I was in on that one. Sad to arrest Santa on Christmas Eve." Trent stuck a brush crosswise into his mouth and spoke around it. "Those kids probably never will trust Santa again."

"Oh, I have to tell the twins. They'll love this one."

"I was hoping you'd let me."

"I'm not sure I'm ready for you to see the boys again, Trent." The words popped out before she thought.

The laughter died in Trent's eyes. His shoulders drooped. He leaned forward, brush poised, but didn't touch any paint to the portrait. Then, for the next ten minutes he painted steadily without saying a word. Finally, he laid down his brushes, and picked up a slender one he hadn't used before. "I've enjoyed the last few days more than you can imagine. This is the last sitting, Holly. I hope you'll find your portrait worth waiting for." His smooth baritone sounded husky.

The deep timbre of Trent's voice sent delicious shivers to her stomach. She blinked. She hated to see Trent look so sad, but she couldn't take back her words. How could she soften the blow? "Did I mention that I have no other pictures of myself? This is truly the best present I've ever received."

He used the brush to sign his name. "No. But having you sit for me means a lot." Trent stepped back from the easel. He straightened his shoulders and his jaw jutted. "Usually I ask clients for one sitting and then complete a portrait from photographs. But with you, I wanted to make certain I caught the real person beneath the beauty."

Heat flooded her face. "You've been sniffing terpenoid, Trent Conway. I'm not beautiful."

He propped a foot on the nearby stool, leaned an elbow on his knee, and dangled the slender brush from his fingers. "You can't see what I see. I know you. You're beautiful inside and out." The cleft in his chin stood out when he smiled.

Her face heated. "Please don't make me feel awkward with

your compliments."

"No embarrassment intended. Holly, I'd like to see you more. To take you on a date."

She shook her head. "I've resisted dating for the past two years." She shrugged. But these last few weeks Shirley and the boys throw every eligible bachelor they meet at me." Holly smoothed the green silk dress where the material clung to her thighs and then flared to the floor. "Life's been crazy."

"Don't be tough on them." Twinkles again lit his eyes. "Just fit me into your schedule. By the way, I named your portrait Christmas Holly."

"Because of my dress?" Yes, she had to give him a chance or she would regret not doing so for the rest of her life. She'd learned to regret the chances she didn't take.

"Partially. But mostly because you have an inner glow that lights up my studio, reminding me of Christmas...and miracles." Trent raised an eyebrow. His lips tilted up. "You're the most beautiful woman I've ever met."

Though she'd dreamed about him for years, the timing was too soon after he popped back into her life. She stood. "I've got to go."

"Don't get upset. I'm sorry. But it's hard to keep my mouth shut. I won't say anymore."

She settled back on the couch. "I hadn't accepted any dates until I moved to Williamsburg. Instead, I dived headlong into my waitressing work, using all my energy. I love what I do."

"You dated Bob."

"I was forced into that date."

"Your friend, Shirley?"

"Right." No more dates. "When I'm ready to date again, my heart will let me know. I don't need a matchmaker. Not even a close friend like Shirley."

"But you'll miss our times together. We could begin by seeing each other as friends." Trent's voice sounded as rusty as an ancient door hinge.

"Perhaps." She wasn't ready to date the man who'd broken her heart. And from her response to his nearness, he could break her heart again. No, he could return to chasing criminals, painting portraits, and blowing his horn. Those activities should keep him out of her hair.

"I'll take that as a yes," Trent mumbled around the brush handle he'd stuck back in his mouth.

She *would* miss the engrossed expression that changed his attractive face into the artist's face. From being easy-on-the-eyes to transforming him into a man with purpose and drive and vision. She loved watching him work. Loved seeing the magic his hands created. Loved talking with him. Especially when they managed a comfortable, relaxed relationship. That's all she could handle. "Okay, friends."

The gleam returned to Trent's eyes. His shoulders straightened. "Finished. You can view the portrait now. I hope you like it."

Did he think she wouldn't? She shot up, almost afraid to look. Her stilettos tapping on the hardwood floor, she glided over to the easel.

"Well?"

She inhaled a long, deep breath. "The portrait takes my breath away. It's like looking into a mirror. I…I love the way you captured my skin tones." She touched a dry portion of the canvas. "Do I look that lovely?" Heat flooded her from her scalp to her ears. "I'm sure I'll be happy with this."

"When will you bring the boys? I'll return to full-time work in a few weeks. We need to schedule the time soon."

Trent seemed to want to connect with the boys.

She had to quit riding the fence. Did she want Trent back in her life?

Chapter 10

Holly frowned. She should be happy or at least content. But, now that the portrait hung in her rented living room above the Christmas-garland decorated mantle, she missed her mornings spent with Trent. Missed their casual conversations. Missed their spirited discussions about God and how He worked in a believer's life.

Probably missed Trent more today because a light snow had fallen on the colonial streets and Christmas lights reflected in its virginal whiteness. Because Williamsburg looked like a miracle on earth. And because Christmas was so very close. She slapped her hands on her hips. Buck up! She'd get over not seeing Trent every day.

She slipped on her coat and hurried to work.

She knocked snow off her shoes on the entryway and opened the door to *Ye Olde Queen's Inn*. The scent of pine and aroma of Christmas cooking welcomed her. Coming to work reminded her that Trent chose to lose his place in *Radioactive* rather than stop talking with her. That had to mean something.

Shoulders back, head lifted, Holly shifted her mop cap so more curls showed and marched to her first table. Her mind still revolved with images of Trent. She dredged up a sunny smile and handed the lone occupant a menu. "How can I serve you?"

"That's a leading question coming from a beautiful girl."

The deep bass voice grabbed her attention. The man settled at her table was body-building large, handsome, and looked sure of himself. Blond crew cut, tanned skin, and bright blue eyes gazed at her with a Santa's-got-a-present-for-you expression.

A chuckle rose in her throat. "What would you like to drink? We serve our own brand of Ginger Ale. And we brew our beer using historical recipes."

"Is your coffee good?" He winked a blazing blue eye.

"Excellent."

"I'll have coffee. What do you recommend from this extensive list of colonial- era food?"

"It's all excellent. We serve traditional dishes like the Game Pye, the Hunter's Pye, and the Peanut Soup. All are tasty." She moved aside for the strolling mandolin player to linger beside the table. Rich notes of *O Little Town of Bethlehem* melted her heart. She hummed.

"Yeah, I like that carol too." The diner thrust out his hand. "Name's John Baxter."

Holly smiled, ignored his hand, and delivered a Williamsburg curtsey. "Nice to meet you, John."

He dropped his hand and winked. "I hear you serving wenches share tidbits of colonial history with us patrons."

"We do." She tucked a finger beneath her chin and tilted her head. "I can begin with facts. Williamsburg became the capital of the Virginia Colony in 1699. Our fair village started as one of America's first planned cities suitable for becoming the capital of the largest British colony in America."

John raised a hand. "Okay. I get the history." He grinned. "And the top-notch ambiance. I dig this place being lit with candlelight rather than electricity. Décor takes me a step back in time." He fingered the pewter pepper pot and lifted the tiny spoon in the pewter salt dish. "What's this for?"

"Well, sir, salt was a major commodity in colonial days. Only the affluent could afford to buy the seasoning. So even the wealthy used salt sparingly." Holly smiled. "Thus, the tiny spoon."

John Baxter laughed longer and louder than her explanation warranted.

Uh, oh. Not just a born flirt. Another patron coming on to her. But this one looked rather interesting.

"What entrée do you recommend?" He flashed a smile that he

must know looked charming and confident.

Oh, the man was a heart-stopper. "If you have a large appetite, the Hunter Pye is enormous…jammed with venison, rabbit and duck. In his day Thomas Jefferson visited the inn. Our oyster dressing was his favorite."

"Sounds perfect. I'll take the Hunter's Pye with a side of the oyster dressing."

"I'm sure you will be pleased." Holly half-turned to leave and spoke over her shoulder. "I recommend the Applesauce Bread Pudding for dessert."

"Whatever you suggest has to be good."

She took his menu and turned toward the kitchen.

"Don't happen to know a couple boys named Rake and Randy, do you?" he bellowed.

Holly halted so fast her shoes squeaked on the wooden floor. She pivoted to face him. "You've met my sons?"

"Not only met them but teach them." He slapped a palm on the tabletop. "Those two red-haired imps ended up in my office this morning. I'm the principal of Matthew Whaley Elementary school."

"Oh, did they misbehave?" She crossed her arms. What mess had they gotten into now?

"Third time this week." His blue eyes twinkled. "So, I got suspicious. Asked them what was going on. You'll never guess."

She sighed. "With them, you're right. I never know."

"The two of them decided I would make the perfect date for your weekend."

Holly almost dropped the menu. "What?"

He hunched toward her, speaking in a low tone. "The three of us brokered a deal. They promised not to act up one more time during the rest of the school year if I ate dinner at *Ye Olde Queen's Inn* and scoped out their Mom."

"You didn't!"

"I did." John Baxter shoved his chair back and stood. "You surpassed all their superlatives." He bowed. "I am formally inviting you to take dinner with me tomorrow night, followed by an evening of ballet at *The Nutcracker*."

Holly brushed a hand across her burning cheek. "Never mind. You don't have to do that. I'll talk with the boys. They won't cause any more problems, I promise."

"A deal's a deal. You want your sons to behave the rest of the year, don't you?"

"That's blackmail."

"Come on. What's the harm? You'll enjoy dinner and love the ballet."

"Since you put my boys at risk if I don't, how can I refuse?"

"Great, I'll pick you up at 6:00."

"I live at—"

"You forget, I have all your information in my files."

Applesauce Bread Pudding
8 slices raisin bread
½ cup chunky applesauce
4 eggs
1 tablespoon sugar
1 ½ cups milk
½ teaspoon vanilla
¼ teaspoon salt
Cinnamon
Butter
Preheat oven to 350 degrees. Butter a 2-quart baking dish. Butter 2 slices of raisin bread. Cut all slices in half diagonally to make triangles and place unbuttered slices in dish. In mixing bowl beat eggs and combine remaining ingredients. Pour mixture over unbuttered bread slices in dish. Place buttered bread slices on top of mixture to decorate. Sprinkle with cinnamon. Bake covered for 30 minutes. Remove cover and bake additional 30 minutes.

Chapter 11

"Shirley, last night was wonderful." Holly stood rocking on her heels at her workstation, waiting for the restaurant to open and the customers to flood in. "John's conversation at dinner was interesting and *The Nutcracker Ballet* was brilliant. I particularly enjoyed the *Waltz of the Snowflakes* and the *Pas de Deux* with the Sugar Plumb Fairy and the Prince."

Shirley's eyes were glued on the front door. "I've never seen the Nutcracker. What's it all about?"

Holly smoothed the white apron over her long dress. "The opening act takes place at a Christmas Eve party in Germany. Clara, the little daughter, receives a special gift. A nutcracker. Clara loves the nutcracker, but her brother Fritz breaks the toy."

"Just like a boy."

Holly nodded. "Clara lays the nutcracker in her doll bed so it will get well." Holly's memory came alive as she talked. "The party ends. Clara and her family go to bed. Clara sleeps, then gets up to make certain her nutcracker is resting." Holly can't resist pirouetting around the dining room. "The dolls and toys all wake to life. Mice run around the nursery. The nutcracker fights the mouse king and loses. Clara throws her slipper at the mouse king and saves the nutcracker's life." Holly performed a Plié. "The nutcracker transforms into a human prince." Holly mimicked an Arabesque as well as she could in her long gown.

Shirley stared wide-eyed. "Now you're cooking!" She clasped Holly around her waist and twirled with her. "I could fall in love with a nutcracker prince."

"Everyone does. So, then the prince and Clara set off through the snowy woods for the Land of Sweets where the beautiful Sugar

Plum Fairy rules. The fairy orders coffee, tea, chocolate and the Russians to dance. The flowers and the Sugar Plum Fairy dance. The ballet ends with everyone dancing." Holly was breathless from her moves.

Shirley scooted off to wait her first table. Order taken she hustled back, her eyes bright. "That plot doesn't make sense."

"You're right. Not much plot. The ballet's about beautiful dancing and out-of-this-world music. These days no one cares that the plot is weak. The Nutcracker's a Christmas tradition." Holly rushed off to serve her first table.

The family ordered the special molasses cookies and hot cider. After she delivered the sweets and drinks, Holly scurried to Shirley's side. "John Baxter said that when the ballet was written critics chastised Tchaikovsky for writing music to accompany such a flimsy plot. The composer had already received acclaim for his music for the *Sleeping Beauty* and *Swan Lake* ballets."

"Your John Baxter turned out to be an egghead, eh?"

"Why not? He *is* Rake and Randy's school principal."

"You liked John?"

"Well, yes. But I felt strained while I was with him because John only sees the boys when they misbehave." Holly shook her head so her brown curls bounced under the mop cap. "Which they haven't done until the last few weeks after they cooked up the scheme to fix John up on a blind date with me."

"From what I saw of the guy at your table a couple nights ago, those rug rats of yours spotted a winner. He's cowabunga! How does he compare to Bob Robinson?"

Holly glanced at the few customers arriving. Except for the family enjoying the cookies, her tables were still empty. Wouldn't hurt to take the work time to answer Shirley, since her friend had set up her date with Bob. She took Shirley's hand. "I'm sorry. I didn't like Bob's aggressive attitude. I really didn't like that he gave Trent Conway an ultimatum."

"Yeah, Bob did seem overbearing. I'm all ears. What ultimatum?"

"Bob told Trent never to speak to me or see me again. If Trent did, Bob would fire him from *Radioactive*."

"Wow. That's heavy. I noticed Trent doesn't play with the band anymore. So, I'm guessing there won't be any more dates with Bob."

"Correct."

Her other tables remained empty. Shirley had serviced her table. Holly had time for more girl talk. "I told you about the portrait Trent painted."

Shirley nodded. "So, to rephrase. How does John Baxter stack up next to Trent Conway?"

"I honestly don't know." Holly rubbed the back of her neck. "Last night, when the Prince entered the stage to dance with the Sugar Plum Fairy, my thoughts jumped to Trent...even though John sat beside me holding my hand."

"Wow! Sinister. Are you going to see John again?"

"I don't know. I'd hate to get involved with him and then sometime in the future break-up. I don't want to hurt him. And John might take his injured feelings out on the boys."

"You're kidding, right?"

Holly frowned. "Partly. But I don't want to chance that happening."

"What about Mr. Artist? Will you see him again?"

"I don't know. He totes a lot of baggage and memories with him. I'm not sure I can handle letting him carry all that back into my life."

"Why don't you admit it, Holly? You're stuck on Trent again. He's your Mr. Dreamy."

"How can I? I'm afraid I'll get hurt again."

"One way to find out. Take a chance! With that dreamboat, I would."

Holly walked to her empty table and whisked a damp cloth across the top, gathering crumbs from the molasses cookies. Did she have the nerve?

Colonial Molasses Cookies

Heat oven to 360 degrees
4 ½ cups all-purpose flour

4 teaspoons ground ginger
2 teaspoons baking soda
1 ½ teaspoons ground cinnamon
1 teaspoon ground cloves
¼ teaspoon salt
1 ½ cups shortening
2 cups sugar
2 eggs
½ cup molasses
¾ cup coarse sugar

Mix together flour, ginger, soda, cinnamon, cloves, and salt. Set aside.

In a large mixing bowl beat shortening until softened. Gradually add the 2 cups sugar, beat until fluffy. Add eggs and molasses, beat well. Add half the flour mixture, beat until, combined. Stir in remaining flour with a wooden spoon. Shape dough into 1-inch balls. Roll in coarse sugar. Place on ungreased cookie sheet 2 inches apart. Bake in a 350-degree oven 12 to 14 minutes until light brown and puffed. Let stand 2 minutes and transfer to a plate.

A half hour later Holly grinned and stood shoulders back, head held high These were her pride and joy.

"Hi, Mom." Rake shouted from across the room as he pranced toward her, his elf shoes slapping the floor.

"Ready for work, Mom!" Randy pushed against Rake in his attempt to reach her first. Rake sprawled, almost hit the floor but regained his balance, and shoved Randy, managing to grab her around the waist seconds before Randy.

"No roughhousing boys." Holly touched her finger to her lips. "Shush. In here we use our quiet voices."

"Look what Mr. Charlie gave us to hand out." Rake opened the decorated Christmas bag he held and showed her the treasure inside. "Candy canes!"

"Wonderful." She selected one and tucked the cellophane-wrapped red and white striped cane onto her apron bib.

"And look, Mom!" Randy displayed a large platter of red and green iced sugar cookies baked in the shape of angels.

"Brother, that was some miracle. Those cookies almost landed on the floor!" Shirley whistled.

"Okay boys. Elves are quiet and soft-footed. They pop up at your side when people aren't looking and surprise them. They do not make loud noises and shove one another." Holly smiled at the identical red-heads with their sprinkles of freckles over pert noses."

Two pairs of hazel eyes gazed at her with naked love. Both heads bobbed *yes* making the green caps with their funnel tops shake and the bell atop jingle. Green felt elf shoes with curled up tips shuffled on the wooden floor.

"Hey guys, those red-striped tights look groovy. I could tell you were elves in the dark." Shirley patted Randy on the back. "You two glow like neon lights."

Charlie walked into the dining room. "Okay boys. No shenanigans or your first day will be your last. Circulate around the room and hand out the treats to people seated at the tables as well as those waiting in the anti-room to be seated." He grinned at Holly. "And if I find sticky fingers, you won't be able to carry any left-overs home tonight."

The boys straightened and put on their obedient faces. "Yes Mr. Charlie. We are elves, not boys. And no sticky fingers. You can count on us."

Holly trembled. This had seemed like a good idea when Charlie approached her. She'd have to keep a strict eye on the boys. In their eagerness, they could burn down the restaurant.

She sighed. But they did look cute. And she loved having them near. She watched her delightful little elves weave between the tables gaining laughs and small talk from the patrons. They were adorable. How long would that behavior last?

Chapter 12

Trent cleaned his brushes. Soothing. Relaxing. Freed his mind to think about important things. After Christmas, his full-time job waited for him. He swirled a brush in terpenoid and watched the red paint whirl in circles until it disappeared. He laid the brush aside.

He had to step up his campaign.

At some point he'd have to confess to Holly. Suck in the embarrassment. Take his bitter medicine. Force out words that had been stuck in his throat. How time flew. He blinked his eyes, and ten years had disappeared.

He cleaned another brush. Sure, by some standards he'd been successful. He'd joined the Williamsburg Police Force and worked his way up to detective. Not much crime, and with time on his hands, he'd created Trent Conway's Portraits. He'd fallen into the brass-playing gigs by accident.

Life was good. He had friends. Enjoyed his work. Hadn't realized how huge a gash his divorce had torn in his life. He pulled the brush from the terpenoid and worked the paint-clogged threads through the artist's soap.

When Holly moved into her apartment in Colonial Williamsburg his good life ground to dust. Became colorless and dead without the woman he'd fallen in love with back in high school.

He rinsed the brush in warm water, squeezing the sable strands between his fingers. How had he fallen into such a trap? Older and wiser now and after the fact. Hindsight. He should have never let her go. He set the brush bristles up in the drying rack.

Even after he confessed, would she take him back? Did she still have feelings for him? If possible, Holly was more beautiful today than she had been those quickly evaporated years ago. And love for her boys had strengthened her. She had grown into a nurturing woman.

What now? The Holly he'd known would never be interested in a player like Bob Robinson. And she didn't seem to have changed. Bob would be no problem.

But that school principal Rake and Randy set her up with looked like serious competition.

He smacked a fist into the palm of his other hand. "I've got to make my move!"

He stored his brushes and paints, pulled on his leather jacket and clambered down the stairs.

Ye Olde Queen's Inn hummed with couples and families. He stood in the receiving area waiting for a seat. *Radioactive* played in front of the stone fireplace. Trent's fingers moved over invisible brass keys along with the notes the quartet played. He hummed *I'll be Home for Christmas.*

He grinned. If he'd ever imagined elves, Rake and Randy personified the mischievous wee folk. The two darted, slithered, and pranced in and out between the tables. Good touch, Charlie. Who could resist returning to the restaurant to watch the elves as much as to enjoy the food?

Randy rushed over. "Have a cookie, Mr. Trent. They're real good."

Trent selected a red-iced angel and touched a thumb to the corner of Randy's mouth to swipe off a few red and green crumbs. "Thanks, Randy."

"Mr. Trent, you and Mom are the only two grown-ups who can tell me from Rake. How do you do it?" Wide hazel eyes above rosy cheeks questioned him as if the safety of the world depended on his answer.

"Easy, Randy. You're a shade heavier than Rake. And your mouth is shaped differently. More like your mom's." Trent ruffled Randy's hair. "Your hair isn't quite as red as Rake's. You look alike, but you're different. Unique. You're your own man."

Randy's chest puffed out, and he stiffened his back. "Mom

says we both look like Dad."

"I never met your dad. But you and Rake have different expressions from one another. You look at life in unique ways. You're the impetuous one and Rake's the quieter one." He tilted Randy's chin up. "It's easy to tell you from your brother."

"Thanks, Mr. Trent. You're the greatest!"

"You better get circulating or Charlie will give you the evil eye."

"Right!" Randy saluted, making his elf's hat tilt and turned back to dance among the tables and offer his cookies. His bell jingled with every step.

Across the room, Rake waved some candy canes and frolicked over. "Here's one for you, Mr. Trent."

He knew Holly hadn't missed the boys' greeting him. She carried a load of empty dishes from a vacated table and glided in his direction.

Now or never. Trent gulped.

Holly approached, looking sweet and more delectable than any food the restaurant served. She smiled. "Hi."

"Great boys you have there! Can I take you to the Christmas Tree Lighting tomorrow night?"

She blinked her big emerald eyes, hesitated, then said, "Okay. I'm off work. What time?"

"I'm not sure when the festivities start. Early I think. I'll pick you up at four."

"Perfect. I'll see you then." She hustled toward the kitchen.

Wow. Ten years erased in a few seconds. She'd said *yes* and looked elated. The tension binding his chest disappeared.

A shoulder bumped his and almost knocked him against an older lady standing next to him.

"Look where you're going!" Trent glimpsed John Baxter moving through the crowded entry toward a table on Holly's side.

Trent grinned. Appeared he'd arrived just in time. Seemed Baxter was after the woman he loved.

Chapter 13

"Remember the time after junior prom that you and I drove to the lake?" Trent squeezed Holly's hand and led her toward the huge Christmas tree in the center of Market Square.

"That was fun. A night to remember." Holly snugged her red coat under her chin and shivered.

"But you were chicken."

"Yeah. But you egged on Ginger and Dick. You talked them into swimming in that dark water. You wanted me to jump in too."

"I was wild and crazy in those days."

"You were. I wasn't about to skinny dip in Rogers Lake with the car headlights spotlighting me." Holly laughed. "Although I did want to see what you looked like under that white tux jacket."

"If the headlights hadn't been shining on the lake, would you have gone in?" Best not to mention how much he'd wanted her to jump in. But he needed to keep her talking about the happy times they'd shared. Remind her how much they'd cared about one another.

"No. I wasn't about to dive into that dark water. Or get my formal messed."

"Remember –."

The piping of fifes and the snare of drums interrupted, drowning his words. Marchers approached, dressed in colonial garb, and high-stepped down the cobblestone street.

Crowds on both sides of the street clapped and cheered, then fell in behind the loud band as they led the way to the giant Christmas tree in the center of the square.

Holly's hand nestled warm in his as they joined the hundreds of people, boots and shoes clattering over the cobblestones, headed toward Market Square. For the first time in ten years his world tilted to its right spot. He whispered, "You're the only woman in the universe for me." Apparently, she couldn't hear over the band piping and the drums drumming. "You fill the empty vacuum inside my heart."

For good or ill, he didn't know which, the band and crowd noise overwhelmed his words. Her eager expression didn't change. With her nose and cheeks tipped red from the cold she gazed at the festive scene, her head tilted back, a happy smile on her lips.

They arrived in time to see the dark, giant spruce spring to life with lights. The tree illuminated joy on the faces of the surrounding people, especially the children.

The drums faded, and the fifes burst into *O Come All Ye Faithful.*

As if led by a choir director, the bystanders merged their voices in singing the beautiful carol. Afterward the fifes played, and they all sang some of the other loved Christmas carols.

With the ringing of sleigh bells, Santa and Mrs. Claus arrived on a horse-drawn carriage. With screams of delight, the noisy, jumping children surrounded the horses, the carriage, and the red-suited couple. He'd invited Rake and Randy, but the twins were attending a birthday party for one of their school friends.

Holly's hand chilled inside his. "Let's go to Rudy's for a wassail or a hot chocolate. It's getting colder."

"Hot chocolate for me." She grinned, her cheeks rosy, and her emerald eyes ablaze.

He steered her down a cobblestone lane. Lampposts strung around with fresh pine branches lit their way until they arrived at the small bakery. "We can watch the fireworks above the Governor's Palace from here." He pulled out a chair at one of the two sidewalk tables for her. "Knowing about this place is one of the benefits of living here."

She smiled. "One of the many. I can't believe I'm spending Christmas in Williamsburg. This place is so romantic."

He counted on the romantic ambiance. They settled at a sidewalk table cupping the warm drinks in their cold hands.

Soon cascades of fireworks exploded in the sky outlining the mansion, the trees and the gardens.

They oohed and awed together.

As red and green tints from the explosions lit her profile, he yearned to reach across the table and touch her soft cheek. Over the years, he'd missed her more than the ache in his heart laid bare.

She gazed at the sky, unaware of his pain, her expression as joyful as a child's.

He reached across and cradled her hand inside his.

After the fireworks climaxed into a giant crescendo, they stood and strolled past a turned-up keg of roasted chestnuts. He stopped and bought a bag from the vendor. They shared the warm nuts as they strolled the festive square.

"Are you cold?"

She nodded.

"Ready to go home?"

She shook her head.

"Let's stop here for another drink."

"Sounds like fun."

He slipped a five into the waiter's hand. The man led the way inside to a table for two beside the roaring fire.

"I love this coffeehouse."

"Yeah, Carlton's is the best." He seated her and ordered two hot scones with butter and two more cups of hot chocolate with chocolate stirrers.

"This has been an unforgettable evening."

Her smile sent ripples through his stomach. "Want to take in the Christmas Homes Tour with me? The ramble takes place all next week. When do you have a day off?"

"I do have Wednesday off work." She played with the top button on her wool coat. "What happens on the tour?"

"The garden club sponsors the event. Home owners in the historic district open the doors to their private residences, and the public pays to stroll through their homes. The décor is Colonial. The decorations Christmas. The gardens behind each home are opened. As well as the sheep, hogs, and goat pens." Trent fiddled with his hot chocolate spoon. He swallowed. Would she want to see him again?

232

"Sounds delightful."

He breathed again. "Okay, Wednesday at two. We could take in a movie after."

"Hmm, Trent. Are you trying to monopolize my time?" She raised the cup to her lips.

"You guessed it. You still know the way I operate. How about the tour?"

"Sounds too lovely to miss."

"Great, two o'clock." He sipped his hot chocolate. Then said, "Hey, do you remember the time I took you rowing on Lake Rogers? You splashed me and soaked my jeans and shirt from head to foot."

"I did." She smiled.

"And I developed blisters on top of blisters on both palms from all that rowing. Couldn't afford to rent a power boat."

They laughed.

"Remember how exotic the gym looked when we had the Cinderella prom theme with the stars and the Disney carriage? Junior year wasn't it?"

"How could I forget? You looked so handsome in your white tux jacket and I wore my red strapless ballerina dress."

"Did I?"

"You were always handsome. Still are."

"You're even more beautiful than you were then. We have closets filled with great memories. Two years of knowing one another."

"Yes, I never looked at another guy."

He took her hand in both of his. "I loved you then and I love you now."

She squirmed and gazed at the door. "We have to leave. The boys will be home from the party soon." She rose and gathered her shoulder bag, a frown marring her smooth forehead. "I trusted you then. Now I don't."

Trent groaned. "What can I do to regain your trust?"

"I'm not sure you can."

Chapter 14

December 20, 1955

"Oh, Trent, thank you. I've always wanted to take this carriage ride around Williamsburg." Holly grasped the hand Trent held out and ascended the three steps into the bouncy carriage and settled on the padded seat.

Trent mounted behind her and perched beside her, his thigh touching hers. He casually laid his arm across the seat behind her.

Joy tripped through her heart. She tugged her red knit cap down around her ears to shut out the cool breeze.

"Giddup." The driver urged his horses.

The carriage lurched forward with Trent's hand grasping her shoulder, holding her steady, until the ride smoothed into a slightly rocking motion as the coach jounced over the cobblestone street.

"I enjoyed our tour of Christmas homes. It was fascinating. So many of the owners shared the history of their homes. I loved strolling through the back-yard gardens, even though most of the vegetation was dormant." Holly gazed at the colonial shops the horses clopped past. "To say I'm impressed with how self-sufficient the people in colonial America were is putting it mildly." Holly bounced on the seat. "Everything any resident needed he grew in his own backyard or the item was manufactured somewhere inside the village. No imports."

They rolled past the cabinetmaker and the cooper. "Like at those shops." She pointed.

"Not many imports anyway." Trent cleared his throat. "Not much money in those days. People bartered for goods they didn't make or grow themselves."

The colonial houses slowly slid by. Almost, she could believe she lived in those by-gone days. They passed the working black-smith shop, with its roaring fire, and the muscular blacksmith in his big leather apron hefting his hammer up and down to clang on the anvil. The blacksmith pounded on something glowing red hot atop the anvil. Holly removed her fingers from her ears once they'd glided by the gunsmith and the silversmith shops.

The carriage turned onto a one-lane dirt road and drove past double-story white-frame houses surrounded with picket fences. They breezed past the book bindery.

"Only the rich could afford books." Trent nodded toward the bindery window.

"That's sad. I love to read. Do you still read much?"

"Mostly historical books and books about politics." Trent shook his head, his dark hair unruly in the breeze. "If Americans don't study our history, we're doomed to repeat the worst part. Knowledge is power." He ran his free hand through his hair. "Don't get me started. I get pretty loud in my opinions."

"I couldn't agree more about knowing history. This is the right place to visit." She gazed into Trent's serious brown eyes. Why was he so intense today? He'd seen these places countless times. What was bugging him? The further they rode, the more edgy he appeared.

As they rolled past, Trent pointed to the brick yard. "Even today this establishment produces bricks for some of the homes."

"Amazing."

He was silent as they drove down another dirt road. The muscles in his arm lying across her shoulders tightened. Something bothered him. Something he'd been thinking about since they settled inside the carriage. "Is anything wrong?"

"Holly, I have something I've been wanting to confess. It's been eating me."

"Oh?" Darn. She didn't want any deep discussions. Wanted to enjoy this ride and not think. Just snug here, warm and comfy, and enjoy the sights and feel the chill wind on her cheeks.

"I was married."

Her heart jolted. She shouldn't be surprised. Trent was

handsome, personable, and as far as she could tell, made a reasonable living with his two jobs. She threw back her head and inhaled the crisp morning air. Sunshine warmed her back while the cool breeze chilled her cheeks. She stiffened her courage. She could handle this. "Okay."

"My senior year at college I married the girl Mom and Dad all but shoved in my face. Julie was pretty, intelligent, and already a rising star in the political world, thanks to her Senator father."

"So, you made your parents happy." She forced life into her flat voice.

"I was wrong to marry Julie. I loved you."

"What happened?" Was Trent over his marriage with Julie or did he still hold feelings for her?

"Our marriage lasted less than six months. Turned out I wasn't what Julie wanted in a husband." Trent shook his head. "I had no interest in relocating to D.C. Nor was I eager to support Julie in her political career with all the parties, meetings, and back-biting." His hand slipped down further and clasped her shoulders. "We have differing political views as well."

"No. You wouldn't thrive living that sort of life. You've never had an easy time keeping your mouth shut when you disagreed with someone's opinion." Holly gazed into the street. At least the old Trent would have hated the political life.

"The straw that broke our marriage happened one night when I asked her if she planned to have children." His smooth voice sounded strained as if he spoke through a tight throat. "We should have ironed that out before we rushed into marriage."

"Oh?"

"Children weren't included in her life plan. I discovered Julie had a high-walled, unbendable life plan. The husband she had in mind was wall-paper. Decoration."

"I'm so sorry."

"Then somehow she discovered I was still in love with you. I don't think that made a lot of difference to her." Trent's voice turned hard. "Julie didn't care who I loved. For her political alliances she entertained quite a number of men. Flirted with them all. Part of her job description Julie explained."

"I made excuses for her, not wanting to accept her behavior." Trent's warm hand squeezed her shoulder. "But, when I joined the police department, she divorced me." He gazed straight ahead. "Police work didn't meet her social standards."

Holly laid a hand on his. The one clasping her shoulder. "So, after your divorce, you remained single all these years?"

He nodded. "Filled my life with my careers and serving the Lord when I could." He tightened his grasp around her shoulders until he hugged her to his side.

She didn't resist or take her hand off his. They rode in silence, his words revolving inside her mind. "Danger and excitement belong in your life. I can't see you happy without them."

"And children. I want a pack of kids. A whole house full." He grinned. "I wouldn't wish being an only child on anyone." He grinned as if he'd unburdened his thoughts and could relax. "Your two make a nice beginning."

She pulled away to stare at him full in the face. "But you chose the life your parents planned for you."

"Yes. I'm older and wiser now." He put his arm around her again. "And so are Mom and Dad."

She snuggled into his side. "Aren't we all." He'd obviously found telling her to be difficult. Listening had been hard as well. Raised more questions. "Your Mom and Dad won't interfere with your life again?"

His voice smoothed into its usual baritone richness. "I can't promise that. When I take you to meet them, and you know I must, they'll fall in love with Rake and Randy and pressure me to marry you."

"Doesn't sound like they are older and wiser."

His deep laugh rang out. "Their pressure will be more subtle. They remind me constantly that they aren't getting any younger."

The carriage jolted to a halt, back at the sidewalk stop where they had started. "Okay, folks. Hope you enjoyed the ride." The driver tipped his top hat.

"We did." Trent hopped out and helped her down. He caught her hand and they strolled down Duke of Gloucester Street.

Holly's heart still beat double-time. Trent had spilled his heart.

238

What should she do?

Chapter 15

Holly gazed out her apartment window at the dusting of snow sparkling in the early morning dawn on the cobblestone street below. She sipped the hot cider in her cup and tried to still her wild thinking.

Trent stirred her emotions like no other man ever had. Not even Vince. She'd loved Vince with all her heart, and they had rejoiced together when their babies were born. Though they'd only had a few years with one another, they'd loved well…until the day the bottom dropped out of her world when the plane crashed. She'd spent two years grieving Vince's death.

Time to close that chapter of her life and flip open a new one. Judging from her sons' actions, they hankered for a complete family again. They yearned for a father.

She paced the small living room, circling the perimeter over and over.

Would Rake and Randy be hurt if she stopped any romance from developing between her and their principal? John was a fine man. If Trent hadn't entered her life again, she would be tempted to further her relationship with John. But her heart already seemed to be taken. Had she ever stopped loving Trent?

She paced, stopping now and again to sip the cider.

She'd already refused one date with John. She'd be up front with him. The sooner the better. The handsome, personable man would have no trouble finding a woman whose heart was not already taken.

Trent had spent eight of the last ten years of his life alone because he loved her, and he'd not made contact because she was married. Then he'd given her time to grieve before introducing himself with that French horn. Leave it to Trent to be creative.

When she spent time with him all the old feelings flooded her with new strength. Now she hated to be away from him.

Trent was older and wiser to the point that he knew how his parents would react if she agreed to meet with them again. How could she not trust him considering his actions during the past years?

Her old love made her heart sing again. Caused joy to pulse through her veins. She adored watching him interact with the boys. Trent seemed smitten with the twins. The boys jabbered less and less about John and more and more about Trent. That meant something.

"The signs of love are all in place. Thank You, Lord. I hear what You're saying. Shirley and my sons are misguided matchmakers. You brought Trent and me together in high school and again in this beautiful city I've grown to love. I'll trust You and will no longer turn my back on the promise of love."

Her telephone rang.

"Oh, hello Trent." Butterflies flitted inside her stomach.

"How about you go to church with me tonight? I guarantee Rake and Randy will love it. The children are performing a pageant."

"Three days before Christmas?"

"A time to be together with loved ones."

Could she get the time off from work? "I don't know."

"The boys will love it."

Trent picked her up at her apartment. The boys were angels, each hanging onto one of Trent's hands, laughing and joking with him. No bad behavior.

She rushed into the bathroom to touch-up her lipstick.

Randy tip-toed in. "Mom."

"What dear?"

He inched over and fingered her powder and the nail polish cluttering the sink's ledge. "Rake and I don't care if you choose Mr. Trent over Mr. John. We like Mr. Trent a lot and really, really want to have a new father." He thrust a small arm around her neck. "We miss Dad." He kissed her on the cheek leaving a tiny wet spot. "But Dad's in heaven and having a good time taking care of kids up there. We need a Dad, so we can have a good time down here."

Holly nodded, crooked his small body in her arms, and kissed his cheek. "Thank you, sweetie!"

"Besides, it's too hard not to get into trouble at school." Randy broke from her arms and whirled in a circle. "And we don't want the principal telling us we're bad at school *and* at home." He giggled and darted from the room.

Holly smiled, gathered her purse and coat, and the four of them left her apartment.

They sat together in church. She and Trent sandwiched the boys between them. Shirley slipped in and established herself in the vacant seat Holly saved beside her.

Contentment stretched over her as strong and sweet as the taffy pulled in the Williamsburg Candy Shop.

As the pageant progressed, all three of the males in her life wore an engrossed expression. Rake nestled close to Trent and Trent had his arm around her son's shoulder.

"Look at that yummy narrator." Shirley whispered loud enough the narrator's cheeks reddened. "He's just the type of hunky male I could go for."

The children filing in and taking their places on the church's small stage quieted Shirley.

The tall narrator straightened his blue robe, cleared his throat, and began speaking. "And Joseph also went up from Galilee, out of the city of Nazareth, into Judea, unto the city of David, which is called Bethlehem; because he was of the house and lineage of David to be taxed with Mary his espoused wife, being great with child. And so it was, that, while they were there, the days were accomplished that she should be delivered. And she brought forth her firstborn son, and wrapped him in swaddling clothes, and laid him in a manager, because there was no room for them in the inn."

The small girl playing Mary cradled the doll in her arms and sweetly hummed.

"And there were in the same country shepherds abiding in the field, keeping watch over their flocks by night."

Three small shepherds filed in, holding staffs, and checking the audience for their parents.

"And lo, the angel of the Lord came upon them, and the glory of the Lord shone round about them; and they were sore afraid."

A small angel with a tilted gold halo hurried down the aisle and joined the shepherds on stage.

"And the angel said unto them, Fear not: for behold, I bring you good tidings of great joy, which shall be to all people. For unto you is born this day in the city of David a Savior, which is Christ the Lord. And this shall be a sign unto you; Ye shall find the babe wrapped in swaddling clothes, lying in a manger."

Other small angels filed up onto the stage, sometimes brushing their wings against one another by mistake. Small giggles mingled with the narrator's words.

"And suddenly there was with the angel a multitude of the heavenly host praising God, and saying, Glory to God in the highest, and on earth peace, good will toward men."

The crowded stage overflowed with shining small faces grinning into the audience and searching for parents.

"And it came to pass, as the angels were gone away from them into heaven, the shepherds said one to another, let us now go even unto Bethlehem, and see this thing which is come to pass, which the Lord hath made known unto us."

Small hands waved from the stage. Small angels and shepherds jostled one another as they crossed the stage to stand in front of the living manger scene.

"And they came with haste, and found Mary, and Joseph, and the babe lying in a manger. And when they had seen it, they made known abroad the saying which was told them concerning this child. And all they that heard it wondered at those things which were told them by the shepherds."

Caught up in the story, the children quieted and some of the shepherds knelt before the mother and baby.

"But Mary kept all these things and pondered them in her heart. And the shepherds returned, glorifying and praising God for all the things that they had heard and seen, as it was told unto them. Luke 2:4-20"

The audience stood to their feet and clapped long and loud for their children. The narrator bowed. The organ played, and all the parents surged to the front of the church to grasp the hand of a small angel, shepherd, or Mary or Joseph.

Laughter and voices mingled.

The tall narrator, his blue robes flowing behind him, pushed through the crowd and strolled over to Shirley. He offered his hand and smiled. "Hello, I'm Seth Johnson. I couldn't help noticing your face in the crowd. I've seen you working at *Ye Olde Queen's Inn* and have been wanting to meet you. That last shaft of sunlight beamed on your golden hair, and I took that for a sign that you might agree to join me for a cup of hot chocolate." He glanced at Holly. "That is, if your friends don't mind."

Shirley beamed, shook Seth's outstretched hand, and nodded. Her voice sounded breathless. "Yes, I'd love to share a hot chocolate with you." She gazed down at her shoes. "I've noticed you eating at one of my tables now and again."

She glanced at Holly, her plain face lit from within giving luminous sweetness to her features. "Do you mind?"

"Of course not. The Village Café is open until all hours. Go. Enjoy." Holly smiled at the tall, rugged-looking narrator. "I know you'll take good care of my friend." She glanced at the manger scene where Mary still held the baby in her arms. "I've discovered miracles still do happen at Christmas."

Seth's deep laugh rang out, "Yep. They do that." He put a hand on Shirley's back and guided her through the crowd. "Did you receive the Christmas flowers I sent you?"

"Yes. But I didn't know you sent them. The flower shop had a mishap with whose flowers went to who. I didn't find a card."

The two left, whispering together.

Holly smiled as she watched them walk out the front door together.

Trent clasped her hand and escorted her and the boys back to her apartment. Together they tucked her sons into bed. All four of them knelt by the twins' beds while the boys prayed their nightly prayers.

"You need to sleep tight, so you can go to work with me tomorrow. No roughhousing. Go right to sleep." She kissed each boy's cheek.

She and Trent slipped back into the living room.

"Fantastic boys!" Trent grinned and settled on the couch in front of the fire.

She brought two cups of hot cider sprinkled with cinnamon, set the steaming cups on the coffee table, then scrunched on the couch beside him.

After they drank, they placed the boys' Christmas presents under the tree. Trent brought out two he had wrapped for the boys.

Holly clasped her hands and gazed at the star-topped Christmas tree. "Thanks for inviting us. We had a joyful time tonight."

"Let's make it even better." Trent slipped down on one knee on the floor to face her. "Holly Belle Silver, I love you with all my heart. I've loved you since I first saw your face in Calculus Class. You walked into the room wearing your pink turtle-neck sweater and plaid skirt with your long hair curled around your face. I couldn't breathe right. I thought you were a dream-walking. Your still one. I know now that I'll never love anyone else. I'll never leave you again. Will you do me the honor of becoming my life partner?"

"Trent, I too believe in love at first sight. The first date I had with you when I had to sit through that horror movie, *Revenge of the Creature*, and you held my hand, I fell in love with you...and never stopped. The boys love you. I love you. I'm sure being the wife of a detective will be wild, but yes. I'll marry you." She grabbed his hands. "Besides, I still need that portrait of the twins."

Trent laughed from deep within his chest. "We could make that a family portrait." He sprang up and swept her into his arms. He kissed her as if he'd been in the desert way too long and she was life-saving water. When he finished he held her at arm's length and gazed into her eyes. "Sorry I don't have a ring. It's my Christmas present to you, but I want you to choose the one you like."

"Pretty certain, were you?" She kissed him. Then plopped on the couch and drew him with her.

He shook his head. "Nope. But I wasn't about to give you up." He pulled a small box from his pocket. "I bought a back-up present in case you refused."

"May I open it tonight?"

"Sure. We'll shop for your real present tomorrow."

She pulled off the wrapping. "Oh, Trent! It's lovely." She shook her head. "But it must have cost a fortune." She held out her wrist for him to attach the diamond bracelet.

"I didn't want to influence your decision, but I made a killing trading stocks over the past few years. If you want to quit work and stay at home raising the boys...and our other children, we can work that out. Your choice."

"I've always wanted to be a stay-at-home mom."

"I don't want to wait long. Seems to me the ten years I've already waited was way too long." He traced a finger over her lips. "Though you're worth the wait. Let's get the license. We can get married at church on Christmas Day and spend our honeymoon at The Magnolia Manor B & B here in Williamsburg. I have to report for duty in one week."

"Do you think your parents will want to attend?"

"I've been talking to them about you and the boys for days. They wouldn't miss our wedding. They'll hire a private plane if they need to."

"What ever happened to taking things slow?" She melted into his arms.

Chapter 16

Christmas Day 1955

Holly stood at the front of the church waiting her cue. "This Christmas has turned out to be so much more joyous than last Christmas."

Shirley adjusted the cap sleeve to her red taffeta ballerina dress. "You had a rough year last year."

Holly loosened her death lock on her wedding bouquet. "My heart still aches, but I'm no longer devastated. No longer feel I can't face the world alone."

"You don't have to. You have Trent…and me."

Holly nodded. "Mom would have loved helping with the wedding preparations." Holly fluffed her veil over her face. "I still miss Mom's caring touch. Time has eased the pain."

"Yeah. Time's good for something besides putting wrinkles in my face."

Holly laughed. "This year I can picture Mom peering out a heavenly window and tossing down blessings and good wishes for a long and happy life."

Shirley turned to face the door and stood at attention. "That's my music." Her dress rustled as she departed to glide down the church aisle.

Trent and his best friend, whom Holly had yet to meet, waited beside the altar at the front. Both tall and striking in their white dinner jackets. Each with a red rose in his lapel.

A friend of Shirley's stood in the alcove beside the organ and sang *Always*.

Tears pricked Holly's eyes.

The organ broke out with the Mendelssohn Wedding March.

The redhaired twins, wearing full white tuxes, rushed to her side, one tripping on the white runner that ran down the aisle. Each grabbed one of her hands and walked her down the candlelit aisle. Randy carried her bouquet. Once the boys recognized familiar faces, they strutted like wooden soldiers, huge smiles lighting their freckled faces.

Holly's white ballerina slippers floated down the aisle between them.

She glimpsed friends on both sides of the aisle. Trent's beaming parents reigned in the front row. Holly and Shirley's fellow workers, neighbors, and friends filled the front section of the church.

Poinsettias bloomed everywhere.

The boys dropped her hands, Randy passed her the wedding bouquet, and they scooted into the pew next to Trent's parents without any mishaps.

Trent welcomed her with a smile that made her heart sing.

Before she knew it, the young pastor pronounced them man and wife.

Tears pricked Holly's eyes as her groom took her into his arms and kissed her as if he would never let her go.

The photographer flashed his camera, popped out bulbs, and flashed again. After pictures of the wedding party and family, they all trooped over to *Ye Olde Queen's Inn* where Charlie presided over a three-tiered wedding cake. He'd opened the doors to the Event Room, so customers could glimpse the wedding reception and sit-down dinner.

The reception was flawless.

Mr. John Baxter approached the wedding table, carrying a plate of bridal cake in one hand and a wedding present in the other. "Best wishes to a fine couple. I'll see you both at parents' conference."

After guests gathered at one end of the long room, Holly tossed her bouquet of white roses over her shoulder to Shirley. Her friend beamed at Seth, who ran a finger around his collar under his tie, but grinned.

Inside the bride's room, Holly changed into a red suit with a white fur collar. After more photographs, she and Trent ran for the silver car trailing cans and old shoes. Someone had scrawled *Just Married* across the back window.

Holly's mouth dropped. "Wow! A BMW. Is it yours?"

"Yep."

A limo stopped at the curb. Mr. and Mrs. Conway motioned for Rake and Randy to join them. Holly had balked at Trent's parents caring for the boys while she and Trent honeymooned. But during the rehearsal dinner, the older couple overcame her concerns and their love burrowed deep into her brimming heart. They'd insisted. She learned they were used to getting their own way. She'd have her work cut out for her standing on her own two feet, but fortunately Trent's parents lived six hundred miles away.

She and Trent ran to the BMW amid a shower of rice. Everyone massed on the sidewalk called "Congratulations!"

She couldn't have asked for a more beautiful or happy wedding.

The BMW slid to the curb in front of an old-fashioned, Federal Style, two-story brick building.

A huge Christmas wreath hung over the door to the Magnolia Manor B & B.

He carried her over the threshold without even breathing hard.

Finally, they faced each other in the bridal suite.

Holly wrapped her arms around her new husband's neck. "I thought I moved to Williamsburg for a few magical months. God had other plans. I fell in love with the village."

"And with me?" Trent's lips nibbled her neck in the tender spot beneath her ear.

She giggled. "Yes, with you. Here, with you by my side, the magic of Christmas will last all year long."

"You're a Christmas miracle yourself! Shall we make Williamsburg our home?" His warm lips travelled to her cheek and then to the corner of her mouth.

"Isn't this where you work?"

"It is." He kissed her long and thoroughly.

When she came up for air, she pulled in a deep, happy breath.

"Then this is home. The boys love it here. And so do I. I can't think of anyplace I'd rather live." She caressed his cheek. "Or anyone I'd rather be married to. I love you truly."

Trent smiled, but his eyes looked dark and serious. "For as long as we both shall live. I'll never leave you."

THE CHOICE

By

Anne Greene

DEDICATION

I dedicate this book to every reader who has ever fallen in love.

As ever, I dedicate this book to my supportive husband, Colonel Larry Greene.

Above all, I dedicate this book to my Lord and Savior, Jesus Christ

Ephesians 3:20-21 – Now unto Him that is able to do exceeding abundantly above all that we ask or think, according to the power that worketh in us, unto Him be glory in the church by Christ Jesus throughout all ages, world without end. KJV – **Felicity's Verse.**

I Corinthians 15:58 – Therefore, my beloved brethren, be ye steadfast, unmovable, always abounding in the work of the Lord, forasmuch as ye know that your labor is not in vain in the Lord. KJV – **Ben's Verse.**

CHAPTER 1

Laramie (in what would become Wyoming) - 1850

"If I wanted to stay single, I'd wait for the perfect man." As she carried the wooden sign toward the large storefront window of Ft. Laramie's only general store, Felicity Daniels' long, pink gingham skirts brushed the floor.

She passed between the barrels of flour and boxes of food clustered on the wooden-plank-floor and the shelves stacked high with dry goods.

Papa's old friend, Jedidiah Adams, planted a hand on her arm and stopped her rush. "Now, jist take some time and think this through."

"I don't have any more time." Felicity gently removed his hand and wended on through the piled-high goods to the front of McVey's General Store. She stared out the huge front window for a second, then bent and pushed several bolts of flannel yard goods out of the way. She shook her head. "No, this is better." And positioned the material so the heavy denim and calico bolts held up her sign.

WANTED: GROOM BETWEEN THE AGES OF 20 AND 30. STRONG, ABLE-BODIED WITH NO DISFIGUREMENT. CHRISTIAN. EAGER TO TRAVEL TO THE OREGON TERRITORY. ALL EXPENSES PAID. APPLY INSIDE. FELICITY DANIELS.

She straightened and set her jaw. She'd given Ben many chances to fall in love with her during the two months she'd been stranded in Ft. Laramie. She'd had no success, and time had run out. Ben ignored every one of her not at all subtle hints. Even said

255

no to her offer to take him for a buggy ride and a picnic. She stood, hands on her hips gazing at her handiwork. "Since it's essential I get married, rather than the perfect man, I'll settle for a good one."

"You could keep on clerkin' here at the gen'l store." Jed stroked his flowing silver mustache.

"That's not an option, Jedediah. Mr. McVey specified this would only be a temporary job until the last wagon train departs and business falls off. The last travelers leave in two days. I mean to go with them."

Jed lumbered to join her at the window. "Even unmarried settlers can claim three hundred twenty acres of that free land in the Oregon Territory. That should be enough land for you." Jedediah placed a heavy hand on her shoulder. "I know. I know. To get the whole six hundred forty acres you gotta have yourself a husband. I'd apply for the job myself, but ain't nobody gonna believe I'm yer husband. Good-looking young gal like you." He blew out a breath. "You best settle for the smaller tract of land. Good husbands don't grow on trees."

"According to *The Donation Land Claim Act,* the authorities won't allow a lone woman to claim that free land." Felicity flipped her long, blonde braid over her shoulder. "Besides, how do you suppose I can stake my claim on that land, cut down trees, build a house and a barn, and plant those acres all by myself?" She tossed her head, swirling her long blonde braid from her back to her shoulder. "I need a man with a strong back and big muscles. If he knows how to string a sentence together so much the better."

"I'm bound to take care of you myself, even with my rheumatism makin' me hobble like an old geezer." Jed gripped her arm. "Why are you so bent on leaving here? Not two months back, yer daddy's dying words asked me to take care of you." He jutted a white-whiskered jaw. "And that's exactly what I aim to do. Right here in Ft. Laramie. I'm not lettin' my life-long friend down. We was like brothers."

Felicity gave Papa's old friend a gentle smile. "Papa and I set out for the Willamette Valley in that Oregon Territory to forge our destiny in a new land." She tugged her arm free. "We've traveled this far to that Promised Land, and I don't plan to be stuck here in the middle of nowhere when I have two perfectly fine prairie schooners still loaded with provisions and the mules to pull them. Those mules are eating me out of Papa's savings. I can't afford to stay here any longer."

"Now, Felly, don't go off like a hog gone wild. Let's think this through." Jed shook his head until his silver mustache trembled.

She stared Jed down. "I'm out of time. I'm through thinking. It's time to act. The last wagon train of the year leaves in two days. Any later trains will get caught by winter. I've got to travel now." She strode to the front door and pushed one of the double doors open.

The bell above the door chimed. Gathering her skirts, she stepped outside into the late August heat.

Jed hobbled through the door and stood by her on the uneven boardwalk. "That's some sign you painted. But I told you, won't do no good to drive a man yer fixin' to corral. Jus' leave yer gate open a crack and let 'em bust in."

"I left my gate open wide with one man. Didn't work. I don't have any more time for those shenanigans. Two days from now, I leave." She glanced up and down the busy boardwalk. "And I've got to have a groom." Stepping back, she admired her hand-printed sign. The white paint on dark wood showed up well, blasting her message to the people bustling by.

"What mule-headed man will answer a sign like that? He'd have to be at the end of his rope to marry-up with you jist to get six hundred forty acres in the Oregon Territory."

"Are you saying a man would be crazy to marry me?" Felicity puckered her forehead and glared.

"Now, now, don't get yer dander up." Jed rubbed a weathered hand on the back of his wrinkled neck and his face sagged. "Yer so purty you look more ornamental than useful. How's that man to know what a strong, capable woman you are?"

"He had two months to find out. He's lost his chance. When the right man applies, I'll know him." She wrung her hands together as if washing Ben right out of them. "I've prayed about this, and God hasn't brought any other solution to my mind." She moved aside so passersby could see her sign. "What's marriage anyway, but two people building a new life together and establishing a home site on wonderful, fertile land? The land I'm sure of, and I'm trusting God will bring the right man."

"Them flyers you put such store by promise green, rolling hills, fenced land, herds of contented cattle, and flourishing crops." Jed swiped a work-hardened veined hand across his mouth. "Mabbe they're pie in the sky and promise more than they give. Ever think of that?"

She smiled as images flashed through her mind of permanence, stability, peace. How she yearned for a home of her own.

The wooden sidewalk vibrated under passing feet.

Farmers with broad shoulders and their big-hipped wives with unsmiling lips, their sun-bonneted heads turned back toward their three or four children, plodded by. Cowboys with guns strapped on their hips and tall hats with large brims dipped low on their foreheads tromped by as if they owned the fort. A few soldiers, their blue uniforms making them appear taller and broader than they were, glanced at her. Several children rolled hoops down the busy street. Wagons raised dust on the road, stirring up the odor of old manure. Everyone who trudged by gaped at her sign. No one turned into the store.

Shouts of team masters and the bustle of wagons wafted over the stockade wall behind the store, coming from the pastures outside.

"Wagon train is fixing to resume its long journey. No way you can find a suitable husband afore they leave." Jeb shook his head, so his silver hair stood out like spokes from a wheel.

Felicity pulled in a deep breath. Oh, the familiar noise brought an ache. She and Papa started out in early April, and they got just one-third of the way before they got stopped here at Ft. Laramie. She'd never forget when the cholera hit Papa. Though she'd done her best to nurse him, he'd not lasted a week. A shiver crept down her spine. If only she could forget Papa's sunken eyes and the clammy texture of his skin as he gripped her hand. He'd been a tall, hardy, healthy man, her strength and the rock of her existence. Nothing seemed impossible for him. As he died, he made her promise to go on to the new land and create a fresh start. But he'd died before he could tell her the reasons why they raced from Independence, Missouri, in such a hurry. Running as if someone chased them.

No matter, she had her suspicions. During the whole journey here, Papa had looked over his shoulder. With Papa's last breath, he'd begged her to get married. He'd said he had many good reasons why she needed to change her last name.

So, she'd promised him.

Nothing in this raw fort town beckoned her to stay. Even without her promise, she longed to leave. When the wagon train moved out there'd be little left here, but the general store and the small fortification garrisoned with twenty or thirty soldiers. No women lingered behind except Sal, running her boarding house, and a couple Indian women who did laundry for the soldiers. All humanity plunged onward to grab a piece of that free land. If she waited until the wagons rolled again next year, the free land would be taken. She'd be too late.

"Well, Felly, when a woman starts draggin' a loop, there's always some man willin' to step into it."

She nodded. "God will send the right man. I hope you're praying with me that he arrives in time and applies." No use wishing her groom had those unforgettable eyes as blue as the sky on a clear summer day. God hadn't answered that prayer.

"I'm a praying you'll change that stubborn mind of yours." Jed patted her shoulder.

"That's not going to happen." Felicity took Jed's hand and gazed into his grey eyes, still lively in their bed of wrinkles. White hair from his bushy brows drifted down over his drooping lids. "You're a godly man, please pray God will send a believing man to help me on my way." She squeezed his fingers. "Wouldn't hurt if he were good to look at."

"Felicity, honey, don't get your hopes high. When yer daddy and I started this pilgrimage together, we both thought we was younger than we turned out to be. But whatever happens, I can't let you go alone. I might be a hindrance, but I'm comin' with ya."

Jed's slow-talking words flew straight to her heart.

She pulled him by the hand back inside the slightly cooler

general store. Throwing her arms around his burly body, she hugged with all her strength. "Thank you so very much, Jed. I love all that beauty inside you. But I don't want to take you beyond what your strength can handle. If anything happened to you, I would never forgive myself."

"Don't you worry none, Felly. There're good years left in this old frame. I might slow you down a tad, but God knows that would probably be best. I'm thinkin' yer goin' off faster than a cat with her tail on fire."

"Just pray, Jed. Just pray for the right man to come inside and apply."

The above-the-door bell jangled. A few men entered, darted glances around the store and then headed toward the back counter. Four more men entered. Then the wood floor trembled under countless boots. A stream of men pushing and shoving boiled into the store.

Her mouth dropped open. She let Jed go and scurried behind the store counter. Good heavens, was it a stampede?

Jed lumbered up beside her and dropped both fists on the counter. "Felly, I'm thinkin' you best charge each man who wants to take you up on yer offer ten dollars apiece jist to apply." The overhead lantern flashed his white hair silver as he nodded. "Or you'll never make headway through this mob."

Men continued to spill into the store and lined up three deep at the counter. The line stretched out the open door and down the sidewalk.

Had she bitten off too big a bite? Oh, if only one of God's Christmas Angels would step in to help. She really needed a husband for Christmas.

Jed emptied a number of one-pound sacks of kidney beans from a basket and slid the woven container over in front of her. He pushed a child's school slate over and handed her a piece of chalk. "Ten dollars each."

"That's a week's wage. Don't you think—?"

"Yep, thet's fair!" Jed climbed up on an overturned wooden box and waved his flannel-coated arms. "Gents, are ye here cause of the sign in the winder?"

Deep throated, tenor, bass, and baritone voices chorused, "Yes!"

"Well, if ye wants to talk with the little lady, ye gots to drop ten dollars in the basket."

Silence for the barest moment, then pushing and shoving men burst forward to thrust a ten-dollar gold piece into the basket.

Felicity gaped. Gold dollars!

"Gold's easier to come by than silver these days. Money's flooding out of California territory, thanks to the gold rush," Jed whispered. "Shut yer mouth and start takin' names."

Felicity blinked. A few seconds passed before she gained her senses. "Stop! Stop!" She gazed at the assorted well-dressed and the motley-clothed crew of men churning in front of the store counter. "I...I won't take your money unless I think you might be a likely candidate. So, please stop tossing money in my basket and form a line. If I think you might be considered, you may deposit your ten-dollar gold piece, and I'll write your name on my list."

She pushed up the fitted sleeves of her pink-gingham dress, took the chalk, and gazed at the man standing first in line. Too slender. She needed muscle. "I'm so sorry, but I'm afraid you won't do. If you gave me a gold piece, please retrieve your money from the basket."

Jed nodded and pushed the basket toward the man.

"Aw, girlie. I need me a missus so I can get an extra three hundred twenty acres. I'll even pay my own way. I just need a wife."

Felicity tossed her head and winked at Jed. Ha! These men wanted a wife for the same reason she required a husband. Beneath her long skirts she tapped a jig with suddenly lighter feet. These men knew exactly what they signed up for.

"You heard Miss Daniels. Next." Jed's deep voice carried the authority he'd used as the foremost blacksmith in Independence, Missouri, before he retired. Many a teamster had quaked at that tone.

The twiggy man fumbled in the basket, his thin fingers closed over a gold piece, and he turned and shuffled out, his mouth pulled down at the corners.

As the next man in line stepped forward, his pungent odor preceded him. Perhaps he'd just arrived and hadn't had time to go to the hotel for a bath. No, several days ago he'd come into the store to buy flour and a new pair of boots. He'd been in Ft. Laramie long enough to clean up. "I'm sorry. Please take your money."

The man frowned and raised a fist.

Jed cleared his throat.

The man lowered his head, dug into the money basket, and retrieved his gold piece.

Felicity gazed at the next man. Clean. Tall. Muscles. Not too old. "You may leave your application fee. Please spell your name, and I'll write it on the slate." She poised the chalk.

He tipped his big hat, spelled his name, and gave her a pleasant smile.

His nose was large, but he had an agreeable look about him. "Next."

Another four men passed her initial exam, and she wrote their names on the slate.

Oh, dear heavenly Father, please send the right man. Seems quite a few men want a wife as well as have their way paid to the Oregon Territory. How shall I ever find the right groom?

All afternoon men either passed or failed her first look. None stood out in her mind. Some wore denims and chambray shirts, some wore cowhide chaps and wool vests and carried leather gauntlets, and a few wore store-bought suits. All wore six-shooters strapped to their hips and carried big hats in work-hardened hands.

Soon all the men looked the same. Was every single man in town lining up in front of the counter? She sighed. "Jed, please use another chalkboard and add that the man must be a Christian who regularly attends church. I'm sure that will cut the list down. I should have thought of that at once."

After Jed added the words and held up the sign, a few men frowned, left the line, and stomped out. Several others sauntered out of the store as if they hadn't wanted to apply after all. One man grabbed a gold coin from the basket, dipped his chin, and slunk out the door.

262

But a good many men stayed.

Those men whose names she'd written on the chalkboard loitered around the store, sitting on barrels, standing braced against the wall, leaning over the counter, or squatting on the floor waiting to see what she required next.

"Oh, dear. What shall I do now? I never thought I'd have more than one or two men who would accept my offer." Her ankle-high laced boots pinched her feet. Her head pounded. How could she find the right man in this horde? Her petticoat stuck to her drawers in the heat of so many bodies. The stays, usually so comfortable, poked her ribs. "There must be twenty men waiting for me to interview them."

"Well, missy, you'll just have to add some more qualifications." Jed slid another small chalkboard down the counter to her.

Felicity gazed at the gang of men scattered around the store. Some tried to appear unconcerned, others looked anxious, and many wore a stony expression to hide their thoughts. She didn't want to live in close quarters with a stranger for four more months, and the more she thought of her scheme, the more she felt like a fool. But she and Papa had faced too many hardships to get this far. She couldn't stop now.

Allowing a man to drive one of her wagons and eat at her campfire would be another affliction she had to face. She knew how to put her shoulder to the wheel and keep on plodding when the going got rough. Hadn't she done that all her life? And the fact that these men pursued a wife for the same reason she hunted for a husband made her deal a lot sweeter. She had a clear conscience.

She promised Papa she would start a new life in the Oregon Territory … so she would. She'd promised him she would marry … so she would.

"If any of you men smoke or chew, please take your gold piece out of the basket. I won't marry a man who smokes." She wrote the new demands on the chalkboard.

Two men glowered at her and reached for their ten dollars.

"I won't marry a man who drinks." She chalked that onto her requirement list.

A lanky cowboy's hand shot up. "Um, Ma'am, do you mean drink just a little now and again, or do you mean get drunk?"

"I mean, I don't want a man who drinks even one small drink of hard liquor at the end of a trail ride. I mean, no drinking at all."

Grumbling, more men moved toward the door. When the door shut on the last one, and the store grew quiet, half the men had taken their money and left.

Felicity pulled in a deep breath. Better. She sauntered out from behind the counter and zigzagged among the remaining men. All strong and healthy-looking. All tall. All passed the smell test. As she swished by each one, the man produced his best smile. All pleasant looking.

She gazed at Jed and shrugged. "I'd prefer a man who is intelligent. Who can carry on a conversation."

"You want a man who can be plenty smart without strugglin' to make a job out of it." Jed shook his head. "Maybe you should write them up a quiz. You were the Assistant Editor of the *Independence Times*. You know how to do thet."

As she hurried over to Jed, Felicity's high-laced shoes tapped the floor. She whispered, "I think it best you don't mention my job or my father as editor. He wanted to keep that information quiet."

Jed bobbed his head, his long hair swinging in his face.

"O.K. men, I'm going to dine at the hotel. I'll meet those of you who are still interested in the job back here in two hours. In the meantime, please consider why you are qualified to handle this position and be prepared to state your case." She held out her arm to Jed and the two of them made their way through the general store and out onto the street.

The hot evening still held some daylight, though most folks had gone to their supper, leaving the sidewalk less crowded.

"Oh, I never expected such a response." Felicity tried not to frown. Seemed every man in Ft. Laramie wanted to marry her ... except the one man she'd prayed would apply. Why hadn't he? From the looks of his worn boots, Ben didn't appear to be rolling in money.

The boardwalk still vibrated with footsteps, but the farm families who would depart with the wagon train had returned to their camps. Wood smoke, with mouth-watering scents of beef cooking over spits and coffee boiling, wafted over the high pickets surrounding the small fort. She motioned in that direction. "I loved those meals by the campfires after a long day of driving the mules or walking beside the covered wagons."

"Seems purty sure you will again. You and me took turns driving one wagon, and your papa drove the other. Reckon your new husband will drive the other wagon now."

She blinked against tears that *would* prickle her eyes and demand to fall. She and Papa had loved sitting by the fire and listening to cowboys' harmonicas and singing hymns before they crawled into their bedrolls. "How can I possibly go on without Papa?"

"Now, honey, you got something started that'd be hard to stop. Don't you fret about yer daddy. We'll find us the right fella." Jed put his gnarled fist under her chin and tilted her head up. "And you don't have to marry him. You and me will sign up for my three hundred twenty acres. See if we don't."

"But Papa wanted six hundred and forty acres. He'd sent our man, Jabez, to scout out the land. Jabez sent word that to be profitable, a man needed all six hundred forty acres."

"And then that slave never came back, did he?"

Felicity shook her head. "He would have been such a help on this trip. But Papa pretty much thought Jabez would take off once he reached the Oregon Territory." She smiled. "Land's not the only commodity free out west. At least Jabez sent back his report."

"Thet slave wouldn't have solved your problem. But he would have been a big help workin' thet land."

Just as the dinner bell rang, she and Jed climbed the wooden steps to the porch and walked through the front door into Sal's Boarding House.

"Say, what about that feller who's staying in the downstairs corner bedroom? I've been studyin' him, and he seems like a good, Christian man. I see him at church every Sunday."

She frowned. "I don't know. There's something about him that irritates me every time I see him." And why not? Ben had not so much as walked her to the new church after she'd dropped a wagonload of hints. Those sky-blue eyes barely acknowledged her when he breezed into the general store to buy provisions. Ben hadn't even gotten excited when she dropped everything dear Mrs. Baxter ordered into a jumbled pile in front of the sweet lady and rushed to wait on him.

But he'd gotten plenty animated choosing which goldmining pan he wanted. He'd chosen one of each. She sighed. He hadn't picked up on her hint of the picnic lunch, the carriage ride, or the pie auction. She'd spent all her spare time baking that pie. Ben had no interest in her.

"The feller's tall. He's so clean and brown, looks like he's been scrubbed with saddle soap. But you ask him where he's from and where he's aheadin', he turns as dangerous as being up a creek with a grizzly. Otherwise, he's right smart to talk with."

"Perhaps that's why I don't like him." Or more likely because he ignored her smiles and attempts at revealing her interest.

"But jist take another look. He favors one of them men in a mail-order catalog."

"Oh, he's handsome all right, with that dark, wavy hair and those brooding blue eyes. But he gives the impression he's not interested in land in the Oregon Territory. He's got Gold Rush Fever."

What a happy day for her *if* she *could* order a man out of the catalog. A mail-order groom. That's what she needed. One who fit all her criteria. She could check off all the things she wanted in a man … and mail him back if he didn't suit her needs. She thinned her lips. Darn if she wouldn't order one who looked just like Benjamin.

She and Jed entered the dining room. Every chair at the double-trestle table held someone except for three empty seats at the far end. Jed seated her and hunkered down across from her, leaving the chair at the end for whoever came in late.

She glanced around the table. Of course, the missing boarder had to be the dark-haired cowboy. "Do you recall his name?" She'd already gone so far as to embroider his name on her pillow slips. Well, Papa always said *'Dreams never amount to much. Just get your hopes high until someone comes along and stomps them into the ground.'* Still a blue-embroidered *BEN* on her pillow winked at her each night before she closed her eyes.

"Ben Bonneville. Cain't think why I didn't mention him to you as a possible. Seems to me he fits the bill, unless he's on the dodge from the law." Jed glanced over his shoulder at the door. "Here he comes. Now don't you go acting as prim as a preacher's wife at a prayer meetin'. I'm thinkin' this Benjamin might be jist the man we're alookin' fer."

Her cheeks heated. Too bad Ben didn't think so.

CHAPTER 2

"Evening, Mr. Bonneville." Felicity hid her irritation and tacked on her sweetest smile.

A crease formed between Ben's dark brows. His azure-blue eyes clouded like a dreary day in winter. "Evening, Miss Daniels, Jed." He tossed his big hat to the peg above the back door and hitched up the chair at the end of the table.

The landlady, Sally Thomas, presided at the head of the two long trestle tables set end to end and bowed her head. All the men, women, and children sitting at the table lowered their heads and closed their eyes.

"Lord, we thank You for the food we are about to partake of and pray You will bless it to our bodies and our bodies to Your service. In Jesus name, Amen."

Amens ranged up and down the table.

Felicity placed her napkin in her lap and gazed at the storm cloud that was Ben Bonneville. "Did you have a bad day, sir?"

"You could say that." He seized a plate of roast beef from the woman at his right and stabbed a slice of meat. "I'd say just about the worst day of my life." He thrust the serving dish to Felicity without looking up from his plate.

What awful manners. Even when grieving Papa's death, she'd tried her best to be civil to people. Her heart had ached so, she'd thought she'd never recover.

"What's the trouble, Ben?" Jed laid a hand on Ben's shoulder.

Jed's soothing voice had helped her through her worst days. Perhaps he could cheer Mr. Bonneville. She smiled at Letty, the lady at Ben's right who passed him the mashed potatoes.

Ben shook his dark head. Bristles shadowed his tan skin as if he hadn't taken time to shave today. "Don't want to bother you folks with my troubles." He glared at her.

Her heart fluttered at that deep-blue gaze. Drat! She'd abandoned hope about Mr. Ben Bonneville. If only the butterflies in her stomach would lose heart as well.

"I heard palaver that some silly woman put a sign up in the general store. Can't think any woman in this male dominated country would be so hard up she had to advertise for a husband."

Felicity lifted her chest, stiffened her back, and tossed her braid over her shoulder. "That is my sign, sir." Her tone could have iced a gallon of sweet tea.

Ben swallowed and choked on the meat. He coughed. His face reddened. "Seems I stuck my boot into my mouth there." He grabbed a drink of water.

"Yep. You did." Jed forked a slab of beef. "Maybe you could tell us what made yer day so bad."

As if he'd lost his appetite, Ben slid his plate, stacked high with food, toward the center of the table and wiped his mouth on his napkin. "Might as well. Maybe save you folks from my fate." He gulped another drink of water, leaned forward, and raised his voice. "I've been robbed." He waved his hands over his blue plaid shirt. "All I have left are the clothes on my back. The thief stripped me of everything else I own."

Felicity gasped. "I'm so sorry."

A murmur ran up and down the table.

"I've got two bits in my pocket between me and starvation." Ben's mouth hung down at the corners.

Questions flew up and down the dining table. Everyone gaped at him.

"Yep. My horse, Salvation's, missing from the stable, too. I got nothing left."

"Seems like you might want to add your name to Felicity's list of prospective husbands." Jed forked some green beans into his mouth and winked.

Felicity's face heated. If only she could slide down under the table. She smacked Jed's free hand lying on the wooden tabletop.

"Well, that sounds like a mighty fine offer for some lucky gent." Ben coughed. "But a wife doesn't fit anywhere into my plans."

"And why not?" Jed's eyes widened like he was as wise as a tree full of owls.

"Not that it's any of your business, but before she died my mother racked up quite a debt with expensive medical bills. I'm obliged to pay them. I'm off to join the gold rush."

"Sounds like an honorable thing to do. But cain't you earn thet money just as well on the acreage Felicity's going to get in Oregon? Might take a bit longer until harvest time. Her way is slower but sure as shootin' surer." Jed sipped his coffee, his eyes staring Ben down, his silver mustache glowing in the candlelight.

"That might be so, but I've heard God's call. When I reach those gold rush towns, I'm going to ride circuit and preach to those miners and prospectors." He rubbed the muscles at the back of his neck and frowned as if he had a massive headache. "And I've never heard of a circuit-riding preacher who supports a wife at home."

Felicity's heart dropped to her stomach to land hard on the dinner she wished she hadn't eaten. Had she only thought she'd given up hope on Ben?

Well, his words pounded the nail into that coffin.

CHAPTER 3

With darkness shrouding Ft. Laramie, Ben, hands clasped behind his back, shoulders hunched, boots thudding like a blacksmith's hammers, trod the wooden boardwalk through the small town. He strode for over an hour, but God remained silent about his predicament.

He passed the general store for the fourth time. Light from a kerosene lantern in the window streamed on Felicity's sign. *Wanted Groom. All expenses paid.* The words flamed a trail into his heart.

Had he trudged here on purpose? Before he left his cold dinner lying on the table at Sal's boardinghouse, he'd jammed his big foot in his mouth about that sign. He'd laughed. But that had been before Felicity acknowledged *she'd* placed the sign in the window.

She'd dropped hints for the past two months that she liked him, but he'd turned a blind eye, and focused his thoughts on obeying God's will for his life. Now everything had changed.

Heart stampeding inside his chest, he closed his eyes. *God, do You want me to marry Felicity?*

The word *marry* felt foreign in his thoughts and rattled around in his mind.

Once on the trail, would the delightful lady change her mind and travel to the gold rush rather than to the free farmland? He had to pay off those medical bills, and a gold rush camp had great need of a preacher.

God, if You want me to wed Felicity, You need to give me solid direction.

Felicity was a beautiful lady. She possessed a sunny disposition. Appeared to be a hard worker. And he enjoyed being in her presence. Had been a hard row to hoe to turn her down.

But he knew nothing about farming. He knew horses and the ins and outs of the part-time sheriff's job he'd taken while attending the University of Missouri. He knew how to preach. He'd had to quit seminary before he received his degree because Mother needed him when her health deteriorated due to the cancer growing inside her chest. But God's calling didn't depend on a degree. Or a wife.

Ben leaned closer to the store window. Quite a hubbub inside the general store. Lanterns glowed on the counters. Moving shadows showed men milling about inside. Golden hair gleamed behind the front counter. A trick of light fell on Felicity's angelic face.

Throat suddenly dry, he gulped. She wasn't waiting until morning. She was at this moment interviewing men to wed! She meant to follow through with her hare-brained scheme.

He pressed his nose to the glass window. Ft. Laramie was one tough frontier stopping-off place filled with desperadoes as well as good men. Perhaps one of those men inside was the thief who stole everything he owned. Another might be a murderer. Maybe the man she chose would be a wife-beater or a wife-deserter? What kind of man would he be to let Felicity fall victim to her own scheme? He was a God-fearing man in need of transportation to the west. He would treat Felicity with kindness. He would protect her. If she didn't know the Lord, he would lead her into God's flock.

Felicity needed him. Any one of those other men could take advantage of such a naïve girl. He would not. He shook his head. Was his change of heart a sign that God wanted him to love and honor that silly girl?

A number of men poured out of the store. Ben slid into the shadows as Felicity and Jed walked from the store and down the sidewalk. Must be she'd finished her interviews.

With Felicity's hand tucked into Jed's arm, the couple headed toward Sal's. Bedtime then. Would Felicity sleep easy tonight with her choice already made?

Ben slipped inside the general store and passed groups of men hunched together and making bets on which of them beautiful, rich Felicity would choose as her husband.

"Okay, fellas, time to head out. Store's closing for the night. Miss Felicity will be back early tomorrow." The owner, Trevor McVey, herded the remaining men toward the door.

So, the compelling lady had not yet chosen a groom. A shadow lifted from Ben's heart.

He hustled to the counter. Pulling one of the child's chalkboards in front of him on the counter, he grasped a stub of chalk and wrote: *I owe you one ten-dollar gold piece. Ben Bonneville.*

God, if this is what You planned for me, let Felicity choose me as her husband. If not, show me another way to travel to the California gold fields. Felicity doesn't look like a farmer's wife to me. But she doesn't belong at the gold fields either. The beautiful lady should live back east ordering about a mansion of servants.

You know I've been praying about her for two months now. I think she should go back to Missouri. Oregon Territory's too rough for a lady like her.

Nevertheless, if Felicity continued on west, he had a mind to be the one driving her wagon. Much as he'd like to charge over to Sal's boardinghouse, beat on Felicity's door, and persuade her to be his wife, he would leave her decision in God's hands.

He strode toward the stable. His landlady, Sal, hadn't wasted any time. She'd kicked him out.

Since he'd already paid for Salvation's stall, he'd spend the night in the empty space.

Probably Felicity would erase his name from the chalkboard. He had little to offer her.

CHAPTER 4

Felicity ambled toward the general store. The gorgeous September morning, so clear the mountains rose purple in the distance, did little to lighten her heart. Today she must choose a husband. She'd tossed on her bed all night and had even hit the top of her head on the iron headboard. Her covers had knotted, and the room stifled her, though she'd thrown both windows wide open.

She'd splashed tepid water onto her face and brushed and arranged her waist-long hair into its usual braid. She'd arrived downstairs before any of the other boarders and eaten a cold biscuit before her stomach rebelled.

Though Ben had been robbed, he'd not appeared at the store last night. Surely after he lost all his worldly goods, God would have spoken to him about signing up to become her husband. Tomorrow she must wed, and today she had to interview the ten men she'd selected. What was wrong with Ben? His chiseled features and broad shoulders had ensnared her heart. His athletic build could work any farm. Was she the problem? Did he not find her attractive?

The bell above the door tinkled, and she strolled into the store. The place looked a shambles. Men last night had moved the kegs they set on into small circles to discuss their chances. Her basket of gold pieces, and the chalkboards still cluttered the counter. Felicity heaved a deep sigh. Well, she would do what she must. Again, Ben lost his chance. She shrugged. Why would she want to wed a man who missed so many opportunities? She closed her eyes and his picture flashed before. Because the man stirred her heart into frenzy each time he came near.

She moved over to the counter and picked up the chalkboard

with the ten names written on it.

Jedidiah lumbered up from the rear of the store. "Are you ready for this, Missy?"

"Yes. One of these men I interview, I shall have to marry."

Behind her, the bell above the door clanged. She turned.

Ben strode in. Two days' growth of dark beard shadowed his strong jaws. His eyes looked blood-shot, and his dark hair stood on end as if he too had spent a sleepless night. His boots clumped across the wooden floor, and he touched a light finger on her hand that held the chalkboard.

"You can add my name to that list."

Her heart leaped like a rabbit to fresh flowers. "Oh? Do you want transportation to Oregon?" She made her voice sound cool and unconcerned, but her stomach fluttered, and her hands turned icy. "I thought you planned to join the California Gold Rush."

"I do." His Adam's apple made an obvious trip up and down his tanned throat. "But I'd like to strike a bargain with you. If you choose me as your husband, after we're married and if you still have your heart set on getting to Oregon Territory, I'll see that you get there. But God might have other plans for us. I'd like you to be open to them."

Ben flashed his heart-stopping grin. "You won't be sorry if you choose me as your husband."

Her cheeks burned. "I promised to interview these other ten men. Shall I interview you as well?"

"That seems fair." He glanced around the store, empty except for Jedidiah standing next to her. "Why not start now? None of the others know you as well as I do. And they're not here." He glanced down at his rumpled clothes and red tinged his cheeks.

Had he slept in them?

"Sorry I look so ill groomed, but I've got nothing to change into, and Sal kicked me out of my room last night."

Her pulse raced. Drat! She *was* his last resort. Certainly not the way she'd hoped to find a husband. Perhaps she'd do better if she chose a man who wanted *her* as much as he wanted his expenses paid to gold rush Territory?

"Then, where did you sleep?"

"Slept in the stable. Still have my job there for two more days."
He smiled.

He did have a warm, charming smile. Still had all his teeth, and
they looked white and straight.

"Okay." She pulled a clean slate over and poised the chalk.
"What are your qualifications?"

Again, his Adam's apple traveled his tan, muscular throat. "My
qualifications?"

"Why yes. I'll weigh your qualifications against the other ten
men and decide which of you would be best suited for a husband."

A bead of sweat formed at his hairline. He did have wonderful,
wavy, dark hair.

"Qualifications?" He dragged a hand through that thick, dark
hair, leaving a racetrack from front to back. "Well, as your
husband..." he hesitated "...un..."

"You've never been married?"

"Of course not."

"What type of work do you do?"

"Preach...sheriff...clerked in stores..."

"Ever saw down trees?"

"Yeah, one or two."

"Build houses or barns?"

"Helped neighbors."

"Plow fields?"

"No."

"Plant fields?"

"No." Another trickle of sweat joined the first one.

The bell above the door clanged, and two muscular men strode
in. Seeing them at the counter, they clomped over. "We're here for
the interview."

Felicity smiled. "Would you mind waiting a few minutes? This
interview shouldn't take long."

The men strode over to an overturned barrel. One sat. The
other leaned against the wall. Both men had shaved, worn new
shirts, and shined their boots. They stared at her, interest stamped
on their faces.

Felicity turned back to Ben. "Now, Ben, is it?"

He nodded.

"You know how to drive a prairie wagon with horses?"

"Yes, I know horses."

"And driving a loaded prairie wagon?"

"Well, no. But I've driven a stagecoach. Can't be too different."

"You have a lot of nos checked against you. What do you do well?"

Ben tugged a hand through his hair again and frowned. "I learn fast."

The doorbell tinkled again. Three burly men clomped in.

"Have you given up your hope to take the Oregon Trail turn-off to California? Or do you still plan to prospect for gold?"

Ben's sea blue gaze turned stormy and dropped to the floor. "I'll cross that bridge when I come to it." He pinched the bridge of his nose and then glanced at her. His broad shoulders drooped. "I'm not a charity case. I'll give you more than my passage in work. By the time we hit the fork in the trail, *if* you still want to get that free land in Oregon, we'll go for it together."

"But in the meantime, you'll try to sway me into heading to California and forgetting about Oregon?"

"I can't lie to you, ma'am. That's exactly what I plan to do."

"And if I still want that land in Oregon, you'll go with me and sign up as my husband?"

His teeth ground. "If that's what you and the Lord want, then I'll take you on to Oregon Territory." Both his hands fisted on the counter, and his jaw clenched until the muscle bulged.

The bell clanged, and a rush of tall, strong men entered the store.

She smiled her sweetest smile. "I'll let you know."

His handsome face tight, his back like a ramrod, Ben turned to leave

CHAPTER 5

"Where's Ben Bonneville?" A loud voice called.

Ben dropped the pitchfork full of hay and strode from Salvation's empty stall. "Right here. Who wants me?"

"Miss Daniels over at Sal's boardinghouse says to come immediately. The Fort Commander's ready to perform the wedding."

Ben's heart thundered. Salvation was gone, but the other horses hadn't been fed and needed fresh water. Still, how often did a man have a wedding? And the beautiful princess chose him. Why hadn't she notified him? If she had, his straw bed last night would have been a featherbed, rather than a torture rack. "Be right there."

He stumbled over to the water trough and splashed water over his head and hands. No mirror, so he finger-combed his hair. He ran a hand over the rough bristles on his face. Fine-looking groom he made. His rumpled clothes smelled. He probably looked as if he'd been on a week-long binge. No help for it. Felicity chose him.

He dunked one boot into the water trough to get rid of the muck, and then the other. He'd give the horses clean water after he was a married man. He shivered. Blasted cold in the stable this morning.

Well, he'd done all he could to get ready.

He opened the stable door.

Outside everything glistened white. Snow layered the boardwalk, the roofs, the buildings, the street, the trees. Washed white. Yesterday had been hot. Today an unseasonable snow blanketed everything as far as he could see. Who knew weather in Wyoming was so changeable? Like the woman he was about to marry.

Yesterday, he'd been certain he'd lost the lottery. So he'd put in another sleepless night praying Felicity would find a man who would treat her well. A man who would protect her. A man who would love her. He'd not told her so in the interview, but if he had to kick the man she chose from kingdom come, nothing would keep him from making sure that man she married treated her well.

He stomped through ankle-deep, fresh, sparkling snow toward Sal's. He should be wearing a fine tailored suit, have a fresh haircut and shave, and be rested and ready to take on Felicity as his bride.

Nevertheless, his heart sang a psalm of thanksgiving. The beautiful, spunky lady with the golden hair would be *his* wife! Fresh cold air stung his cheeks as he marched through the heavy snow. Had been the hardest task of his life to avoid her and refuse her offers of courtship. He'd thought the Lord wanted him to pan gold alone. But having a woman to bring gold nuggets home to was so like God. God always gave more than he expected.

Snow tumbled from the roof overhanging the boardwalk onto the back of his neck. He needed his jacket, but the thief swiped that too. Yet he thanked the thief. How else would he have known God wanted him to wed Felicity?

The wind crawled through his summer shirt. He shivered. Only a few more blocks to Sal's. Inside would be warm. Big, round flakes fell on his face. Slow at first, then heavier and thicker. Beautiful, but cold. He broke into a run, his boots sliding on the snowy boardwalk.

~

Felicity waited at the top of the wooden staircase at Sal's. The Commanding Officer of Ft. Laramie waited, Bible in hand, in front of a roaring fire in the good-sized living room. Men who had hoped to be chosen as her husband filled every available chair and stood in groups at the back. Perhaps they hoped Ben would not show?

Felicity shifted her weight. Her new white kid lace-up boots pinched. She smoothed her white dress, the only one available in

Ft. Laramie, though the garment was only a white print with tiny white flowers. She'd ironed the flowing gown hastily. Still the garment fit well and looked smart.

But where was her groom? Had he left Ft. Laramie last night when he thought he'd not be chosen? Where could he have gone with his money and horse stolen? She'd remember today's date, September 2, 1850. This would be her wedding date, and she would celebrate this day until she went to be with the Lord. Oh, how she prayed she'd made the right choice. Every one of the other men had more to offer. But only Ben caused her pulse to race and her heart to warm. Not to mention the butterflies that flew in her tummy each time she gazed into his azure-blue eyes.

She turned to look out the tall window behind her. Where was Ben? No Ben, but the Lord sent the glorious snowfall as a promise of a new life with a new husband, and a new, permanent home of her own.

Was Ben perverse enough to make her wait as she had made him wait? The moment he entered the General Store last night, she'd known she would choose him. Why hadn't she told him then?

She tapped her foot. She'd give him five more minutes, then she'd—

The front door burst open, blowing in cold wind and snow. Ben stepped inside, put his shoulder to the door and forced the rough plank closed behind him. He blinked, gazed around the room, and then his sapphire eyes shot up to meet hers.

Cold blasted his handsome face red, he wore no jacket, and snowflakes melted into wet spots on his summer-weight shirt, outlining the athletic frame beneath. He pulled off his big hat. The dark hair below glistened as if he'd just had a shampoo and bath. His summer blue eyes held a light she'd never seen. Even the dark curtain of whiskers shadowing his face didn't detract from the grin that spread across his face. Did his bristles hide dimples? Oh, she had a lot to learn about this breath-taking man.

"Leave your guns at the door." The CO's booming voice probably carried all the way to the stable for the horses to hear.

Ben's hands moved so fast, his guns hung on the peg by the

door before Felicity had even begun to admire Ben's lean hips and muscular legs.

"Thank you, Father God," she breathed. Didn't hurt that her groom was the best-looking man in the room. Didn't matter he'd never plowed or planted. He could learn.

His intense eyes blazed a trail up the stairs to her.

She started her slow descent to him.

A muted "Umm" rose from the men gathered in the lobby below. The men stood.

She had eyes only for Ben.

As her best man, Jed stroked his silver mustache and cleared his throat.

She met Ben in front of the CO. The fire's warmth reached out to meet them.

"Please face each other."

They already were.

The preacher placed their hands together. "Please hold hands."

His hands felt icy, but his lips smiled.

"Dearly beloved, we gather together to see this man and this woman united in holy matrimony…."

He'd never looked at her that way before. *Oh, thank you, God. This is the man you've chosen for me.*

"…I now pronounce you man and wife. You may kiss the bride." The CO moved away from the fire as if the blaze had been warming his backside too much.

She'd never kissed except that one time when she was ten and stepped under the mistletoe by mistake, and the neighbor's boy had run over and smacked his lips on hers. Ugh. She'd wiped that kiss off in a hurry.

Ben planted his arms around her as if he would never let her go and moved his lips ever so slowly down to hers.

She entwined her arms around his neck and kissed him back until her body tingled.

Men around the room expelled a breath.

His cold lips warmed against hers and were soft and tender, full of promise. He lifted his head far too soon. When she opened her eyes, a deep flush darkened his face.

Her pulse whistled through her veins like a windy night full of snow. This was no mistletoe kiss. This was a forever kiss.

The men were supposed to clap, but a deep silence filled the room.

She was Mrs. Ben Bonneville, and she would own land in Oregon and have a permanent home for the first time in her life. And she'd be bound to the vibrant man standing beside her for as long as they both lived. She inhaled a shaky breath. What would marriage be like for them? She really did not know what kind of man Ben actually was.

A strong masculine odor filled her nose. He needed a bath. But she liked his scent.

The tall clock in the nearby nook chimed ten.

Outside huge flakes of snow fell silently against the window, whirling away into whiteness.

One by one the unchosen men filed out of the living room until only the four of them remained. She, Ben, Jed, and the CO.

"Um, I've got some things to attend to. If you need anything else, Ma'am, just send for me." The CO clasped his Bible in one hand and shook Ben's with the other. "Congratulations, man, you've married a fine woman."

"Thank you, sir. That I have."

Jed shook Ben's hand. "You take care of this woman, or I'll shoot a hole in you big 'nough to drive a wagon through."

"Yes, sir. You have no worries on that score. I'll take care of this angel with my life."

Jed nodded, then backed out of the room, his stern eyes never leaving Ben's face.

Then she was alone with a man for the first time in her life. Not just any man, but with Ben. Her husband. What would they do now?

The way he gazed at her sent delighted shivers all over her body. Might she invite him to her room at Sal's?

Or should she tell him their marriage would be in name only?

CHAPTER 6

Felicity gazed at the man she'd chosen to wed. Handsome, personable, and now penniless, he owed everything to her. No farmer, but by the looks of him a man who could carry his own weight physically. Extremely attractive and with a last name Pa's enemy couldn't trace back to her.

And he needed a bath.

He sat next to her on the horsehair settee. Behind them the floor clock ticked loud in the silence.

The other residents at Sal's kept peeking through the doorway from the dining room and gazing down over the banister from upstairs. "The other boarders would like to use the sitting room, but they are polite enough to give us time alone." She unclasped her tightly gripped hands where they rested in her lap and gazed at her ringless fingers.

"Uh huh." His face heated until even his ears turned scarlet.

"Should we go upstairs to my room?"

He shook his head as if he'd awakened from a dream. "Maybe I could head on over to the Purple Sage Saloon and mosey into the back room where they keep tubs and run baths for two bits a soak."

She nodded. "That's a fine idea. You would probably return by lunch time, and we could meet at Sal's dining table." Was he as reluctant to be alone with her as she was to be alone with him? True she knew Ben slightly better than any of the other groom applicants, but he was almost a stranger.

He sat, hands splayed on his jean thighs, back straight, face scarlet, gazing into the fire.

When he didn't make a move to leave, she stood. "Well, I shall meet you at lunch then."

He rose and dipped his head. "I'm sorry to ask, but do you have two bits for the bath and shave?"

"Oh!"

"I'm sorry. I can take a cold bath in the stable. Forget I asked."

"But just look outside. It's snowing huge flakes. I'm nervous the snowfall won't allow us to get started along the trail tomorrow." She glanced around the sitting room. Where had she left her glass-beaded reticule? She could ask Sal for a tin bathtub and hot water, but then Ben would have to strip and bathe in her small room. That simply wouldn't work.

Oh yes, there her purse was, on the mantle shelf where she'd deposited the small bag when she'd gone upstairs to make her entrance for her groom. "I have just what you need here." She took her purse, found the twenty-five cents and placed the coins in his hand.

"Thank you." He clinked the money in his big palm. "I'll pay back every cent I borrow." His jaw tightened. "I've never been in this position before, and I won't ever be in this position again." He turned on his heel and headed for the front door. "Snow won't stick. We'll be on the road tomorrow at dawn."

The door shut behind him with a decisive bang.

She pulled in deep breaths. Well, he was a proud man. She'd learned that much about him. That trait could be either good or bad. Weak-kneed, she plopped down on the settee.

Jed made enough noise to scare a deaf deer as he entered the sitting room from the dining room. "Well, honey, how's it feel to be a married lady?" He slid down to sit beside her, his familiar form as comforting as a mug of mulled cider on Christmas Day.

"Now that we're married, I don't know what to do with him. The situation feels so awkward. I don't know Ben at all."

"Don't you fret, honey. I wouldn't let you marry a man I didn't think measured up. From all I've heard about Ben, he'll stick with you until they cut ice in Death Valley. He's a good man."

"Thanks." She reached for Jed's hand.

"Most men are like a prickly hedge. They have their good points. My take on young Ben is that he's got a oversupply of good points. Where'd he go?"

"He went to the Purple Sage for a bath and a shave."

"You sent him *out* for a bath?" Jed shook his head until his silver mustache flew straight out.

"Yes." Felicity straightened her back. "I'm not ready to be alone with him."

Jed rubbed her hand. "Well, honey, that's yer business." He winked. "Ben's good around horses and drives the stage from time to time when Wells Fargo needs a substitute driver, so he won't have no trouble driving yer prairie schooner." He smiled, showing the gap where he'd lost a tooth on the bottom. "Make sure you get plenty of sleep tonight. We head out at dawn tomorrow." His gray eyes twinkled.

Heat burned her cheeks. "We'll be ready. Everything's packed in my wagon except the clothes I'll need tomorrow. I'm anxious to be on our way. The snow won't stop us, will it?"

"Naw. Soon as the sun comes out this afternoon, snow will melt. I've got all our supplies and water loaded. Jist need to hitch up those mules, climb aboard, and we'll be on our way."

"Good. We can't leave soon enough for me."

"Ben looked as jumpy as a bit-up bull in fly time when he left here. Is he getting cold feet?"

"No. He had to borrow money for his bath."

"Shoulda guessed that. A good man always wants to throw his own lasso. Well, honey, I'm out to check those wagons. You notice the man had no jacket?"

"Yes, I did. Perhaps I'll run over to the mercantile and make some purchases. What size do you estimate he wears?"

"Looks like an extra-large to me." Jed stood and patted her shoulder. "I'm on my way." He smiled. "You look like a jackrabbit about to bolt into tall grass. Being married's nothing to be a scared of. Easy as fallin' off a log. Jist releax. Everthing will work out jist fine."

~

Lunch had been awkward with everyone shooting glances at her and Ben and grinning like expectant sparrows watching a worm hole.

The glistening snow outside had turned to slush, and when the sun peeked through the clouds, melted into pools of dingy water. Much like Felicity felt. Worry lines crinkled her forehead. She had to get this understanding with Ben over with so she could breathe free and set her mind on tomorrow's trip.

As if Jed read her mind he said, "Felly, I aim to spend the afternoon checking out the wagons. Looks to me like you and Ben have some talkin' to do to iron out this marriage thing." He scooted back his chair and rose from the dining table. "I'll see you at the crack of dawn tomorrow out at the wagon train. We drew numbers ten and eleven in the procession. I'll drive behind you and Ben."

Ben nodded his dark head. His freshly cut hair waved back from his forehead. "Good spot. Not too much dust to choke on and far enough back in the line to be sure the trail ahead is drivable."

Felicity raised her brows. "Have you traveled by wagon train before?"

"Of course. I had my own wagon and mules before someone stole them. I did some scouting and hunting for Jason Seemont, the wagon master." He shrugged. "But Jason's train continued on a couple months ago. I stayed behind to earn enough money to carry on to California. Had everything I needed to join Caleb Grant's wagon train until robbers stole my stash." He fisted his hands. "Somebody sure wanted to go back east because I checked with Caleb and no one signed onto his train with my gear."

Felicity cringed inside. She knew nothing of Ben Bonneville except he was tall, strong, and so good-looking he made her nerves tingle every time he came near. And he did seem to have some redeeming qualities that would help Jed and her travel on to secure that land in Oregon. But would he steal one of her wagons and take off to the California Gold Rush when they reached that fork in the trail, or would he keep his part of their strange bargain?

"I hear Caleb Grant runs a tight train. He's a good wagon master, and he's been over the Oregon Trail several times. We're in good hands." Ben seemed more comfortable talking with Jed than with her. Perhaps he hadn't been around women much.

Jed nodded and turned to leave. "Looks like Felly's in good hands, too." His worn boots clicked on the wooden floor until he shut the boarding house door behind him.

Felicity sighed. She'd hoped the others would leave the table as well, but they roosted in their chairs like brooding hens and appeared as if they wanted to stay and watch the newlyweds. "Shall we go up to my room?"

Ben jumped up from his chair as if a scorpion had crawled down his neck. "I'm ready if you are." He helped her shove back her chair and offered his hand.

As they left the dining room and strode up the staircase to the rooms for the boarders, he held her hand. They strolled the long hall to her room at the end, his boots and hers tapping on the bare wooden floor.

Once inside the small room, Felicity folded her full skirts and perched on the edge of the double bed. She nodded toward the straight-backed chair. "Please sit down."

Ben turned the chair and straddled the reed seat, his brilliant robin's-egg blue eyes sizzled across the small space and fastened on her.

How to start? She'd thought downstairs was awkward! She couldn't meet that expectant gaze. Instead she glanced at the familiar rose wallpaper, the dresser with the washbasin, the cheval mirror, and down to the patchwork quilt on which she sat.

"You wanted to talk before—"

"Yes! Yes." She grabbed a hand full of her white gown and worried the soft material. "There's one small matter we need to clear up."

"And that is?"

He had a beautiful smile. Straight, white teeth. Slight impressions like dimples in his lean cheeks.

"Um, yes. This is rather delicate to put into words."

"Go ahead. I'm your husband. You can tell me anything. Whatever you need, I'll take care of it."

"I'm so happy to hear you say that. I do have rather an urgent need, and you are the only one who can ..." She hesitated. "... take care of it."

"Whatever you want. I'm your husband, and I'll provide it." His face beamed.

He really seemed to like her. How different his attitude had been when she'd tried to entice him into courting her. He scarcely seemed the same person. His vibrant presence overwhelmed the room. Seeing this charming, attentive side of him jolted her pulse to race so fast he must see it beat in her throat. She raised her hand to hide her throat. Was her heart hung in her throat because she was alone in a bedroom with a man for the first time? She wet her dry lips.

He arose and moved toward her, his hands out, his eyes wide, his mouth smiling.

"No, please sit. Hear me out."

He backtracked, dropped his hands, and straddled the reed-seated chair.

Would he grow angry? Would he hit her? The muscles she wanted for felling trees and planting crops bulged beneath the sleeves of his folded-back shirt sleeve. Would he use that strength to end their marriage before it even started? She'd heard stories in the evenings on the wagon train. And seen bruises.

No help for her predicament. She'd made her bed, now she had to sleep in it. "There's just one thing I need to tell you?"

A shadow crossed his face.

Was he a violent man? Jed was over at the wagon train, too far to help. He wouldn't look in on her until breakfast. Had she been too strong-willed and mule-stubborn? Had she made a terrible mistake?

His strong hands gripped the back of the chair with white knuckles.

"I don't know how to put this." Her voice trembled.

"Look, if you need a day to get acquainted, I can wait." His voice rasped as if the mellow baritone came from a tight throat.

"No. No. That's not it."

His taut face relaxed into another beautiful grin. "What's the problem then?"

"I should have told you before we said our vows."

His face darkened. "Are you expecting a baby?"

"No. No. Nothing like that. Far from it."

A frown formed between his dark brows. He leaned so far forward she hoped the chair wouldn't tip over. "Then what's the problem? Did you get robbed too?"

"No. Please, just relax. You're making this difficult."

He settled into the seat. His face hardened. His hands fisted around the chair back. "O.K., I'm relaxed. Tell me what's eating you."

He didn't look relaxed. Every muscle in his body stood on alert. Oh, she was handling this all wrong. She gazed down at the wad she'd made of the lap of her gown. His magnetic presence in her small room distracted her. She must pull herself together.

CHAPTER 7

Ben rubbed the back of his neck. His head pounded. The delicate, lovely young lady, by some miracle of God, his wife, sat in her virginal, white dress on the bed. He was alone with his wife. His wife! And he didn't dare touch even a shining strand of her glorious blonde hair until she got off her chest what bothered her.

He clenched his teeth. He would wait until she confessed whatever dark sin separated them before he took her in his arms, caressed her silky hair, and kissed her beguiling lips. But nothing she said would keep them apart. They had an entire lazy afternoon to themselves for their honeymoon before they drove out in that wagon train at dawn tomorrow.

Last night after he'd allowed his heart to feel, he'd known with every fiber of his being that he wanted Felicity as his wife. What warmed his heart must be love. And that deep ache that made him want the best for her, even if she didn't choose him had to be love. Certain last night, and even surer this morning that he wouldn't be chosen, shards like glass shredded his heart thinking of Felicity choosing first one and then another of the men he knew by sight and hearsay. All good men. She did know character when she saw it. Not a one of the potential grooms a murderer, thief, lazy, or mean. Each man had more to offer then he.

But she'd chosen him.

His heart thundered. Despite the chill in the room, blood ran through his veins so hot and fast he perspired. His head swam. But he must be patient. Whatever bothered her appeared difficult for her to put into words. Was she fearful? "I will never hurt you."

"I thought not."

"I will always be faithful."

"I'm certain you will."

"As I get back on my feet, I'll provide for you, and I'll protect you."

"Thank you."

He jackknifed off the chair and knelt at her feet. "I realized last night that I love—"

"Stop!" She rose and turned her back to him. "I can't …"

He sprang to his feet, went to her, and touched her arm. "Go on."

She spun to face him. "My father insisted I marry. I need a driver for one of my wagons. I need a husband to gain the land I want."

"Yes, I understand all that." He cupped his hands around her upper arms. His hands tingled with her warmth.

She gazed up at him with wide, beautiful, hazel eyes. Frightened eyes. His heart hammered. She feared him! "Tell me."

"I prefer this marriage to be in name only. For the purposes I mentioned."

His arms dropped to his sides. Time ended. His world tilted.

"You need me, and I need you. We shall help each other. And that … is … all."

The silent room closed in like water drowning him. She didn't want him.

"Do I have your word?"

He shook his head, but the whirling inside wouldn't stop. He was married for life. But not married? What limbo was this?

"Do I have your word?"

CHAPTER 8

Felicity walked beside the moving wagon. As a wife, for propriety's sake, she trudged by her husband's team and took turns with him at driving the mules. All day they'd plodded across a plain, so hiking hadn't been difficult.

She pulled in a deep breath of fall-scented air, mule odor, and axle grease. So wonderful being on the move again. The unseasonable snow had melted, and the day stayed pleasant with the thudding of hooves and the creaking of wheels and the wind whispering against the white canopy top of their prairie schooner.

The nine wagons ahead barely stirred up dust and strung out like a wavering ribbon in front of them. In the wagon behind, Jed's silver head and mustache bobbed as the older man nodded on the driver's seat, the reins loose in his hands.

A family walked beside the wagon in front. Their milk cow, tied to the rear of the wagon, ambled obediently in the shade of the wagon, tail switching back and forth. Pots and pans hanging from hooks along both sides of the canvas clanged a cheerful tune. Two little girls in gingham dresses looked enough alike to be twins, their long braids bouncing against their small backs as they walked. The mother, looking as if she were again in the family way, strolled at their sides.

Ben slapped the reins against obstinate black backs as her mules pulled to the side to nibble fresh, green grass. He wrestled them away from their grazing.

God was in charge, and the world looked fresh and clean with snow dripping from the branches of the pine trees they passed. She was finally on her way to gain that free land in Oregon.

But try as she would to rid herself of them, restless thoughts swirled inside her head. She retied the ribbons of her sunbonnet and peeked around the blue material at the man driving her team. Ben had appeared tireless and cheerful all day. The irresistible man started a conversation with her each time she glanced up at him. When they changed places, he walking and she driving, he handed her up into the wagon and down from the wagon in a most courteous manner. No one could have asked for a more desirable companion. Even easy-going Jed seemed cranky in comparison. And Ben took great care of the mules. He held the reins with a gentle hand and hopped down and led the eight ornery beasts when the column of covered wagons traveled up a long hill.

Mules weren't the only recalcitrant creatures she traveled with. Yesterday she'd glimpsed Ben's obstinate side. Mule-headed that's what he was. Stubborn to a fault. After a stunned silence when she'd delivered her news, his face had turned to stone. She'd insisted he promise her.

But he hadn't. With bulging jaw and narrowed eyes, he finally said, "I promise to court you until you love me as much as I love you. Until you do, I promise not to touch you."

A thrill flashed through her veins even now. How magnificent he'd looked. His blue eyes steeled to grey with purpose, his expression determined, his head thrown back as if nothing could stop him. Her heart had answered. But she'd stood toe to toe to him and neither had backed down.

Ben could be so easy to love. But would he insist on splitting from the wagon train at Fort Hall and heading south to the California gold fields? He needed that quick money, and she needed that Oregon land for her permanent home. So far, she'd not been able to persuade him. And she refused to go to California. Were his needs greater than hers? No. She'd ached for a home of her own since Mother died when she was born, and Dad had dragged her around the country on his quest against outlaws.

So why, when Ben left her room with the excuse that he needed to work in the stable and earn a few last dollars, had she felt so alone? And yet, how relieved not to have him inside her bedroom.

She spent her wedding day ironing the warm clothes she

bought him. And hoping no one noticed her new husband slept in the stable.

Felicity shook off her thoughts. Today was a new day. She glanced at the cloudless sky and smiled. The ex-sheriff with a grudge against Daddy that he'd exposed in a letter to the editor of the *Independence Times* would never find her as Mrs. Ben Bonneville. She'd escaped his clutches. And the revenge of whomever else tailed her father west. She had no idea who else or how many more. But they no longer worried her.

Still, if anyone should track her and uncover her past, Ben appeared more than able to protect her. What joy to have that burden lifted off her shoulders. Dear Jed would have risked his life for her, but her old friend was no match for men intent on vengeance.

With the sun dipping low in the west, she gave a little skip. God loved her, and life was good. With Ben acting more like a brother than a husband, she could endure the rest of this long journey.

If only she could rid herself of the nagging guilt. She should have told Ben before they wed that she had no intention of consummating their marriage. But somewhere deep inside her heart, she'd known he wouldn't have married her if she'd revealed her entire plan. So, she'd kept silent. He must not discover her deathly fear of childbirth.

She pulled off her sunbonnet and let the breeze stir her hair. Mama died when she was born, leaving her terrified to become with child. She'd planned never to wed. Only her desperation drove her to Ben. But guilt grew stronger each day as he attempted to win her love.

He was so captivating.

"Wagons circle. Wagons circle." Caleb Grant, the wagon train master, called as he trotted by on his sorrel mare.

The welcome word relayed down the long line of wagons. She'd soon have a fire going and prepare the evening meal. Perhaps they would sing hymns around the campfire as they had when Daddy traveled with them. Perhaps they would dance.

She shivered. How would she feel dancing with Ben? Was he

graceful and quick-footed or awkward? Would he like dancing with her as the square dance master called the steps to *Nobody's Darlin' But Mine*?

Did he dance the Schottische or the waltz? How she loved to dance after a long day's trek. Her worn feet took on new life when she unlaced her walking boots and shoved her feet into her dancing slippers. And tonight, after two months stuck in Ft. Laramie, her feet begged to dance.

Had Ben danced with many women? He was so attractive he was certain to have enjoyed many girls' attention. She caught her breath. Yet he'd said he loved her. How had that happened?

Her gaze wandered to where he was unhitching the mules, giving them a good rubdown, and leading them to a meadow with a stream where he would hobble them, then carry them some grain. Watching him was pure pleasure. Funny she'd never thought other men looked so easy on the eyes while being efficient in their work. He glanced at her now and again and offered a warm smile and a wave of his masculine hand. The red-checked shirt she'd bought him fit his broad shoulders as if the flannel had been tailored to his size.

Each time he smiled, her stomach fluttered, and she discovered a return smile on her face.

Oh, she must stop staring and get the beans she'd half-cooked in the kettle over the fire and the coffee in the pot. Plus, she had to soak tomorrow night's ration of beans.

The man was so helpful. Immediately after he'd pulled the mules to a halt and set the hand brake, he'd raced to the river and carried back two pails of water for her to use.

She, Jed, and Ben made a warm family group as they gathered around the campfire she'd built, and ate from their tin plates, and drank hot coffee from their tin cups.

Ben brought in more kindling and fed the fire while he and Jed talked with deep, resonant voices about men things.

She rested on a blanket, bracing her back against a fallen log, and enjoyed gazing overhead as stars peeked out one by one, shifting the black sky into a twinkling blanket of beauty.

In the center of their circle of wagons, the fiddlers tuned their instruments. Tonight they played hymns rather than square dances. She discovered Ben sang with a musical baritone and knew all the hymns she knew plus some she did not. They sat side by side on a log in a huge circle with the other families. Jed sprawled on the grass next to her.

Would Ben hold her hand? She laid her fingers near enough to touch his knee, and he took her hand in his warm, masculine fingers. How pleasant to have a big man hold her hand as if he treasured it. Tonight, she didn't even miss Papa.

Ben was proving to be a wonderful man. She'd made the right choice.

Maybe Papa had been wrong when he preached *Dreams never amount to much. They just get your hopes high until someone comes along and stomps them into the ground. Get you some land and work out your own dream. Quit stargazing and come down to earth.*

Being here with Ben was no longer a dream. This was lovely reality. Together, they'd file for that free land, move onto the lush acreage, and make the opulent land their own.

Only one thing could shatter her dream.

An obstinate husband.

CHAPTER 9

Ben grunted. They'd been on the trail six weeks now, and, as far as he could tell, his courting Felicity hadn't made any headway.

He wiped perspiration from his forehead from straining his shoulder against the slippery wheel. He'd worked a good half-hour helping the mules get the wagon across the muddy creek bed. He arched his back. Not easy work. He bent to the task.

He showed her every way she let him that he loved her. But she didn't appear convinced.

The wagon rocked.

"I should climb down and walk. You don't need my extra weight in the wagon." Felicity's anxious face, shaded by her blue sunbonnet, gazed down at him.

He loved her beautiful hazel eyes. Never seen any others that came near to that clear, honest color. "No. You'll get wet and muddy. You don't weigh enough to make a difference in lightening the wagon. Stay put and don't fall if the wagon tilts."

He grunted and strained until the sucking mud let the wheel loose and the wagon jerked and slanted on across the wide stream. He pushed against the rear end until Felicity's wagon moved up the slippery riverbank, then turned back to help Jed's wagon cross the mud that clutched like giant hands.

He'd be exhausted by nightfall. That was good. Took every ounce of strength he had to keep his hands off his bride. When she climbed into the wagon to turn in for the night, her hair spilled down her back in a magnificent waterfall of blonde curls. He had the right to caress those curls, but she didn't love him yet. So, he couldn't even touch one wisp. He pulled in a deep breath. Maybe she never would.

Each night he tossed and turned on his bed of pine needles

beneath the wagon thinking of her just above, just out of reach. His own wife, and he couldn't even touch her hair. Drove him wild. Kept him awake until exhaustion took over. Then she filled his dreams.

She was so beautiful with her delicate face, large hazel eyes, pert little nose, and luscious lips. His fingers ached to stroke her silky skin. He wanted to draw close to her as only a husband and wife could. Each day she seemed to look forward more to his presence. The nights around the campfire tested him to the utmost. Dancing with her so light on her feet, and his arm around her tiny waist, singing hymns, harmonizing with her lilting soprano, or just sitting around the crackling fire with friends chewing the fat, made no difference. He wanted his wife. Would she never accept him? Time blundered to a halt, waiting for her.

No matter how hard the trail, she never complained, though she had to be worn out at the end of each day's long haul. As the country grew rougher, she walked most of the day. She didn't have the expertise to drive the wagon over the mountains and down into the valleys. Keeping the mules in line and on the trail and the wagon from dropping off a mountain was about more than he could manage. Fortunately, Jed had driven mules all his life. Ben valued any advice the old man gave.

Ben called, "Get up there, Jenny. Get up there, Jake. You mules get back on the road." He worked the eight heavy reins, getting the mules back on the trail. He'd been afraid for Felicity that time the Indians made a surprise visit. But she'd stayed calm, even when the leader strode over to touch her hair. After that, when Indians rode into camp or beside the train, she whisked her hair into a knot and tied her sunbonnet on, hiding her hair.

His empty stomach rumbled. Felicity cooked some mighty fine beans, fried taters, and cornbread over the campfires. Tonight, she would cook the brace of quail he'd shot. Food fit for a king. He slammed his Stetson back on his head. Felicity outshone all the other pretty ladies on the train. He'd had to give warning to a couple fellas who eyed her like she was a Christmas Plum Pudding.

In all his twenty-four years, he'd never given a thought to

taking a bride. Now every waking minute she monopolized his thinking. He hadn't even thought about preaching to the people accompanying them on the train. He was remiss. Sinful, not to be about the Lord's business. But Felicity jammed his thinking.

And that land in Oregon, you'd think that was the Promised Land the way she carried on about it. Would she choose to go with him to California? Two weeks ago, he'd been certain she would fall for him faster than chain lightning with a link snapped and be happy to follow him to the gold fields.

Now he was far from certain.

He wiped a muddy hand over his face. He *had* to pay off Ma's debts, half of which built-up due to the hired help she'd needed. The debt rode like a four-story building on his shoulders. He owed seventy-five dollars to various medical people. Take a farmer years to pay off that debt. More likely when the bill collector came, he'd lose that free land Felicity so wanted. He'd never farmed. Never wanted to. He could fell trees and build a credible log cabin. But putting his shoulder to a plow and knowing when to plant and when to harvest … like a foreign language to him. He was a preacher. And he needed gold, not grain.

Wind whipped his Stetson off again. The Stetson she'd bought.

He wrapped the reins around the brake handle, jumped from the driver's seat, and took off running to catch the ten-gallon hat. The brim caught on a prickly pear cactus. He wiped his muddy hands on his filthy pants and used two fingers to disentangle the big hat from the cactus and set his possession back on his head. He couldn't control his life, but he could sure control his hat.

He gazed up as heavy clouds blanked out the sun. Lowering skies crackled with lightning.

Where had that storm come from so suddenly?

He raced back to the wagon train. The procession crawled in front like a twisting snake up a mountain. Big drops of rain stung his face. Sleet.

Felicity must have shimmied up to drive in his place to keep the wagon in line. "Felicity, I'll drive now. You climb back into the wagon and stay dry. Looks like a storm's kicking up."

The wagon slowed. Felicity's face showed relief. She called,

"Whoa. Whoa there." The mules stopped, and she set the brake.

He leaped up to the driver's seat, gathered up the two hands full of reins, and watched her maneuver into the wagon under the canopy, her full skirts whipping in the wind. In the wagon ahead, that entire family of girls jumbled up in their wagon peeked over the tailgate. They didn't even stop their slow-moving oxen while the older son dived onto the driver's seat beside his father.

Closing the gap between their wagons, he shivered. Temperature had dropped at least twenty degrees in the last half hour. This promised to be a big storm. The afternoon grew darker than a blacksmith's apron.

Rain spit from the sky as if nature were mad enough to fight like an Indian on the warpath. The deluge wet him through to his skin in seconds. The brim of his hat hung low, flattened by splattering sleet. Fresh scented air whipped his wet shirt against his skin. The mules lowered their heads, laid back their long ears, and plodded on. If this downpour kept up, even the double canvas rubbed with linseed oil wouldn't keep the sleet out, and Felicity and all her goods would get drenched. He could do nothing but keep the ice-slicked reins clutched in his fists, hold the ornery mules on the trail, and hunch against the pounding sleet. He could barely make out the wagon moving ahead.

On this mountainside there was no place to pull aside and camp. Their train had no choice but to keep moving. And with these sleet-slicked roads, the way down would be treacherous.

CHAPTER 10

Felicity huddled beneath a quilt. How had it gotten so cold so suddenly? Would this sleet turn to snow? Darkness grew inside the wagon so she could barely make out the trunks and barrels. Had life been too easy? Dreams been so close as to seem to come true. Would the whole train die on this mountain? Had Papa been right about dreams?

Lightning creased the sky. Thunder immediately boomed. A tree snapped and fell not far away.

Above the hissing rain came another sound. Was that Ben's teeth chattering? She lifted the front canvas flap and peeked out. His whole body shivered. He would catch pneumonia. When the next flash lit the sky, she groped in the trunk and fished out the winter jacket she'd bought for him. Inching forward over the trunks, barrels, and boxes she picked her way over the packed goods to the front opening.

"Put this on," she shouted over the noisy torrent of sleet.

He turned his sky-blue gaze on her.

Those eyes etched a path directly to her heart.

He shook his head, sending streams of water flying in all directions. "I'm too wet. I'll ruin that good coat."

"Then crawl back here and dry off. The train's moving so slow you'll be on the driver's seat again in no time."

Actually, the train had stopped. The mules stood, heads lowered, ears almost touching the ice-crusted mud beneath their feet. A thin blanket of sleet coated the mud.

Ben wrapped the reins around the brake and climbed inside. The wagon tilted with his weight. He slithered over some barrels, leaned on the corner of one, the coat held out to keep the heavy

308

material from getting wet. Rain dripped off his face and clothes into a puddle onto the floorboards. "I hate to get this fine sheep-skin coat wet."

"I won't abide you catching pneumonia. Take off that wet shirt." She handed him a towel.

His long fingers shook as he tried to unbutton his shirt.

She pushed his hands aside and unfastened the buttons.

He peeled off the wet flannel and handed the dripping shirt to her. She opened the back canvas drape, leaned her arms out, wrung the shirt over the mud, and then draped the shirt over a trunk. All the while trying not to watch how Ben's muscles flexed as he dried his torso. She handed him his dry shirt, and he slipped the green, checked flannel on. She buttoned his buttons. He shrugged into the coat.

Then he leaned over, cupped his cold hands around her face, and kissed her. His lips were cool but grew warm and tender. The lightning that flashed was inside her heart, not outside the prairie schooner.

Astonishing new feelings burst through her. His kiss promised, he had not lied. He loved her.

Too soon he moved away. "That's thanks for the coat!"

Was her imagination running amuck, or did his voice shake?

Almost as soon as the storm caught them unawares, the rain ended.

He crawled back out onto the driver's seat and slapped his dripping Stetson on his head.

She tried not to think of the hungry look in his eyes or the satisfied smile on his lips.

She opened the canvas flap in time to see a perfect rainbow arch across the eastern sky. Such delicate colors. Her heart reflected the beautiful colors. And she so enjoyed his kiss. Her lips still felt warm. And sweet. She couldn't stop thinking of the wonder of being close to him.

The wagon jerked, slid and bumped. Soon the wagon bed tilted downward. They were descending.

She'd heard of mountaintop experiences with the Lord. She'd just had a mountaintop experience with Ben. Was she in love with the incredible man?

Her turn to drive, but she couldn't manhandle the wagon down the slippery slope. She had not the experience or the strength. With the sleet ended, she folded back the flap to catch more of the fresh, clean air.

Ben worked, feet braced against the floorboard, right hand grasping all eight reins, left hand alternating between the chain lock and the log drag, his face taut, his jaw set. At times, the wagon slid crosswise on the muddy trail and threatened to skid down the mountain. Ben kept control and worked the wagon back to the center of the road.

~

Their journey continued.

Felicity encountered new adventures day after day. Too soon they would reach the split in the trail at Fort Hall where a few of the wagons would turn south and lumber toward California. The rest of them would rumble north toward Oregon and the free land.

Ben kept his promise about swaying her to go to the gold rush with him. Each night before she retired to the wagon, and Ben crawled underneath to his cramped bed amid the spare parts, spokes, tongues, and axles slung under the wooden wagon bed, he talked about their traveling to California. He spoke of the rich nuggets waiting to be captured from the cold, rushing streams. He spoke of paying off his mother's debt. He grew passionate about preaching to the needy souls drawn to California by the lure of gold. He promised that after the debt was paid, he'd take her on to Oregon Territory to claim her six hundred forty acres of prime farmland.

She frowned. But, of course, by then all the free land would be claimed. They would be too late.

Through every day on the trail, Ben remained adamant they should travel on to gold rush country. The man continued to be mule stubborn.

What should she do? That single kiss made her soul sing until her silly heart flew right out of her breast and landed at his feet.

Could she follow Ben to an uncertain future? There was nothing in California for her. No land. No permanent home. No roots. Nothing but warring men killing themselves to dig up riches from the earth. Bawdy women. Lawlessness.

He promised to pay back every cent he owed her. He promised to take her to the Willamette Valley in Oregon if she was still bound to go. But he let her know he sure didn't want to go. He owed all that money. And God called him to preach.

How could she be selfish enough to insist Ben give up his dream to make her own dream come true? But Papa preached that land was the only reality. Everything else was stargazing. Papa made her promise to go on to Oregon and start a new life with Oregon land.

The night wind blew pungent odors of horses, unwashed men, wood smoke, and supper cooking over campfires to remind her.

Time had run out. She must choose between her heart and her head. Her dream and harsh reality.

CHAPTER 11

Ben shrugged his aching shoulders. Tomorrow the wagon train would split. If he drove her wagon south to California, would Felicity ride with him or would she choose to ride on to Oregon with Jed?

He'd promised if she didn't change her mind, he'd take her on to the Willamette Valley in Oregon and help her homestead that free land. His stomach roiled. Never wanted to farm. Didn't like the loneliness of living in the middle of nowhere, grinding a living from the dirt. God called him to preach. In order to deliver sermons, he had to be among people. Live in a mining camp or at least a town. He craved excitement. And he had to roll that debt off his back. Lots of men would write off that obligation and forget the responsibility. He couldn't.

But he had an obligation to Felicity, too.

He gazed down at her hiking along like a pioneer woman. Each day they drew nearer Oregon Territory, her face brightened until she glowed. Her contagious smile made his heart sing. Her happiness bubbled over.

When she was happy, so was he.

They'd barely completed the rough trek over the mountains before snowflakes drifted from the sky. The small boots Felicity wore trudged ankle deep in wet whiteness. Probably ice flows clogged the Snake River. At best, crossing that treacherous river at the ford near Ft. Hall was dangerous. He'd make certain Felicity crossed safely before he broke off from the train and headed southwest to California.

~

Felicity stared up at Ben sitting tall on the driver's seat with his Stetson low on his forehead, the four pairs of reins held in one hand. Which way would he choose to go?

Ben shifted on the wagon seat and glanced down. "That sun sure is welcome. I hear that much sunshine in November is unusual."

"I love feeling the warmth on my face."

"Yeah, feels good. But our train had too many delays along the trail, what with broken wagon wheels, and trading with the Indians to keep them from attacking."

"That was scary. But that bout with cholera that stopped us all for several days frightened me more." Thank God, neither she nor Ben nor even Jed had caught the fever.

"Right. We lost too many friends." Ben's words sounded clipped.

He'd lost several buddies to the awful diarrhea and had hovered over her until he made her uneasy.

"Snake River's looking angry this late in the season."

"Yes. Are we too late to cross?" If they had to camp this side and wait for spring all the good land would be claimed before she reached Oregon.

Ben gazed across the Snake River to the other side. "Still a long way to California." He glanced at her. "And to the Oregon Territory. Nope, we'll cross today. Got to. Might be our last chance."

Several chunks of ice rushed along the rapid current of the river. Felicity shivered. How would they pass through such a treacherous mountain of water? How could this raging current be the best ford? If only Moses were here to send them across on dry land.

"Scared?" Ben called down from his seat on her wagon.

"Yes. I can swim, but that looks icy and too swift for me."

"Looks bad, all right. But I'll see you and Jed safely across."

"Thanks!" But then what? He'd not given an inch on insisting they go to California, and she wasn't ready to ask about that again.

"Whoa, whoa there. Whoa, Jenny. Whoa, Jake." Ben halted the

team of pig-headed mules. He climbed down to station himself beside Felicity as the wagon train halted parallel to the swiftly flowing river. "Probably take us all day, but we'll float the wagons across, and the teamsters will swim their livestock to the other side." His jutting chin turned toward her. "People have crossed at this point for several years." He touched her shoulder. "Some wagons get snagged and float down the river and are lost. Some hit boulders in the stream and overturn. I won't kid you, some people die here." He smiled. "We won't. I'll make sure both your wagons and you and Jed make it safe to the other side."

Tears pricked the back of her lids, and she blinked rapidly. "How can you promise such a thing?"

"I've been praying about this crossing and the split trail up ahead. God has work for us to do, so he won't let anything happen to us. He'll keep us safe."

Her heart skipped so many beats she felt faint. "I do hope you remember your promise. I've not changed my mind about going to Oregon."

He grunted. "Nor have I about hightailing it to California."

She lowered her head and pulled in some deep breaths. "What sort of work would God have for me in California?"

His eyebrows shot up, and his mouth tightened. Then he walked to each mule and spoke in an ear, running his hands over the places where they liked to be petted.

"Please tell me?"

He half-turned from the mule named Julie, one hand rubbing her ear. "You'd stay inside our tent and cook for me." He snatched off his Stetson and ran his fingers through his thick, dark hair. "You'd do our washing."

"At that icy stream you spoke of?"

He heaved a deep sigh. "Yes."

"Cook over a campfire?"

"Pretty much."

"And what shall we do with both wagon loads of household items?"

"We'd only prospect for a few months."

"What if you don't find any gold?"

"I will."

"What will I do when you are out preaching to the miners? I hear those mining towns are rough, and few women live there."

He frowned.

"What will you do when those bawdy, gold-digging women proposition you?"

Red flamed under the dark bristles on his cheeks. "You don't need to worry about any other women. I'm a married man. I won't look at a one of them."

She hmphed. "And if those painted ladies pout their lips and tell you they need to be saved from their sinful life, you'll turn away?"

"No. I'll tell them how Jesus died for them, and no matter how much they've sinned, He loves them and will forgive them."

"And if these fallen women repent, what kind of work will they find to do in a mining camp?"

He shook his head. "You've really thought this through, haven't you?"

"Yes, I have, sir. And I'm certain a mining camp is no place for a God-fearing woman. Nor do I think that turbulent place suitable for a married man and his wife."

He shifted his stance, gazed down at his boots, scrunched his dark brows and avoided looking at her. "We'll have to talk later. It's our turn to cross. I have to drive the wagon down the bank and unhitch the mules." His sky-blue eyes clouded. "We need to hire some of those Indians to help float our wagons across." He turned and scrambled down the steep riverbank to talk with a group of dripping Indians emerging from the river.

Jed moseyed up to plant his worn boots in the grass beside her. He stared at the wagons floating across the river and pulled on his silver mustache.

"Bless the man, Jed. Ben still thinks I'll go to that gold mining camp in California. Can you talk some sense into him?"

"I've been a talkin' a blue streak, Felly. The man's more stubborn than all our mules combined. He's so obstinate he wouldn't move camp for a prairie fire." He rubbed his silver-whiskered jaw. "Man's been reelin' round like a pup tryin' to find a spot to lie down. He wants to please you, but he's obligated to pay off that debt."

"Do you think we should go to California for a few months and then travel on to Oregon?"

"I wonder if we didn't make a big mistake when we chose Ben as your groom. Maybe should have chosen one of those other good men."

Perhaps Jed was right. Perhaps she'd made a huge mistake. But Ben had made a bargain.

And she wouldn't change her mind.

CHAPTER 12

Ben smothered the fear in his chest and plastered on an unconcerned expression.

"Climb on Jenny. She's the safest, most obedient mule in your team. Hang on to the reins, and Jenny will do the rest. She's a great swimmer."

He made a foothold for Felicity with his hands and boosted her onto Jenny's slender back. "I'll be praying the entire time you're in the river. The water will be icy, and you're bound to get numb, but Caleb Grant has a fire going on the other side. Head directly there." He held Jenny's bridle in one hand and rubbed her ear with the other. "After you cross, I'll get the rest of the mules across. After that, I'll join you at the fire." He laid a warm hand on her dress-covered calf, and then squeezed her booted foot. "The others have had no problems, and the river's fairly calm. This time of day is the best time to cross."

"But what about our wagons?"

"After you and Jed and the mules cross, I'll work with the Indians we hired to float our wagons across. The first nine wagons and teams made the crossing just fine. No reason we can't."

Except Felicity looked more delicate than any of the farmer's wives. And she was *his* wife. Almost his wife. He'd done his best, but he hadn't crossed that barrier yet.

"Stay calm, keep your reins loose and give Jenny her head. Leave the rest to me."

She smiled down at him, her creamy complexion pale, her cinnamon eyes begging him for his strength and protection. He'd ride with her if two on Jenny would help, but he'd be too much weight for Jennie in that swift-moving river. A cold knot squirmed all the way through his chest and wound around his heart. Crossing the Snake River was no place for the sweet woman he'd allowed himself to love. If anything happened to her ...

She gazed at him, trust in her hazel eyes. Her luscious lips formed into a delightful smile. But fear showed in the way her hands gripped the reins too hard and her knees strained around Jenny's barrel stomach.

"I'm praying for you, Felly." Jed straddled Joseph, their biggest mule, who thought he was a clown, but remained a steady, reliant beast. "I'll be side by side with you, Felly. No need to be frettin'."

Fear worked its way up to freeze Ben's brain. He had to cross that icy river with the other three mules, then cross with both wagons, then cross again, five trips. But even prolonged frigid water wouldn't keep him from protecting Felicity.

If Felicity had the slightest trouble during her crossing, he had Jake reined and ready to ride. He couldn't stand the thought of Felicity's bright head going under water in that icy river. He hopped on Jake. "I'm crossing with you too. I'll ride on your upstream side."

Felicity nodded, gave him a wavering smile, glanced at Jed, and kicked her heels into Jenny's sides. "Get up, Jenny. We're going for a swim."

As Jenny's hooves touched the cold water, Ben's stomach clenched into knots. Felicity gasped as her legs submerged. Her long dress floated up over her knees, then grew wet and lumped down over her legs. A few steps more and water swirled around her waist.

He spurred Jake to the upside where the current blasted the hardest.

Jed moved to her other side. The mules lunged forward until they had to swim. He drove Jake next to Felicity, their mules almost touching. He must get his wife safely across.

Once he delivered her over to the warming fire, he'd hitch the other three mules together and swim them across, then return to work with the Indians floating the two wagons over the river.

He'd probably have to thaw out by the fire between each

crossing.

He fastened his gaze on the two mules lunging beside him, one with a silver head bobbing above the mule swimming through the water and the other with a blonde head bobbing above the near mule, her long dress billowing out on both sides, plowing through the current.

Icy water swirling around his chest took his breath away.

Jenny stumbled, slipped, and started floating sideways, Ben grasped Jenny's reins so hard, the leather bit into his fingers. He grabbed Felicity's arm.

She gasped. Her hazel eyes widened, and she screamed.

CHAPTER 13

As Jenny, her short tail wafting on the water behind her, Felicity clinging to her back, floated downstream toward the rapids, Jed's mule stumbled. Jed slid into the bone-chilling water, and his mule strained forward toward the bank. Jenny and Felicity swept downstream and out of Ben's reach.

Ben grasped Jed by the collar of his jacket and pulled him halfway onto Jake.

"Never mind me! Go for Felly!" Jed gasped and pushed himself off the mule. "I can swim the rest of the way."

Ben turned Jake's head downstream and kicked the big mule in the sides. Jake caught sight of his mate, Jenny, being carried downstream by the current and pricked his long ears toward her. He needed no more urging.

The big mule swam hard toward where Felicity grasped both arms around Jenny's neck. She managed to stay astride the struggling mule. Both must have been dunked underwater because Felicity's hair hung wet and stringy, and she'd lost her sun bonnet.

He and Jake caught up with Felicity. Her head lay against Jenny's neck, but the rest of her body dragged beneath the swirling brown water.

A cold hand squeezed his heart. Could he save both Felicity and the mule? She'd pasted herself to the mule's back. *God, please help her retain her hold.*

He urged Jake to swim downstream until they worked their way to Felicity's side. Her wide hazel eyes showed white. Water dripped from her hair and face, and her open mouth gasped for air. She looked half drowned, but she clung to the mule's slick neck, hands intertwined in Jenny's short mane.

Ben directed Jake to push against Jenny's side and turn her toward shore. The big mule seemed to understand. He pressed his weight against Jenny. Ben's and Felicity's legs mashed together between the mules, but Jake made progress in halting Jenny's flight downstream. Both mules struggled toward shore.

As they reached more shallow water and the mules' hooves touched ground, Felicity's hands loosened. She swayed.

He dropped Jake's reins and slipped his arms around Felicity's waist. She slid off Jenny's back and would have gone under water, but he used every ounce of strength he had and pulled her in front of him onto Jake. The mule grunted but pumped his legs until his hooves touched bottom, and he scrambled up the steep mud bank.

Felicity lay against him, eyes closed, body shaking. He directed Jake toward the huge bonfire, and Jenny trotted behind her mate.

"Ben."

He leaned his head down and almost missed what she said, her teeth chattered so.

"I ... I ... will go ... to ... to California ... with ... you."

CHAPTER 14

The crossing had been tougher than Ben expected. He hunched on a log shivering by the fire as Jed paid the Indians who had helped. After Felicity's narrow escape, he'd wrapped her in a blanket and carried her close to the fire. The first settlers across brought her a hot cup of coffee they'd brewed.

With the sun starting its descent in the west, he'd not taken time to warm himself. He'd plunged back into the Snake River, crossed over on a mule one of the other families offered, and swam his remaining three mules, tied together head to tail, across. He'd tethered them where Jake and Jenny each rested on three hooves, Jake's head hanging over Jenny's bowed neck.

Then he'd warmed himself at the fire a few minutes.

"I'll bring that second wagon over." Jed stood from where he'd been sitting beside Felicity.

His hands trembled and he'd lost his Stetson.

"Better you stay here and look after Felicity. Make sure she doesn't take a chill." The old man sure didn't look like he could manage another crossing.

"I'll stay, but I'm dressing those quail you bagged last night. They'll taste mighty good tonight."

"Good idea. Roast quail is just what we need." Ben descended back into water so cold his bones ached. He had to float the first wagon across before the sun set.

With paid Indian help, he finally managed to float both wagons across. Drained and shivering, he straddled the log beside Felicity and Jed, warming his shivering body at the bonfire. The golden sun touched the horizon in a blaze of reds and oranges.

"Made it across just in time. Rest of the wagons will have to wait until tomorrow." Hot coffee warmed his insides, and soon Felicity, with Jed's help, would serve them all a nourishing supper.

She looked pale, but dry and competent as she turned the spit to brown the roasting quail. Aromas from the campfire set his mouth to watering. His drying clothes smelled like wet dog, and his stomach growled. He twisted around on the log to warm his back.

He should be happy. And he was. But mostly grateful. They'd crossed the most dangerous spot on the trail west, and they'd carted all Felicity's goods safely.

Felicity had promised to go southwest with him to California. He'd stake his claim and make enough money to pay off Mother's debt. Then if Felicity still wanted, he'd journey with her to the Oregon Territory.

But he had to face the gnawing doubt that grew inside his mind with each passing day. What if he didn't strike gold? What if he took Felicity into a crude mining town only to file a claim for a stake that held no gold? What if he bought a dud? Then there was the added expense of mining tools, and supplies. In the back of the wagon, Felicity's burlap bag of beans sagged only half-full. What if he'd have to resupply their food? How could he do that? Everything he owned, she'd purchased.

He owed her everything.

He'd never visited a mining town. Maybe Felicity was right. Maybe the town was too rough for a good woman. He had to consider his wife and her needs, not merely his own problems. He frowned and dropped his head into his hands. Women had so many needs. They wanted a home. And permanence. They needed to be protected. And loved.

Oh, he loved her all right. Lot of good that did him.

Seeing her carried down the river and thinking he'd lost her had been the worst moment of his life. Yeah, he loved her.

Would she ever love him?

CHAPTER 15

Felicity stirred the beans she'd soaked in a covered pot all day in the wagon, and then placed the kettle over the campfire. She rotated the spit with the beautiful quail turning a lovely shade of golden brown. How normal everything was. How peaceful. How full of life and living.

She'd almost died.

She owed her life to Ben. Dear Ben. In the instant his arms wrapped around her and pulled her against his broad chest, she'd realized she loved him. And she had for some time.

Probably ever since that kiss.

So, tomorrow morning she and Jed would turn their wagons south, taking the fork to California. What would a mining camp be like? Would the town be as raw and bawdy as she'd heard? Surely not. Perhaps other women followed their husbands to the gold rush. Probably many wives worked alongside their husbands to pan gold.

She shivered and took a long gulp of hot coffee. Papa would be disappointed she'd not completed her journey to Oregon and homesteaded those six hundred forty acres of prime farmland. He'd preached that dreams were stargazing, and land was reality.

But she'd discovered a loving man fulfilled her dreams. He'd promised to love, honor, and protect her. And he kept his vow. Ben was the finest man she'd ever met. *Thank you, Father God, for bringing him into my life. Thank you that you do make dreams come true.*

Yes, she'd still love to own that lush farmland in the Oregon Territory. Yes, she'd still love to own a snug, permanent home. Yes, she still yearned for peace and serenity. But more than any of those dreams, she wanted to be with Ben. He was her husband. Where he went, she would follow. Like Ruth in the Bible, his people would be her people, his land her land. Of course, Ben didn't have any people of his own, but the rough miners would be his flock, and she would accept them as her people.

Despite her terrible fear, her husband would become her husband. Not every woman who delivered a child died like Mother had. She would trust God. Her God Who did exceedingly, abundantly above all she asked or thought. He would be with her in that California Gold Rush town.

She loved Ben and wanted to please him every way she could.

~

Ben jumped from the driver's seat and scuffed through the light snow that had started falling. Large flakes drifted down on his Stetson and shoulders, obscuring the late afternoon sun. His stiff fingers hurt as he unhitched the mules from the two wagons.

"Wagons camp." Caleb rode his sorrel toward them and waved his hat. "Wagons camp." The wagon master reined up next to where Ben led the eight mules to a patch of grass already dotted with snow. "Never reached this fork so late in the year before, but November's not too late. Tomorrow we split trails. Your two wagons will pull off at the South fork." Caleb pointed toward a distant diverging path. "Most of the rest of us will travel on northwest to the Oregon Territory." He reached out to shake Ben's hand. "I sure will miss you. You've been a help sharing your extra game to feed some of the other families."

Ben shook the offered hand and grinned. "Nope, you won't miss us at all. I aim to go on with the train to grab some of that free land in Oregon Territory. My wife wants a farmer for a husband, not a gold miner."

Felicity gazed up from where she'd been gathering the few pieces of kindling poking through the snow. Her pretty mouth gaped, and her beautiful hazel eyes, that turned his insides into mush, stared at him. A snowflake touched her pert nose and melted.

He'd wanted to surprise her, but not this way. "Excuse me," he said to Caleb Grant." He finished hobbling the last mule and headed toward the rear of Felicity's wagon.

He skirted the back of the wagon and looped his wife in his arms. Slowly he lowered his head and tasted those luscious lips for the second time. With a soft swish, her sunbonnet fell into the snow, and golden hair cascaded down her back.

She kissed him back. Thoroughly. And melted into his arms. Her hands wound around his neck, and her lips responded in a way that weakened his knees.

With his mouth still discovering the joy of her lips, he caressed the silky strands of her glorious hair.

Sure, he still loved adventure. But he held adventure in his arms. She was as much excitement as he could handle. Maybe more.

Sure, he loved to preach. But with his lips melded on hers and hers responding with secrets he hadn't imagined, he'd found his calling. Her body in his embrace answered warm and sweet, giving as much love as he could ever desire.

When he raised his lips, her cheeks bloomed, and her eyes sparkled. He would keep that sparkle in her eyes, no matter what it cost.

"I'll build that permanent home and farm those hundreds of acres. I'll preach to those farmers like they'd never been preached to." He gazed into the gold caramel of her laughing eyes. "So long as you remain at my side."

"I'll never leave you."

"Somehow I'll pay off Mother's medical debt. With you at my side, I can do anything. My labor will not be in vain in the Lord."

She gazed up at him, those beautiful coppery eyes clear and brimming with admiration. "Ben, I love you. Let's celebrate an early Christmas. Will you sleep inside the wagon tonight with me?"

A lump jumped into Ben's throat. He swallowed hard. She loved him! She wanted him. His heart thundered like a herd of buffalo plowed through, forever altering the rhythm. Every shred of fatigue dissolved. He could jump over the silver moon rising in the dark sky.

Christmas had arrived three weeks early. The best he'd ever anticipated. *Thank you, Father God.*

He kissed her again, long and slow and filled with the pent-up yearning of the last few months. He didn't even need the mistletoe he'd climbed the tree to pluck late this afternoon while snowflakes silently fell. When he lifted his head, he gazed at her captivating face, flushed and beaming, and held the mistletoe over her head. "Guess I won't need this."

She reached up, took the mistletoe, and cradled the greenery in her open palm. "No, you won't need this, but bringing this symbol to me was such a sweet thought. I'll save this to put over the doorpost of our new home." She tucked the mistletoe into the pocket of her skirt. Her laugh twinkled out. "Though I don't think *we* will need mistletoe." She stood on her tiptoes and kissed him thoroughly, then breathed a contented sigh. "I'll brew that hot mulled cider I've been saving for Christmas. We'll sip a warm toddy before we go to bed."

"Merry Christmas." Ben cupped her face in both his hands and kissed her lightly on the tip of her nose. Then on her ear lobes. Then the corner of her mouth.

"Silent night, holy night, all is calm all is bright." The song drifted from the wagon ahead where the twin sisters sang to celebrate the soon arrival of Christmas and the end of their two-thousand-mile journey.

"We've just begun our journey together as man and wife," Felicity whispered. "Love is worth waiting for, don't you think?"

He'd waited a long time. "You're right. I'd not have had our journey begin any other way." Now that he knew how precious she was, he had a new priority in his life. God, Felicity, and then preaching.

Was that only a cow bell ringing, or the chimes of Christmas day?

A silver moon in the darkened sky cast shimmering diamonds on the new fallen snow.

The twins in the wagon ahead of them sang, "Joy to the world. The Lord is come."

The scent of cloves and nutmeg in simmering mulled cider combined with the odor of pine wood burning over the campfire. He inhaled deeply.

He'd always remember that scent and this night. Christmas was God's gift to the world.

Thank you, Father, for the gift of your Son. I've learned it's so much more blessed to give than receive.

"Thank you, Felicity. Thank you for this shining moment in our lives."

"Yes," she murmured. "And we have our very own Christmas angel. God sent him to bring us together."

Dear Reader,

I hope you enjoyed this anthology as much as I loved writing it. I'm certain you will love my other stories.

I find it such a pleasure to speak with my readers. Please visit with me at www.AnneGreeneAuthor.com, and www.facebook.com/AnneWGreeneAuthor. You can also subscribe to my newsletter so we can keep in touch. I enjoy discovering what you think about my books.

Please consider telling your friends or posting a short review on Amazon or Good Reads. Word of mouth is an author's best friend, and much appreciated.

ANNE GREENE delights in writing about alpha heroes who aren't afraid to fall on their knees in prayer, and about gutsy heroines. Read her latest release, *Shadow of the Dagger.* Enjoy her *Women of Courage series* which spotlights heroic women of World War II, first book *Angel With Steel Wings.* Read her *Holly Garden Private Investigating series, Handcuffed In Texas,* first book *Red Is For Rookie.* Enjoy her award-winning Scottish historical romances, *Masquerade Marriage* and *Marriage By Arrangement.* Anne's highest hope is that her stories transport you to an awesome new world and touch your heart to seek a deeper spiritual relationship with the Lord Jesus.

Visit with Anne at www.AnneGreeneAuthor.com www.facebook.com/AnneWGreeneAuthor

LINKS TO BUY ANNE'S BOOKS:

If you're an electronic reader, click on the following links to learn about Anne's other books. If you are a print book reader, you will find all her books listed on my website, http://www.AnneGreeneAuthor.com or on https://www.amazon.com/Anne-Greene/e/B004ECUWMG

Shadow of the Dagger

Angel with Steel Wings

Holly Garden, PI: Red Is for Rookie

Masquerade Marriage

Marriage By Arrangement

A Texas Christmas Mystery

A Christmas Belle

The California Gold Rush Romance Collection: 9 Stories of Finding Treasures Worth   More than Gold – The Marriage Broker and the Mortician

Keara's Escape (A Spinster Orphan Train novella)

Daredevils

Spur of the Moment Bride

A Groom for Christmas

Avoiding the Mistletoe

A Rebel Spy

Lord Bentley Needs A Bride

Mystery at Dead Broke Ranch

Her Reluctant Hero

A Crazy Optimist

Texas Law

Recipe For A Husband

A Williamsburg Christmas

Made in the USA
Coppell, TX
24 November 2021

66383792R00198